MW01611557

SUSAN MALLERY

ONLY HIS

ISBN-13: 978-1-61129-833-8

ONLY HIS

This edition published by arrangement with Harlequin Books S.A.

Printed in U.S.A.

To my friends at Facebook.com/SusanMallery:
You have helped shape Fool's Gold.
You've named characters, helped me
brainstorm plots, and even served as
the Fool's Gold cheerleading squad.
Thank you for your friendship and support!

ONLY HIS

CHAPTER ONE

NEVER AGREE TO A JOB INTERVIEW in which the interviewer has seen you naked.

Nevada Hendrix was confident that nugget of advice had been sewn on a pillow somewhere, or made into an inspirational poster. Unfortunately, no one had shared it with her before. Now, facing Tucker Janack for the first time in ten years, she discovered it was very, very true.

She'd had a plan. That's what killed her. She'd polished her résumé, practiced her answers to different interview questions, had bought a new blazer and had even paid an extra seventeen-fifty to get some stupid gloss treatment to make her hair look shiny. She who avoided all things girly whenever possible. Done in by a formerly naked guy and gloss treatment.

"Hello, Nevada."

"Tucker."

She was careful to keep her game face in place—whatever that meant. All she knew was that having her mouth drop open and gape in astonishment wasn't going to make her look capable.

"I was expecting your father," she admitted. After all, the call she'd received about the final interview had specifically said she would be speaking with Mr.

Janack. Not a name she associated with a guy she'd known back in college.

"I'm running the construction and doing all the senior hiring personally on this project," he said, motioning for her to take a seat, which she did.

They were in a conference room at a hotel in Fool's Gold. Ronan's Lodge, known to locals as Ronan's Folly, was a beautifully constructed building with hand-carved woodwork and elegant furnishings. Things she might have stopped to appreciate under other circumstances. As it was, she couldn't see much past the man who'd taken a seat across the table from hers.

Time had been kind to Tucker. He was still tall—which shouldn't be a huge surprise. So few men shrank these days. His hair was dark, with just enough curl to keep him from looking too pretty. The dark eyes, square jaw and hint of a smile on his kissable mouth were exactly as she remembered.

Um, no, she told herself firmly. Not kissable. Far from kissable. He was her potential boss. Or not, depending on how he remembered the past.

She swore silently and wondered why old man Janack couldn't have kept control of just one more project. But when it came to Tucker, she'd never been able to catch a break.

"It's been a long time," he said, giving her that slow, easy grin of his. The one that had made her feel like the most special girl in the world. That had been a complete lie and had broken her heart to the point that it had almost not healed itself.

She drew in a breath, pushed all memories of a younger Tucker out of her brain and squared her shoulders. "As you can see from my résumé, I've been busy. After college I worked in South Carolina for a couple of years, learning all aspects of construction from the ground up, so to speak. We did mostly commercial spaces and, before I left, I was in charge of a five-story building."

It may have sounded small to him, but it was something that made her proud. "We came in early and under budget, with the cleanest inspection record the company had experienced."

He nodded as if he already knew all this. That, if he'd read her résumé, he did.

"Why didn't you stay?" he asked. "They can't have wanted to let you go."

"They didn't, but I wanted to come home."

"Roots?"

"Yes." She did her best not to remember that he'd never experienced what it was like to settle in one place. He'd grown up all over the world. After all, Janack Construction was multinational. She remembered Tucker talking about summers in Thailand, winters in Africa.

She sensed the danger of getting personal and reminded herself she really wanted the job.

"Since returning to Fool's Gold, I've handled mainly smaller projects. Some residential. I have experience working with crews of different sizes and understand state and local building codes." She continued talking, giving examples of her various skills.

"The team that will be working here is one of our best," Tucker told her. "They've been together a long time and they don't take well to outsiders."

"Do you mean outsiders or do you mean women?"

Tucker leaned back in his chair and flashed that killer smile again. "Janack Construction is an equal opportunity employer who complies with all state and federal employment guidelines."

"How very politically correct. I'm not afraid of a team of men, if that's what you're getting at. I grew up with three older brothers."

"I remember. How is Ethan?"

"Good. Married. Happy. If you're going to be around for a while, you should look him up."

However, if the powers that be actually liked her, then Tucker was only in town to hire and would soon be jetting off to another part of the world.

"I will. I'm going to be here through the initial phase of the construction."

Damn. So much for being liked by a higher power.

"You work for Ethan," Tucker said. "Why do you want to come work for me?"

She didn't. She wanted to work for his father, but that wasn't an option. "I'm looking for a challenge," she said, admitting the truth.

"You've seen the scope of the project?"

She nodded. Janack Construction had bought over a hundred acres north of town. They were building a resort and casino complex on tribal land. The company had leased additional acres to a developer that specialized in outlet malls—a fact that had the female population in the area quivering in anticipation.

"We should talk about it," he said quietly.

Nevada stared at him, wondering why the project

could warrant the slightly furrowed brow. And then she knew. The "it" in question wasn't work related.

"No, we shouldn't." She fought against the urge to stand and possibly back up, putting more space between them. "It was a long time ago."

"Nevada," he began in a low voice.

"Don't. It's over and done. It was meaningless."

He raised his eyebrows. "Really?"

Why couldn't he be like every other guy on the planet and want to avoid talking about anything remotely uncomfortable? Did they have to rehash the past?

"Tucker, it was ten years ago. Five difficult, awkward minutes out of my life. Seriously, it doesn't matter."

He shifted in his seat. "Is that how you think of it?"

"That's what happened. You were drunk, I was…" She pressed her lips together. No way was she going to say the words "a virgin" during a job interview. "Let it go."

"It wasn't five minutes. I've never—"

"Oh, my God!" Unable to stop herself, she stood. "This is about your ego? You can't handle the fact that our brief sexual encounter a decade ago was a bad memory? Grow up, Tucker. It's not important. I don't think about it. I came here to have a job interview, not…" She stopped herself, but had a feeling it was a little too late. "We were friends then, too. Can't we remember that instead?"

He stood, as well. "You didn't think of us as friends. Not after."

She wasn't a screamer, which was the main reason

she didn't shriek at him. Instead she forced herself to sound completely calm and in control. "Did you have any other questions about my work experience?"

"No."

"Then it was great to see you again, Tucker. Thank you for your time."

With that, she turned and walked out of the conference room. She kept her head high and her shoulders back. No one looking at her would guess that on the inside she was both humiliated and defeated.

Having to relive that embarrassing night with Tucker was bad enough, but to lose the chance at her dream job was even worse. She'd *wanted* the opportunity to work with Janack Construction. They were a great company and she would have been able to stretch herself professionally without having to leave Fool's Gold. Life didn't get much better than that.

Instead he was going to dismiss her without considering her qualifications, which was just like a man. Talk about unfair.

She spun on her heel and marched back to the conference room. The door was still open. She saw Tucker slipping a folder into his briefcase.

Her folder, she thought grimly. Sheets of paper representing her hopes and dreams.

"I'm good at what I do. I work hard and I know this town," she told him when he looked up and saw her. "I understand the people and I could have been an asset to you. But that's not going to happen, is it? All because of a meaningless act that took place years ago. So much for integrity."

Tucker watched Nevada turn her back on him for the

second time in less than a minute and walk away. The door closed firmly behind her, cutting off his view of her cropped blond hair and stiff back.

"Not a bad exit," Will Falk said, coming through a side door. "When did you two have sex?"

Tucker glared at the other man. "It's none of your business."

"You think I wanted to hear all that? Based on what she said about your performance, you need to do something." Will, a forty-two-year-old friend of the family and Tucker's assistant, grinned. "Five minutes? Pretty humiliating."

Tucker ground his teeth together. "Thanks for the recap."

He wanted to shout that it had to have been longer than five minutes, even though, technically, he couldn't remember much about the evening. As Nevada had pointed out, he'd been drunk. Not to mention out of his mind, lost in a tempest named Caterina Stoicasescu. Unfortunately, Nevada had also been caught up in the hurricane of Cat's life, however briefly.

"You really blew it," Will offered helpfully. "I thought she had potential."

"She does. I'm not done with her."

Will chortled. "Seriously? You think she'll come work for you now?"

"She wants the job."

"No. She wanted it. Past tense being the key here. Now she knows it means working for you. Hell, Tucker, five minutes?"

"Would you let go of that?"

"I guess I'm going to have to. Still, you were a smart

kid, not ugly enough to crack a mirror. I figured some woman somewhere would take pity on you and show you the ropes. Guess I was wrong."

Tucker pointed to the door. "Out."

"Or what? Going to pull my hair?"

Will was still snickering when he limped out of the room.

If it had been anyone else making fun of him, Tucker would have been pissed. But Will was practically family. Barely ten years older than Tucker, Will had been working for Janack Construction since he'd left high school, and Tucker had always thought of him as the older brother he'd never had. Will had quickly moved up the ranks, until an accident six years ago had broken both his legs and fractured his back.

The company medical insurance had taken care of the bills, and Tucker's father had kept Will on the payroll. Even after a year of healing, Will hadn't been able to go back to working at a site.

Right about then Tucker had started running projects on his own. He'd offered Will the job as his right-hand man and they'd been working together ever since. They were a good team, which was why Tucker was willing to take so much crap from his friend. All of which was interesting, but didn't solve the Nevada problem.

The casino-resort project was huge. The biggest one he'd ever run. He needed a good team in place and Nevada brought a lot to the table. The fact that he knew her and trusted her made him unwilling to let her simply walk away. But how to convince her to let go of the past and come work for him?

As he followed Will out of the conference room,

he realized once again the trouble in his life could be traced back to Caterina Stoicasescu. Cat had always been hell on wheels. Those around her had the choice of ducking out of the way or being run over and left broken and bleeding on the side of the road. He'd been run over plenty of times, until he'd realized he was done being a fool for love. The emotion wasn't worth the trouble. Unfortunately, Cat had left him one more mess to clean up.

NEVADA STOOD OUTSIDE of the hotel and wondered where to go next. If she returned to work, Ethan, her brother, might be there. He would want to know how the interview had gone, which was a pretty reasonable question, given the circumstances. Unfortunately, the answer wasn't easy. What, exactly, was she supposed to say? Ethan might consider Tucker a friend, but there was no way he was going to take kindly to the fact that Tucker had slept with his baby sister when she was an eighteen-year-old virgin.

With work out of the question, she searched for another retreat. Going home was an option, but she didn't want to be alone with her thoughts. That way lay madness, or however the quote went, she thought grimly as she started down the street.

Ten minutes later, she entered Jo's Bar. As always, the open bar was well lit and female friendly. Until recently, Fool's Gold's guilty secret had been the town's lack of men. Jo's Bar took advantage of that fact and catered primarily to women. The appetizers came with listed calorie counts, the TVs were tuned to reality shows and shopping channels, and low-calorie versions of drinks were offered whenever possible.

At a little after three, in the middle of the week, there weren't many customers. Jo Trellis, the owner of the bar, had moved to Fool's Gold about four or five years ago. She'd redone the place, ignoring conventional wisdom that said bars should cater to men, and opened her doors to great success.

No one knew very much about Jo's past. She was tall and muscular, pretty, in a quiet way. The only thing everyone knew for sure was that Jo kept a shotgun behind her bar and she knew how to use it.

Jo came out from the back room and spotted Nevada sliding into a booth.

"You're here early," the bartender said.

"I know. It's been one of those days when getting drunk seemed like a sensible option."

"You'll pay for it in the morning."

While the advice was sound, right now morning seemed a long time away. "Vodka tonic. A double."

"Want anything to eat?" Jo asked, sounding more like a concerned parent than a woman who made her living serving liquor.

"No, thanks. I don't want to slow the process." If she drank enough, she would forget. Right now, forgetting seemed really smart.

Jo nodded and left, only to return seconds later with a large glass of water.

"Hydrate," she growled. "You'll thank me later."

Nevada dutifully sipped the water until her drink arrived and then carefully gulped about half the contents. Now it was just a waiting game, she thought. Waiting for the vodka to cloud her brain and make her awful afternoon fade away.

As a rule, she was a big believer in facing her problems head-on. Figure out what was wrong, come up with several solutions, pick the best one and act. She'd always been a doer. She did her best to keep her complaining to a minimum and to be a team player. That meant exactly jack shit when it came to Tucker Janack.

She couldn't fix the past. There was no game plan for going back in time and undoing a bad decision. The reality was, she'd been crazy in love with the man and she'd acted rashly. The fault was hers. She could accept that. What really fried her was having to pay for it now.

She finished her drink and motioned for another. Before it arrived, the door to the bar opened and her sisters walked in. A quick glance at her watch told her that less than fifteen minutes had passed since she'd sat down in the booth.

"Impressive," she called to Jo.

Her friend shrugged. "You know how I feel about people drinking alone."

"It's medicinal."

"If I had a nickel for every time I heard that."

Nevada turned her attention to the two women walking toward her. They were exactly her height, with the same blond hair and brown eyes. Hardly a surprise, considering they were identical triplets.

When they'd been kids, telling them apart had been a nightmare for nearly everyone, including family. But they'd since cultivated distinct differences, including how they dressed and their personal style. Montana wore her hair long and curly, favored flowy dresses and all things soft. Dakota went the more tailored route, although the fact that she was currently pregnant would make identification even easier.

Nevada had always considered herself the more sensible sister—her present condition notwithstanding. She spent much of her days on job sites, where jeans and work boots were a requirement rather than a fashion choice. She made smart decisions, thought things through and did her best to avoid having regrets. Tucker was the biggest bump on the otherwise smooth, slightly lonely course that was her life.

"Hey," Dakota said, sliding into the booth across from her. "Jo called."

Montana slid next to Dakota and tilted her head. "She said you were drinking."

Nevada waved her empty glass toward Jo. "Maybe a quesadilla, too," she called.

"I thought you didn't want to eat."

"I changed my mind."

"Good." Jo walked toward her and grabbed the empty glass, then took orders from Dakota and Montana. "If only you were smart enough to stop while you could still avoid a hangover."

"Sorry, not happening." Nevada waited until Jo had left, then looked at her sisters. "You two got here faster than I expected."

"It's this new invention called a phone," Montana told her. "It speeds up communication."

Dakota placed both her hands on the table. "What's going on? This isn't like you. You don't drink in the middle of the day."

"Technically, it's past the middle." Nevada squinted. Ah, there it was. The faintest of buzzes moving through the back of her brain.

"Fine. Normally you would be at the office, but instead…" Dakota sighed. "Your interview. That was today."

"Uh-huh." She glanced toward the bar, wishing Jo would hurry.

"It had to have gone well," Montana said, loyal as always. "Didn't Mr. Janack realize how qualified you are? He needs someone with your experience to deal with the local factor. Plus, you look really nice."

Nevada inhaled the scent of grilling tortillas and cheese. Her stomach growled. She hadn't eaten lunch— nerves about her interview had caused her to work instead.

"What happened?" Dakota asked, apparently less interested in Nevada's appearance than her sister was. "Why do you think the interview didn't go well?"

"What makes you think I believe that?" Nevada asked, the buzz getting stronger by the second. Even so, when Jo brought the second drink, she took a big gulp.

"The drinking was my first clue."

Having a trained psychologist as a sister was a double-edged sword, Nevada thought. "I don't want to talk about it. If I did, I would have come to see you both. But I didn't. I'm here, getting drunk. Leave me alone."

Her sisters exchanged a glance. If Nevada put her mind to it, she could probably figure out what they were thinking. After all, they were genetically the same. But right now all that concerned her were the smells drifting back from Jo's small kitchen.

"Nevada," Montana began, her voice gentle.

That was all it took. A single word. Nevada shook her head. Why couldn't she be like other people and hate her family? At the moment, a good estrangement sounded like the perfect plan.

"Fine," she grumbled. "The interview wasn't with Mr. Janack, aka Elliot, the father. It was with Tucker."

"That's the guy who was friends with Ethan all those years ago?" Dakota asked. She sounded as if she wasn't completely sure of her facts. That was reasonable, considering her only encounter with Tucker would have been over a summer, back when they were kids.

"I don't get it," Montana said. "He's in charge now?"

"Running the whole project," Nevada said, still watching the door leading to the kitchen.

"Why is he a problem?" Dakota asked.

Nevada abandoned her hope for food anytime soon and faced her sisters. "I know Tucker. When I went off to college, Ethan told me to look him up, which I did."

"Okay," Montana said, sounding confused. "But isn't knowing him a good thing?"

"I slept with him. Let me just say, that makes for an awkward interview."

Jo appeared with the quesadilla and several napkins. She set herbal tea in front of Dakota and gave a diet soda to Montana. After placing a basket of chips and bowl of salsa in the middle of the table, she left.

Nevada picked up a slice of the quesadilla and took a bite, ignoring her sisters' wide-eyed stares.

"Not today," Montana said in a whisper. "You're not saying you slept with him today."

Nevada finished chewing and swallowed. "No. I didn't have sex during my interview. It was before. Back in college."

She ate some more while her sisters stared at her expectantly. Montana cracked first.

"What happened?" she demanded. "You never told us this."

Nevada wiped her hands on a napkin, then took a sip of her drink. The buzz was stronger now, which would make exposing her secret easier.

"When I left for college, Ethan asked me to look up Tucker. He was working in the area."

Although she and her sisters had been extremely close, they'd made the decision to go to three different colleges. The four years apart had given them the chance to solidify their identities, or some such crap, she thought hazily. While it had seemed like a good idea at the time, now she wondered if things would have gone better with one of her sisters around.

"I wasn't especially interested in spending time with a friend of his," she continued, "but he kept bugging me, so I did. I called Tucker and we agreed to meet."

She still remembered walking into the huge open room in the industrial complex. The ceilings had probably been thirty feet high, with light spilling in from all the windows. There'd been a huge platform in the middle and a beautiful woman wielding a blowtorch. But what had caught Nevada's attention was the man standing by the platform. The grown-up Tucker was very different from the kid she'd remembered.

"It was one of those things," she said, taking another bite of the quesadilla, chewing and swallowing. "I took one look at him and fell head over heels. I didn't have a chance."

Montana leaned toward her. "That's not a bad thing, right?"

"It is when the guy in question is madly in love with someone else. He had a girlfriend." If one could give Cat such a pedestrian title. "I was crazy about him, and he was wild over her and she wanted to be my friend. It was hell."

"Who was she?" Dakota asked. "Another student?"

Nevada shrugged. "It doesn't matter." No way was she going to say the name. There was a chance they would recognize it and Cat wasn't anyone Nevada wanted to talk about.

"I hung out with them a few times," she said. "Then I couldn't stand it anymore, so I pulled back. One night I heard they broke up and I went to see Tucker. He was seriously drunk and we had very bad sex."

She didn't mention that she'd basically thrown herself at him. And that, looking back, she was a little surprised he'd even remembered it was her. After all, he'd called Cat's name at the crucial moment.

She sighed. "It was a mess. They got back together, I was crushed and that was it. I never saw either of them again. Until today."

There was so much more. The fact that Tucker had chosen Cat over her. Not a surprise, really. Cat was beautiful and larger than life and they'd been together first. Still, Nevada had been heartbroken and humiliated. Plus, the sex really had been awful. So bad that she'd waited nearly three years before risking getting intimate again.

"I wanted the job," she said, picking up her drink. "I wanted the chance."

"You don't know he won't hire you," Montana told her. "You're the best candidate."

"I don't think that's a deciding factor."

Dakota sipped her tea. "Was it hard to see him again?"

"It was a shock. I was expecting his father. But that's not what you're asking, is it?"

"No."

Nevada considered the unasked question. "I'm over him. It was a long time ago and I was young and foolish. Everything is different now."

"There aren't any lingering feelings?" Dakota asked.

"Not even one."

Nevada spoke as firmly as a nearly drunk person could. The good news was, she was pretty sure she wasn't even lying.

CHAPTER TWO

TUCKER HAD NEVER THOUGHT much about small-town America. Mostly his work took him to remote places, where they had to create their own infrastructure to get the job done, or to urban areas, often those that were crumbling. He wasn't used to cheerful storefronts and friendly people strolling along clean sidewalks. In the ten minutes it had taken him to get from his hotel to the center of town, he'd been greeted multiple times, told to have a good day, asked if the weather could be any better and nuzzled by a tiny toy poodle in a pink sweater.

He'd been to Fool's Gold before, back when he was about sixteen. Tucker's mom had died when he was pretty little, so his dad had taken him along on construction jobs. He'd grown up all over the world, getting his education through local classes and tutors. His dad had worried that he wasn't socializing enough with kids his own age, so every summer Tucker was sent to a different camp in the States. One year it was space camp, another had been a drama camp. The year he'd turned sixteen, his father sent him to a cycling camp, where he met Ethan Hendrix and Josh Golden.

The three of them had hung out all summer. Josh and Ethan had both been serious about cycling. Josh had gone on to make a career of it. Tucker had gone into the family business, and went where the next big project was. Ethan had stayed in Fool's Gold.

Tucker crossed a narrow street and saw the sign for Hendrix Construction. Back in high school, Ethan had planned to go to college, then get the hell out of Fool's Gold. He and Tucker had talked about Ethan coming to work for Janack Construction. They'd daydreamed about a dam they'd build in South America or a bridge in India. Instead, Ethan's father had died, leaving Ethan responsible for running the family business. As the oldest of six kids, with a heartbroken mother, Ethan hadn't had a whole lot of choices.

Tucker opened the door to the construction office and smiled at the receptionist sitting behind the desk. "I'd like to see Nevada, please."

He'd arrived early enough in the morning to catch her before she headed to a job site, but still expected to be asked if he had an appointment. Instead, the receptionist pointed toward a door at the rear of the big room.

"She's in her office."

"Thanks."

He circled around a couple of empty desks and knocked on the open door.

Nevada stood with her back to him, pulling out a file drawer. In the second it took her to turn, he saw she wore jeans and a T-shirt instead of the trousers and blazer from the day before. Heavy work boots added a couple of inches of height, bringing her closer to his eye level. She was tall and lean, with curves in all the right places.

Attractive, he thought absently. Sexy. And she'd

probably been back in college. Not that he would have noticed. Being around Cat had been like looking at the sun—he couldn't see anything else. Life would have been a whole lot easier if he'd fallen for someone normal like Nevada instead of Cat.

As Nevada spun to face him, he noticed she wasn't wearing much in the way of makeup and her face was pale.

"Good morning."

She blinked at him. "Maybe for you."

Her eyes were red and looked a little puffy. Judging by the shadows underneath, he guessed she'd had a difficult night.

"Hangover?" he asked, keeping his voice low.

"I don't want to talk about it."

Had she been out drinking because of him? Well, them. He hoped he was the cause of her morning pain. If only for proof that their meeting had affected her as much as it had affected him.

"Whatever you're thinking, stop," she told him.

"Why?"

"You're looking smug. It's annoying. In fact, you should go away. Why are you here, anyway? Are you looking for Ethan?"

"I'm looking for you."

She touched her forehead, as if trying to rub away pain. "I can't imagine why."

"Sure you can."

Despite the dark circles and her pallor, she was still appealing. He liked Nevada in jeans and a T-shirt, rather than dressed for an interview. These clothes were more like the woman he remembered.

"I want a do-over," he told her. "The interview," he added, just in case she thought he was talking about sex. Not that he would say no to a chance to prove himself.

"I have nothing left to say to you. You have my résumé. That's enough."

"You're right. It is. I want to hire you as a construction manager."

"Go to hell."

"Is that an 'I'll think about it'?"

"It's a go to hell. I'm not interested in being played."

"Why would you think I'm playing you?"

"You're only offering me the job because I said you were lousy in bed."

He winced, hoping her voice wouldn't carry. "This is a project worth tens of millions of dollars. Do you think I'd risk that because of my ego?" He moved toward her. "You're more than qualified, which is important, but as you pointed out yesterday, you're a local. You know how things are done around here. You can help us avoid making mistakes."

It was a lesson he'd learned the hard way more than once. Paying attention to the seemingly foolish rituals and expectations of the locals could often mean the difference between coming in on time and on budget and blowing through all projections.

"I know you're interested," he continued. "Otherwise you wouldn't have bothered applying or showing up for the interview."

"It was supposed to be with your father," she snapped. "Not you. I never wanted to see you again."

"I'm the one in charge."

"Exactly. Which is why it's okay for you to leave now."

As rejections went, she was more than clear. He didn't like it, but he wasn't going to beg. He nodded once, then left, still confused about what was going on. He got halfway across the parking lot when a pickup pulled in next to him.

"You're a long way from the Amazon," a familiar voice called.

Tucker saw Ethan climbing out of the truck and grinned.

"What are you doing here?" Tucker asked.

He and Ethan shook hands, then slapped each other on the back.

"I run the place," Ethan said, pointing at the sign. "Not that I'm here much these days. I'm over with the turbines."

Tucker knew his friend had become involved with turbine construction. Wind energy was a growing field and Ethan's product was in high demand.

"I have some names for you," Ethan told him, pulling a worn briefcase off the passenger seat. "Good guys you'll want to think about hiring. A couple work for me, but I'll let them go. With Nevada leaving, there's going to be less construction work."

"Leaving? Where's she going?"

"To work for you." Ethan looked surprised. "I know she applied."

"She did. I just offered her a job, but she turned me down."

"I don't get it," Ethan told him. "She was excited about the opportunity."

"I wanted her on board."

There had to be something else going on, Tucker told himself. It couldn't just be the past. Assuming what she'd said was true, that their time together had been…awful, even that shouldn't be enough to keep her from coming to work for him. He wasn't some jerk of a boss.

"I was planning on giving her a team of my best guys."

Ethan frowned. "Let me talk to her."

Tucker shook his head. "Don't. She either wants the job or she doesn't. It needs to be her choice."

"Okay. But don't think this means you're going to be in town and avoiding me. I want to have you over for dinner. You can meet Liz and the kids. See all you've been missing with your nomadic lifestyle."

"I like my nomadic lifestyle."

"That's because you never were as bright as the rest of us."

NEVADA DID HER BEST to ignore the pounding in her head. She'd taken as much aspirin as she thought was safe and had hydrated enough to water fifteen acres of corn, but she still felt as if she would have been smarter to shoot herself that morning.

Jo had tried to warn her, she reminded herself. She'd been very specific on the consequences of drinking that much—especially for someone who generally limited herself to a single drink. But had she listened? Of course not. Now she was paying the price with a pounding headache and a body that hurt everywhere but her eyelashes.

"I can't believe you turned down the job."

The loud words came unexpectedly, causing her to jump. She glanced up and saw her brother standing in the doorway to her office. Tucker had filled up the space nicely, she thought, remembering how good he'd looked and how that had pissed her off.

"I don't want to talk about it," she mumbled, wondering when the last of the alcohol would finally get out of her system.

"You're going to talk about it. This is what you wanted. You said you were interested in a challenge. Tucker's offering all that. He thinks you'd be good for his team."

Telling her sisters what had happened was one thing, but explaining the details to her brother wasn't a place she was willing to go.

"I'm not interested anymore."

"Why? I don't get this. Are you scared?"

"No."

"Then, what?"

Ethan was a great big brother. In school, he'd looked out for his baby sisters, and as an adult, he'd put his own dreams on hold so he could run the family business and put his younger siblings through college. He'd grown Hendrix Construction into a much larger company and had started a successful turbine business as well. He was a good guy.

That was why she couldn't tell him about her sordid past with Tucker. Ethan would feel the need to do something, which would only complicate the situation.

"Ethan, I love you. Let it go."

He stared at her for a long time, then shrugged.

"Tucker's a great guy. Why wouldn't you want to work for him?"

"I just wouldn't."

"You're being an idiot. You know that, right?"

"Yes."

"Okay. It's your decision."

He walked away.

Nevada was left alone in her office, her head pounding, the past threatening to bubble over into the present. She tried to busy herself with work, but could not stare at her computer screen. Not with her headache. Giving in to the inevitable, she left for the day and walked home.

Late summer was a beautiful time in the foothills of the Sierra Nevada. Fool's Gold sat nestled at about twenty-five hundred feet. Just high enough for them to have all four seasons, but not so high that they still had snow until June. To the east were the jagged peaks, to the west were the vineyards and the highway that led to Sacramento.

Nevada took a slightly longer route home, mostly because she wanted to be on quieter streets where she was less likely to run into anyone and have to make conversation. Between feeling like roadkill and having a very unusual urge to cry, she wanted to simply be, without any expectations.

As always, catching sight of her house made her feel better. It had been built in the 1920s by a man who loved all things Victorian. The three-story house rose well above all the neighboring homes, a fussy dowager out of place among more modern offerings. She'd bought the place three years ago and had done all the remodeling herself.

The new exterior paint had toned down the pink-and-yellow trim to a soft white. The house itself was a pale gray. Turrets stood on either side. One was her master bath, the other was part of the guest room.

She'd turned the main floor into two small apartments she rented out to college kids. This year her tenants were grad students who did something with computers. She wasn't sure what, but they were quiet and paid their rent on time, which worked for her.

She climbed up the main staircase to her place—a spacious two-floor unit. After passing through her living room, she took a second set of stairs up to the third floor and walked into her bathroom.

She'd spent most of her time and budget on this bathroom and the kitchen and loved how both had turned out. The bathroom was huge, with a separate shower and a reproduction claw-foot tub. Big stained-glass windows let in plenty of light while giving her privacy and, when she stretched out in the tub, she could see the fireplace in the master bedroom.

Now, her head still pounding, she turned on the water and threw in a handful of jasmine-scented bath beads. In a matter of seconds, the soothing smell had combined with the steam, already relaxing her.

She walked into the bedroom and took off her boots, then stripped off her clothes. She shrugged into a robe and returned to the bathroom to wait for the tub to fill.

Without wanting to, she remembered the first time she'd met Tucker. She'd been maybe ten and Ethan and Josh had brought him home with them from cycling camp. The most exciting thing about his visit was his father's flying to pick him up in a private jet. She'd found that far more intriguing than Tucker himself.

Eight or so years later, when she'd gone off to college, Ethan had told her to look up his old buddy. She'd made the duty call and was surprised when Tucker was enthused about seeing her again.

He'd given her directions to an industrial complex by the Los Angeles airport. She remembered being surprised by the location. The address was for a building nearly as big as an airplane hangar. The first thing she noticed when she stepped out of her small truck was the sound of music. The pounding rock beat had made the windows rattle.

She'd knocked on the half-open door, but no one had answered. Probably because no one could hear her. She pushed opened the door and stepped inside.

The open area was huge, maybe ten thousand square feet, with soaring ceilings. Big windows allowed the L.A. sunshine to illuminate everything. The floor was concrete, and the music was even louder here. The bass caused her chest to vibrate.

But what caught her attention was the scaffolding in the center of the massive room. Reaching nearly as high as the ceiling, it was a complex framework with platforms and railings. It surrounded a gigantic, twisted piece of metal.

The piece seemed to curl in on itself, yet reached up at the same time. As Nevada studied it, she felt as if the shards had been ripped open by a blast, then hastily put back together, but not in the right order. There was tragedy in the work. A sense of loss.

After a few seconds, she noticed a woman stood near the top of the scaffolding, welding sparks showering her. From this distance, Nevada couldn't tell much about her, except that she was tall and thin.

"You made it."

The voice came from her left, a shout to be heard over the music. She turned and saw Tucker. Only this guy wasn't the tall, skinny teenage boy she remembered. This guy was broad and handsome, with an easy smile and eyes that beamed with pleasure at seeing her. Despite the loud music, the strange building and the unusual artwork, everything disappeared. The world became a pinprick of light, expanding again until there was only Tucker.

Nevada had never believed in love at first sight. Never thought it was possible for one soul to recognize another. Never knew what it was like to have the very breath stolen from her body. She stood rooted, unable to move or speak. She could only stare at the man she knew she would love for the rest of her life.

He said something. She saw his lips move, but couldn't make out the sound. He laughed, grabbed her arm and pulled her outside.

"Hi," he said when they were in the relative quiet of the parking lot. "You made it."

"I did."

He hugged her, his body warm against hers. She wanted to lean in, to get lost in his strength and heat, but he straightened too quickly and she wasn't ready to let go. Not yet.

"How's college?"

"Good. I'm settling into my classes."

"You're okay in the dorm?"

He sounded more like a parent than a friend, but she nodded anyway.

"Ethan's good?"

"He's dealing."

The humor faded from Tucker's face. "I'm sorry about your dad."

"Thanks."

Over the summer, her father had unexpectedly died, leaving the whole family shocked and devastated. Although she and her sisters had protested going off to school, their mom had insisted. Ethan had been the only one to put his dreams on hold, to take over the family business.

"It's complicated," she said. "I still can't believe he's gone."

Tucker put his arm around her and kissed the top of her head. "I want to tell you it will get better, but right now that's pretty meaningless, huh?"

"I know it won't hurt so much later, but it's hard right now."

He stared into her eyes, making the emptiness kind of fade into the background. He still had his arm around her, another amazing concept. Had he felt it, too? The connection?

For once she wished she had more experience when it came to men. In high school, she'd never much seen the point. There had been the occasional guy, but no real boyfriend.

"Want to get lunch?" he asked.

Her heart gave a little jump. Okay, it wasn't a date, but it was close. "I'd like that."

"Good." He dropped his arm. "Let me go see if Cat wants to take a break." He shook his head. "She has the classic artistic temperament. I never know when she's going to go off on me, so don't be surprised if you hear a lot of screaming."

He sounded more excited than upset by the prospect.

"Cat?" she asked, remembering the female welder.

But Tucker was already gone, walking quickly into the building.

Nevada walked to the door and watched as he gracefully climbed the scaffolding. When he reached the welder, he touched her on the shoulder. The sparks stopped and the woman removed her protective gear.

Even from all the way across the building, Nevada could tell she was beautiful. Long, dark hair tumbled halfway down her back in cascading waves. A classically beautiful face—wide eyes, high cheekbones and a full mouth. The woman stepped out of a jumpsuit, revealing a cropped T-shirt and shorts, long, perfect legs and a waist small enough to belong on a model.

She and Tucker descended the scaffolding together.

Once again Nevada was unable to move, but it wasn't Tucker who held her in place—it was her own sense of insignificance. The woman was older than Nevada, and probably a couple of years older than Tucker. Even casually dressed, she had an air of sophistication. Men wrote songs for women like that, went to war for them, loved them.

As the couple approached, Nevada wanted to run. She forced herself to stand there, knowing she would probably trip over her own feet if she tried to get away.

"So, you're Tucker's friend," the woman said, her

voice low and sultry, with a slight accent. "I'm delighted to finally meet you. I'm Caterina Stoicasescu." She held out her long, slender hand.

"Nevada Hendrix."

Nevada shook the strong, scarred hand, doing her best to keep her mouth from hanging open. Her gaze went from the woman to the sculpture and back.

Caterina Stoicasescu? She was famous all the way to Fool's Gold. Talented, gifted. She'd been discovered when she was little. Maybe before she was a teenager. Her sculptures were supposed to be brilliant beyond words. Nevada knew her work was displayed all over the world, that Caterina was well-known and wealthy.

"You are from a small town, yes?" Caterina asked.

"Fool's Gold. It's in the Sierra Nevada foothills. It's pretty. Quaint. Probably different from your regular life."

Caterina smiled, her piercing green eyes tilting up at the corners. "So you've heard of me. That's good."

"I'm not an expert, of course, but yes. Your work…" She motioned to the sculpture. "It's very beautiful."

Caterina moved next to her and they both faced the piece. "Tell me. What does it make you feel?"

Nevada swallowed. "I, um… I don't really know what you're asking."

"When you look at it, what do you think? What did you think when you first saw it?"

"I'm an engineering student," she began, feeling herself blush. She glanced at Tucker, hoping he would rescue her, but he wasn't looking at her. Instead his gaze was locked on the other woman.

"You're smart, I can tell. What did you feel?"

Nevada swallowed. "Sad. Like something bad had happened."

Caterina threw up her hands and turned in a circle. "Yes. That is it exactly." She grabbed Nevada by the shoulders and kissed her on each cheek. "Thank you."

Nevada blinked a couple of times. "You're welcome, Ms. Stoicasescu."

"Cat, please. All my friends call me that." She linked arms with Nevada and motioned to the metal. "It is the end of war. Not something likely to happen, but I made it as a reminder of the pain we all feel. I didn't plan what it would be. I don't. I am only the vessel. The art comes through me."

Cat turned to her. "So, tell me everything about yourself. I know we are going to be great friends."

Nevada was taken aback. "What do you want to know?"

"All. Start at the beginning. I am from Romania. Do you have brothers or sisters? Yes, you must because that's how Tucker knows you. We must do something together soon. Perhaps go to a party."

"I thought we could get lunch," Tucker told her.

Cat released Nevada and turned to him. Her head tilted slightly, causing her blue-black hair to tumble over one shoulder.

"I thought we would stay in."

The simple words were quietly spoken, yet when Cat said them, everything changed. Electricity and heat filled the air. Nevada had been staring at Tucker, so she saw his eyes dilate and his shoulders stiffen.

Still staring at the beautifully exotic woman between them, Tucker said, "Rain check, Nevada?"

Even with her complete lack of experience when it came to men and sex, Nevada knew what had happened. What *would* happen the second she left. They would make love, right there, on the floor. Because they were together and Cat was the kind of woman who inspired a man to incredible passion.

"Sure," she whispered, already heading for the door.

She felt foolish and young and out of place. Her heart ached as she was forced to accept that Tucker hadn't felt the connection. He thought of her as Ethan's baby sister. He loved Cat.

When she stepped outside, her eyes burned in the bright sunlight. She wanted to go back, to tell him he was wrong. That he should give her a chance.

She turned then, new feelings giving her courage, only to see that Cat and Tucker were already in each other's arms. Their kiss was more intense, more passionate than anything she'd ever seen or imagined. His hands roamed her body, touching, claiming.

Embarrassed, Nevada closed the door behind her and hurried to her truck. Once she'd driven away, she told herself it didn't matter. That she would never see Tucker again. Whatever she'd felt for him would fade as quickly as it had come. In a couple of days she would forget all about him.

CHAPTER THREE

"YOU KNOW I DON'T LIKE TO INTERFERE," Denise Hendrix said as she poured chocolate chips into a bowl.

"If only that were true." Nevada leaned against the counter and watched her mother mix up cookie batter. "You love to interfere."

"No. I love to be right." Her mother smiled at her. "There's a difference."

"A subtle one."

They were in her mother's kitchen, at the Hendrix family home. Nevada had grown up here. There had been various renovations over the years, the most recent a kitchen remodel, but nothing could ever change the fact that this was the home of her heart.

Her mother took the bowl to the cookie sheets and began scooping batter into neat rows. "Do you want to talk about it?"

"There's not much to say. The interview went badly. I was expecting Elliot Janack and I got Tucker instead."

"I thought you liked Tucker."

Nevada thought about how desperately she'd been in love with Tucker all those years ago. Not real love—but she'd been young and foolish and caught in a world she'd been unprepared for. Cat had been as much a revelation as Tucker himself.

"Liking him isn't the problem."

She briefly explained about their short past, the lone sexual encounter, sparing her mother the details. "I was embarrassed about what had happened between us, but he kept bringing it up. I swear, he only wants to hire me now to improve his reputation. I'm not interested in that. The job is a great opportunity, but not under those circumstances."

"Did he ask you to have sex with him so he could redeem himself?"

"No, but I don't want a pity job."

Denise put down the spoon and faced her. "You're saying he wants to give you a job to make up for being bad in bed?"

Nevada winced. "It made more sense when I was just thinking that in my head. With you asking the question, it sounds stupid."

"There's probably a reason for that."

Denise Hendrix had married young and had three boys in less than five years. Determined to have a daughter, she'd gotten pregnant one last time, only to find herself having triplets. She'd handled the shock with her usual grace and humor, raising six children with an ease that left most people amazed.

A widow for the past eleven years, she'd finally started dating. But her social life didn't keep her so busy that she didn't have time to tell her children exactly what she thought. That was both a blessing and a curse.

"If Tucker was genuinely worried about his reputation, he wouldn't hire you," her mother said. "He would run as far and fast as he could, or try to sleep with you now and move on. Why would he risk you telling the entire crew about your night together?"

"He knows I would never do that."

"Does he? It doesn't sound as if he took the time to know you at all."

"Things were complicated back then," Nevada mumbled, not wanting to get into the whole Cat situation. Sure, Tucker had been lousy in bed, but Nevada had been the one throwing herself at him the second she'd found out he and Cat had broken things off. She'd practically begged him to sleep with her. Unfortunately, their brief encounter hadn't won her anything and had instead broken her heart.

"If your dreams matter, then you've been given an excellent opportunity. I'd hate to see you miss it and have regrets later. They can be the hardest thing to live with."

Nevada stared at her mother. "Do you have regrets?"

"Not very many. I've been lucky—I had a wonderful husband and I have my children."

"We are pretty amazing."

Denise laughed. "Yes, you are." She touched Nevada's arm. "This is what you said you wanted. Why let a single night get in the way of that? You're both adults. You can agree to put it behind you and move on."

"You're being rational. That's always unnerving."

"It's important to keep you guessing."

Nevada drew in a breath. "You're right. I do want the job. And it was just one night. Hell, it was five minutes. I should be able to forget that."

Instead of returning to her cookies, Denise walked

to the cordless phone and picked it up. "You can call right now."

Nevada groaned. "This reminds me of the time I took Pia's Teen Talk Barbie and snuck it home. You made me go right back and apologize."

"And you were the better for it."

"Maybe." She stared at the phone. "Okay. I'll call."

Knowing thinking about it too much would only make things harder, she pulled Tucker's business card out of her jeans pocket and dialed. Two rings later, she heard his familiar voice.

"Janack."

"Hendrix," she said before she could stop herself. "Um, it's Nevada."

"Hey. What's up?"

She cleared her throat. "I thought we could finish our interview."

Silence stretched between them. Her insides clenched. Damn him, he was going to tell her no. He was going to say he'd changed his mind.

"Great. You free right now? I'm heading to the job site. I'd like to show you what we're doing."

She opened her mouth and closed it. "Um, sure. I can meet you out there."

"See you in twenty minutes."

He hung up.

Nevada did the same, then set the phone back in the charger. "I'm meeting him at the job site. We're going to talk."

Her mother grinned. "Are you sure that's all you'll be doing?"

"Mo-om."

Denise laughed, then hugged her. "You'll be fine."

"You can't know that."

Denise smiled. "I'm pretty sure."

TUCKER STOOD BY THE SIDE of the road. The first work done by his crew had been to clear an area for parking and heavy equipment. Now with that finished, the real effort would begin. Building a casino-hotel resort would take hundreds of thousands of man-hours and millions of dollars over nearly two years. His plan was to come in early and under budget. For that he needed the right team and a fair amount of luck.

He turned as a light blue Ford Ranger drove toward him. Nevada pulled in next to him and climbed out.

She looked good, he thought, taking in the jeans and T-shirt. Sensible, but sexy. One of his favorite combinations. Not that he would say that to her. He wanted her working for him and that meant they would be spending a lot of hours together. The best way to get through that was to act professionally. Besides, he'd long ago learned that finding any woman irresistible was a disaster. He didn't need to go there again.

"What do you think?" he asked, nodding toward the vast expanse of land.

"It's a hundred acres, right?"

"Yes." He pointed to the east. "We go about a third of the way up the tree line." He indicated the rest of the track. "We'll cut into the mountain."

"Won't that provoke the spirits?" she asked, her brown eyes bright with humor.

"You're forgetting I'm one of them. They're delighted to see me."

"That's right. You're part of the Máa-zib tribe through both your parents?"

He nodded. "About an eighth, give or take a little."

"So technically you or your dad had to be the ones to buy the land. A company couldn't own it."

"Right. We've leased it back to the corporation for the project."

"You're a land baron."

"I'm part owner."

"Still, it's impressive."

"Are you impressed?" he asked.

She grinned. "I could be."

"Tell me what else it would take."

"You could show me the plans for the place."

They walked to his truck and he pulled a copy of the plans out from the backseat. After opening the tailgate, he spread them out.

"We're using every inch of land," he said. "There'll be a road circling the entire development. The casino is here, along with the hotel."

He watched her trace the different elements of the plan.

"You're keeping the grove of the oldest trees," she said, not looking up at him. "I like the walking trails." She moved her finger to the mountain. "This is going to require some serious blasting to remove that much earth."

"Ever done any blasting?"

She turned to him. "No, but I'd like to."

"Stick with me, kid."

"Tempting."

He wasn't surprised she could be wooed more by

the promise of a big explosion than a corner office. Nevada had always been like that—eager, interested. Smart. He remembered her ability to call him on any bull. They had stayed up late a few times, arguing about everything from politics to sustainable construction. She was someone he'd enjoyed talking to, when he'd surfaced from the Cat-induced haze long enough to have a conversation.

He wanted to tell her he was sorry about what happened between them. Not the bad sex, although that was damned humiliating to think about, but the rest of it. He'd wanted to be her friend back then but hadn't been able to think of anyone but Cat.

"I thought there was going to be an outlet mall," she said.

He pulled out another large roll of paper. "We won't be developing it. It's too small a project."

"Aren't you the snob."

"The last project I worked on was a thousand-meter suspension bridge in Africa. No, I don't build malls."

One corner of her mouth turned up. "Of course you don't."

He leaned against the truck. "You're not mad anymore."

"I wasn't mad." She straightened. "This is a great opportunity. You're bringing a lot to the town."

"We appreciate their cooperation."

"Don't you always get that?"

"Some towns aren't interested in change or growth."

"Fool's Gold isn't like that. This project will bring a lot of jobs and tourists. We already get a decent tourist trade, but nothing like the numbers this will bring in."

"Why'd you come back? You could have found plenty of jobs in other places."

"This is my home. I grew up here. My family founded this town." She smiled. "In a settler kind of way. Obviously the Máa-zib tribe was here first."

"Obviously."

He understood the concept of roots, he just couldn't relate to it. He'd never had anywhere particular to call home. His dad had always kept a condo in Chicago but they'd rarely been there. His home was wherever the next project was.

"Want to hear about your team?"

"Sure."

He told her about the guys who would be working for her. She would be in charge of clearing the construction area. When that was done, her team would shift to working with several others on the hotel.

"I'm also interested in having you as a liaison with the town," he said. "If we run into trouble."

"I don't think you will, but sure. I can talk to whomever you like."

"You know the guys might give you a hard time at first."

She shrugged. "I have three brothers. I'm not sure there's much they can do to shock me. Plus, I've been in construction a long time."

He wanted to say he would be there to protect her, but didn't. Not only would she have to figure it out herself, *protection* implied a level of caring inappropriate for a work relationship. They were colleagues, nothing more. The fact that he could breathe in her soft, sweet scent was immaterial. As was the way the sun turned her short hair into a hundred different colors of blond.

It was being around her again after all this time, he told himself. He'd worked with lots of women over the years and had never noticed one of them as anything more than a coworker. In a few days, Nevada would just be one of the guys.

"We start the surveying on Monday," he said. "Want to be here for that?"

"Are you offering me the job?"

"I already did. You turned me down. Are you going to make me beg?"

"I probably should."

"I'm not very good at it."

She gave him a slow smile. "Then you need to practice more."

"Is that what this is? A coaching opportunity?"

"I like to help where I can."

He pushed off the truck and moved in front of her. "Nevada, I would like to have you here as one of my construction managers. Yes or no?"

"That's not exactly begging."

"Maybe not, but it's sincere."

"We're both going to pretend the past never happened," she said, rather than asking a question. "We'll start over."

"Agreed."

"Then I very much want the job."

Pleased, he held out his hand. "Good. Let's head into town and talk about the details."

She placed her hand in his. He was unprepared for

the brush of her skin, the feel of her fingers, the jolt of awareness that sizzled its way to his groin.

After squeezing once, he released her and did his best to act casual as he stepped back. Well, dammit all to hell, he thought grimly. He could have gone a lifetime without feeling that.

Nevada appeared unfazed by the contact, which made him doubly stupid.

"Are you going to be staying in a hotel while you're here?" she was asking. "If you want a house to rent, I could ask around."

"I prefer a hotel. It's easier."

"Because someone else does the cooking and cleaning?"

"Of course."

"Typical guy."

"Most days." He walked her to her truck. "Meet me in the lobby of Ronan's Lodge in twenty minutes. I'll bring the employment agreement."

She nodded and climbed into the cab, but didn't close the door. "Do you ever talk to her? Cat?"

The question surprised him. "No. Not in years. Not since we broke up. You?"

Nevada shook her head. "Cat wasn't my friend."

"She liked you. As much as she could like anyone."

"There's a statement."

"You know what she was like."

Nevada looked at him then. He saw something flash through her eyes. Unable to read the emotion, he could only wonder. Hurt? Anger? No way he could guess. Feelings were a complication lost on most mortal men.

A truck drove up the road and parked next to them.

"That's Will," Tucker said. "You need to meet him. He's my right-hand guy, although he'll tell you he's in charge."

"I am in charge," Will said, walking toward them. "Ask him how many times I've saved his ass."

"Can anyone count that high?" Nevada asked, climbing out of her truck and grinning.

Will winked at her, then turned to Tucker. "I knew I'd like her. Tell me she said yes."

"She did."

"Welcome to the team," Will said, shaking hands with her. "Will Falk."

"Nevada Hendrix."

"Tucker was going to give me the employment contract to look over," Nevada said. "Want to come watch me sign?"

"There's nothing I'd like better," Will said. "Meet you in town."

Probably for the best, Tucker told himself as they got into separate vehicles and headed back into Fool's Gold. Until he figured out why touching Nevada had impacted him, the last thing he needed was to spend time alone with her in a hotel. Now that they were working together, anything personal was off-limits. Of that he was sure.

"WHAT?" ETHAN ASKED. "There's something wrong."

Denise Hendrix looked at her oldest son. She still remembered the day she'd brought him home from the hospital. She'd been married all of a year, had barely turned twenty and didn't have a clue what she was doing. Her mother-in-law had still been alive. Although the two women had never been close, Eleanor had shown up within fifteen minutes of Denise and Ralph bringing their baby home.

"I'm here if you need me," the somewhat stern, large-boned woman had announced. "I know what you're going through, but I don't want to interfere."

Denise had assured her mother-in-law that she would be fine. That level of bravado lasted until the next morning, when Ralph went off to work and Ethan started to cry. He wouldn't stop, wouldn't eat, and although he didn't have a fever, Denise had panicked. She'd called Eleanor and begged her to come over.

It had taken Ethan's grandmother all of two minutes to quiet the baby. She'd stood by while Denise had struggled to get her newborn to nurse, had offered sensible advice and never said a word to Ralph about her daily visits.

"I miss your grandmother," Denise said.

Ethan stared at her. "That's why you came by my office? She's been gone twenty years."

"That's not why I stopped by. But I was thinking about her. She was wonderful to me. Do you remember her at all?"

"Sure. When we spent the night with her, we got to stay up as late as we wanted and we could watch anything. Every single time, I picked some horror movie you wouldn't have let me see, and I scared myself so much I couldn't sleep. Then I crawled in bed with her and Grandpa and she would sing to me until I wasn't afraid."

Denise smiled. "That sounds like her."

"But she's not why you're here."

"No. I'm not sure what to do about Tucker Janack. I need your advice." Neither statement was true. She knew exactly what to do about Tucker, but she didn't say that to Ethan. Better to let him come to his own conclusions.

Ethan frowned. "About what? Nevada's going to work for him. She told me she was accepting the job."

"I know and I'm glad. It's just…" She drew in a breath. "They have a past. Remember when Nevada was in college and you asked her to look up Tucker?"

"Sure. I thought he would be a good person for her to know. In case something happened, or she needed advice about school. Engineering's a tough major, and he'd already been through it."

"She did go see him. They were friends. Then…" She waved her hand. "Never mind. I shouldn't discuss this with you."

Ethan's frown turned into a scowl. "Too late now. What happened?"

"He got drunk and they slept together. He was involved with someone else, but they had briefly broken up. He took advantage of Nevada and then went back to his girlfriend. Nevada was crushed, of course. I get sick when I think about it. That man and my little girl."

In truth Denise wasn't happy about what had happened, and she did want Tucker punished. She also believed that sometimes children had to learn by making mistakes and living through the consequences. But Tucker had gone too far.

Ethan nodded once. "I'll take care of it, Mom. Don't worry."

"I knew I could count on you. You've always been there for me and for everyone else in the family."

She rose. Ethan stood as well and walked her to the door.

"Don't worry," he repeated and kissed her cheek.

"Thank you."

Relieved and not the least bit guilty, Denise walked out of the office. There were those who wouldn't agree with what she'd done, but she didn't care. No one messed with her family.

JO TRELLIS LOOKED at the boxes piled in the back of her SUV and wondered if maybe she'd gotten a little carried away. She supposed part of the problem was that she was excited about the thought of her friends having babies, and that she would get to watch those kids grow up. She didn't have any children of her own, nor was she likely to. So she would live vicariously through her friends—Aunt Jo to the new generation in Fool's Gold.

Within a few months, Charity's daughter would be crawling and some months after that, Pia's twins would join her. Dakota's daughter was nearly nine months old already, and Dakota was pregnant with her second child. That explained the various toys Jo had bought.

She'd already figured out that the back corner of the main room would make the perfect play area. Ethan had sent over one of his guys to install removable posts. She'd bought child-safe fencing, to keep the kids in and her customers out. With a little rearranging, she could have tables right by the play area, so moms could visit, their kids could play and everyone would be happy.

She picked up the smallest of the boxes and carried

it inside easily. But the carton with the toddler-size kitchen was going to be a problem.

"Need some help?"

She glanced over her shoulder and saw a tall man moving toward her. He had a slight limp, but powerful shoulders and arms. His sandy hair was just long enough and his dark blue eyes brightened with amusement.

"That box is nearly as big as you."

Her instinct was to tell him she was fine. It was her policy to avoid conversations with strange men. She would say with *all* men, but that wasn't an option in her line of work. So she'd learned to be friendly without ever letting anyone cross the line. However, she'd been in Fool's Gold long enough to know that life was all about community. Over the past few years she'd learned to trust other people and, most importantly, herself.

The man paused by her SUV. "Will Falk," he said.

"Jo Trellis." She studied his worn jeans and chambray shirt. "You're with Janack Construction."

"That's me." He reached for the box and drew it out easily.

Remembering how she'd struggled to get it into her SUV, she tried not to be bitter. Men naturally had more upper body strength than women.

"Where do you want this?" he asked.

She led the way in through the back, passing from the storage room to the main part of the bar. She pointed to the corner she'd cleared.

"Over there."

Will set down the box, then straightened. "Kid toys in a bar?"

"A lot of my customers are having babies."

"They bring them to a bar?" He sounded shocked.

She allowed herself to smile. "I get a big lunch and afternoon crowd. They're here to socialize rather than get drunk. I'll put the toys away before the evening customers arrive. Don't worry. No one in Fool's Gold is corrupting infants."

But Will wasn't listening. Instead he was turning in a slow circle, taking in the mauve walls, the big TVs tuned to a marathon of *America's Next Top Model,* and the comfortable chairs with backs and hooks for purses up by the bar.

"What is this place?" he asked.

"It's a bar."

"I've been in plenty of bars."

"You men have a room in back. It's very traditional. Dark colors, a pool table and plenty of sports."

He still looked lost.

"Fool's Gold has a large female population," she explained. "Most of the businesses cater to women, including mine."

"I see," he said slowly.

She laughed. "If you're going to be here awhile, you'll need to get used to it."

She walked back to her car. He followed.

"Don't get me wrong," he told her. "I like women. I've never known a bar that catered to them, but I'm good with that."

She thought about warning him that just because there were a lot of women around didn't mean he would

find it easy to interest one of them. Most of her customers came to hang out with their friends and talk about
their problems. They weren't all that worried about
meeting guys. But he could figure that out on his own.

Will helped her carry in the rest of the boxes. Just
when she was about to thank him and suggest he leave,
he started opening cartons with a pocketknife.

"You're in management, aren't you?" she asked.

He laughed. "Kicking and screaming I was dragged
there. Why?"

"You're taking charge."

"Want to tell me no?"

"I appreciate the help," she admitted, aware she
wouldn't have had time to unpack everything before
her lunch crowd arrived.

"Happy to give it." He pulled out a brightly colored
plastic refrigerator. "Cute."

"I thought it would be fun."

The tiny stove came next.

"How long have you lived here?" he asked.

"A few years now. It's a good town. Friendly people." People who had accepted her without asking a lot
of questions. She knew they were curious, but no one
pushed. She appreciated that.

"Good. We're here a couple of years with the new
project. A place like this beats a bridge-build in the
middle of Africa. I love being outdoors as much as
the next guy, but every now and then I really want a
burger."

"You move around a lot?"

"It goes with the territory. Janack Construction is
multinational. I've been working with them since I

graduated high school. Known Tucker since he was a kid." He moved on to the next box, which contained a toddler-size tricycle. "Now he's the one in charge of what we're doing here. Time flies."

Jo would guess Will was in his early forties. "What does your family think about you being gone so much?" She asked the question without thinking, but as soon as the words left her mouth, she realized how they could be interpreted.

Will straightened and faced her. "There's just me."

She nodded and found herself glancing away from his steady gaze. An unfamiliar nervousness ripped through her. The second she recognized the feeling, she wanted to hold up her hands in the shape of a T and demand a time-out.

No, she told herself firmly. No boy–girl chitchat for her. No smiling, no getting involved, no caring. She'd been down that path and it had led to a disaster she was still paying for. Relationships were dangerous. For some people, they were lethal.

"That would make the travel easier," she said, taking a step back. "I appreciate your help. If you'll excuse me, I have to get ready to open."

She retreated behind the bar. The long expanse of wood made her feel a little safer. Sometimes something as simple as a physical barrier helped remind her that she was in control of her life now.

Will quickly finished unpacking the toys. He broke down the boxes, storing them in the largest one, and took them out back to her recycling bin. Then he came back to stand by the bar.

"Thanks for your help," she began.

"You're welcome. I was thinking I'd have lunch here."

He appealed to her. She couldn't deny that. The man had kind eyes and she long ago learned that kindness was a vastly underrated trait in a person.

"You seem like a perfectly nice man, but the answer is no."

One eyebrow rose. "You're assuming a lot."

"Maybe, but I'm not changing my story."

He stood there, all tall and friendly. Nice. That was it. Will Falk was a nice guy. He'd helped her and she'd blown him off.

The reasons were legitimate, but he didn't know that. She sighed.

"It's not personal," she said. "I don't get involved with men."

"Playing for the other team?"

Despite the uncomfortable situation, Jo smiled. "No. I'm not a lesbian."

She waited for him to say they didn't have to get involved. That it could just be sex. In her gut, she knew that kind of offer would tempt her. It had been a long, long time since she'd been with a man.

The door to her bar opened and several women from city hall walked in. They waved at Jo before finding their way to a table by the window. In the next minute, twelve more customers came in, including a couple of guys she didn't recognize, but who appeared to be from the construction site. They called out to Will, but settled in a booth.

"I can see you're busy," Will said. "We'll pick this up later."

"There's no point."

"I'm not so sure about that."

The door opened again and Ethan Hendrix walked in. He glanced around the bar, then walked over to the table with the construction guys. One of them stood. Before Jo realized what was happening, Ethan drew back his arm and punched the guy in the jaw.

Jo glanced at the clock. It wasn't even noon yet. Looked like this was going to be a very long day.

CHAPTER FOUR

TUCKER ADJUSTED THE bag of ice on his jaw. The bartender—Ethan had said her name was Jo—watched him warily.

"I said I'm not going to hit him back," he said, knowing he'd deserved the punch and more.

"Forgive me if I don't believe you," she said, then turned her attention to Ethan. "You do that again and you're banned from here."

"I didn't break anything."

"You know how I feel about fights in my bar. Do you want me to talk to Liz?"

"No," Ethan told her, quickly, looking a little panicked. "Don't tell my wife. I won't do it again."

"You'd better not." She walked away to serve a customer.

"Strange bar," Tucker muttered as he felt along his jawline. It didn't hurt too much. He was hoping the ice would keep down the swelling and bruising. Two crews were showing up in the next few days. He didn't want to have to explain a bruise to any of them or listen to their speculation about why he'd been hit.

Next to him, Ethan clenched and unclenched his right hand. "Damn, that hurt."

"You're not getting any sympathy from me," Tucker told him. "What the hell were you thinking?"

"Want me to ask the same question?"

"No. If I had a sister, I would have done the same thing."

"Damn straight you would have." Ethan glared at him. "I expected you to protect her, not sleep with her."

"You realize it happened ten years ago."

"Do you think that matters?"

Tucker set the bag of ice on the bar. "Probably not. For what it's worth, I didn't mean for it to happen. I was drunk."

Ethan's gaze turned cold again. "You want to tell me the details?"

"Uh, no. You're right."

Ethan slugged him in the arm. "I trusted you."

"I know."

"You let me down."

Guilt crawled all over Tucker. "I'm sorry. I don't know what else to say." Bad enough that Ethan knew about that night. Worse if he knew the circumstances.

"My mom thinks it was her first time."

Anyone who said words could cut like a knife was wrong. Words were a hammer to the gut. Tucker sucked in a breath as the potential truth of that statement hit him upside the head.

A virgin? No. She couldn't have been. He groaned, knowing that would make what had happened a thousand times worse. Bad enough to take her while he was skunk drunk, but to have fumbled and called out Cat's name to a virgin...

"Kill me now," he muttered, putting his elbows on the bar and resting his head in his hands. "Wait." He straightened. "Your mother knows?"

"She's close to her daughters."

"Apparently. Who else…" He shook his head. "Don't tell me."

Nevada a virgin? She'd been eighteen. It was possible. With his luck, it was likely.

He couldn't remember much about that night except that it had been quick and pretty bad. How was he supposed to apologize for that? What was he supposed to say? He'd been caught up in the storm of loving Cat. Everything else had been a blur. Sure he'd learned his lesson—never be a fool for love. But that didn't excuse anything, especially his behavior with Nevada.

Jo walked over and placed beers in front of both of them. "Better," she said. "Looks like you two have made up. Are you eating?"

"Lunch is on me," Tucker said weakly.

"You bet your ass it is," Ethan told him, grabbing both beers. "We'll get a table in the back. Burgers okay?"

Tucker nodded and followed his friend.

They left the main part of the bar and went into a space that reminded Tucker a whole lot more of the bars he was used to. TVs mounted on the walls were tuned to baseball games. There were round tables, chairs without padding and a big pool table in the center.

"Interesting place," Tucker said as they sat across from each other.

"Home," Ethan said simply. "Except for college, I've never lived anywhere else." He passed Tucker one of the beers. "You must get tired of traveling all the time."

Tucker grabbed the beer and took a swallow. "It's all I know. Tell me why this is better."

Ethan gave him a slow, satisfied smile, then reached into his back pocket and pulled out his wallet. He passed over a picture. It showed Ethan with a beautiful redhead. She was looking at him the way every man fantasized about being looked at. A combination of love and pride and contentment.

"You don't deserve her."

Ethan chuckled. "Tell me about it. Liz is incredible. Sexy as hell, smart, a great mom. She loves with everything she has. I don't know why she picked me, but she did and I'm not letting go."

The simple words, honestly spoken, made Tucker feel uncomfortable. As if he'd accidentally walked in on something intimate, something he wasn't supposed to see. He couldn't imagine feelings like that. Loving someone and being loved in a way that was supportive and safe. In his world, love was a trap. A man could get lost in love, and sometimes getting away meant chewing off an arm.

"Then there's these three."

Ethan handed over a second picture. This one showed three kids—two girls and a boy. The girls were redheads, the older, maybe fourteen or fifteen, was probably already causing havoc at high school. The younger was an adorable carrottop with freckles. The boy, about the same age as the younger girl, was all Ethan.

"You've been busy," Tucker said, passing back the picture. "Did I know you've been married that long?"

"Liz and I got married last summer. Tyler's mine. Long story. The girls are her nieces. Their mom is dead and their dad's in jail, so we have them now." He put the pictures back into his wallet. "If you'd told me about taking in two kids a year ago, I would have said if they're not yours you can't love them as much, right?"

Ethan shook his head. "I couldn't have been more wrong. Those girls keep me up nights just as much as Tyler does. Melissa wants to start dating. I want to lock her in her room until she's forty." He grinned. "We're working on a compromise."

"You sound like you're happy."

"I am." Ethan picked up his beer. "It doesn't get better than this." He stared at Tucker. "You ever going to settle down?"

"I'm not the type. I move around too much."

"When you take over the company, you'll travel less."

"Maybe. I'm not sure I want to change. I like living all over the world, seeing new things."

"Don't you get lonely?"

Tucker leaned back in his chair. "There are beautiful women everywhere, or are you so married you've forgotten."

"Just not interested. Why go looking when you have the best of everything waiting at home?"

The fervor of the freshly converted, Tucker thought. He'd seen it before. Guys who were newly in love wanted everyone else to have what they did. The problem was they didn't see that love would turn them all into fools until it was too late. Cat had done it to him, and his dad's women did it to him on a regular basis. Tucker had learned his lesson.

Except now, talking to Ethan, he felt a hint of something that might be envy. Roots could be good. A place to call home. Someone waiting.

No way, he reminded himself. He'd tried that once. Cat had nearly destroyed him. Not by anything she'd done, but his reaction to her. He'd allowed her to become everything. He'd been little more than her love slave. By the time he'd managed to escape, he barely recognized himself. No. Love was for idiots who didn't know better.

"You're going to be around here for, what? A year?" Ethan asked.

"About that. I won't stay through completion, but I'll want to make sure the major elements are in place."

"Ever spent any quality time in a small town before?"

"No."

Ethan laughed. "Brace yourself. It's not what you think. Within a month, everyone will know who you are, what you do with your day and who with. You won't be able to make a move without running into someone you know. Stay clear of the local women. They'll eat you alive—and not in a good way."

"Sounds worse than construction in a rain forest. Why do you stay?"

"Because there's nowhere else I want to be. I grew up here. I belong. I want to know my neighbors, have them watching out for the kids and letting me know when a friend is in trouble. They have my back and I have theirs."

"I can't relate," Tucker admitted.

"You'll get a taste of it. Be sure to head into town every weekend. Fool's Gold is known for its many festivals. They happen regularly. The food is always good. Come winter, we can head up the mountain and go skiing."

"I'd like that. I haven't skied in a couple of years."

"Good. If you think you can handle it, we'll have you over to dinner. Or is that too domestic?"

"I can survive a few hours."

Ethan grinned. "We could even invite a couple of the local single ladies. Let them fight over you."

"You said to steer clear of them."

"Maybe you want the challenge. As long as it's not my sister."

Tucker thought about Nevada. "Hands off. You have my word."

"I'd better."

Tucker took a swallow of his beer. Thirty minutes ago, he would have considered Nevada a hell of a temptation. Now, not so much. While he still found her intriguing, he'd already crossed the line once. He wasn't a jerk. He knew when to back off, and with her, that was now.

NEVADA WAS SO EXCITED that despite not having slept, she needed no coffee to be completely wired for her first day of work. She arrived on the job site nearly an hour before she was expected and hung out in the main trailer, opening and closing the empty drawers in her new desk and going over the schedule for the week.

The first order of business was to get equipment in place and start clearing. A part of that would include blasting a section of the east hillside. She flipped through the pile of paperwork required by the city, county and state. She saw that the Fool's Gold Fire Department had to be notified of the blasting and have a representative on-site. At least that was something she could help with. She knew all the firefighters.

Once the land was cleared, the plumbing would be next. Water in, sewer out. Due to some seriously impressive long-term planning on the part of the city nearly fifty years ago, the resort would be able to tap into the city sewer and water system. That would be a huge savings in money and effort for Janack Construction. The downside was a lot more permits, but they were worth it.

She'd just started reading the environmental impact study when she heard footsteps on the trailer steps. Will Falk walked inside.

"Someone's here bright and early," he said before taking a long drink from the coffee carryout cup he held.

"It's my first day. I couldn't help it."

"Enthusiasm is good. It makes me feel old, but it's still good." He held open the door. "Come on. I'll introduce you to the guys you'll be working with."

She rose and grabbed her hard hat, then followed him outside.

While she'd been acquainting herself with the project, about a dozen guys had arrived for work. Pickups lined the small cleared area by the trailer.

The men stood together, dressed in jeans, work boots and T-shirts. It was still summer in Fool's Gold and, even out here, the temperatures would climb to the low eighties.

As she and Will approached, the men grew silent,

watching her. She kept her head up and her shoulders back. Project confidence, she told herself. No one had to know about the butterflies kickboxing in her stomach.

"Morning," Will said. "I'd like you to meet our new construction manager, Nevada Hendrix. She's local, so if you're having any trouble in town, she's the one you go to. If you're making trouble in town, she'll be the one kicking your butts." He glanced at her. "You good with that?"

"I can kick butt," she said firmly.

The guys ranged in age from early twenties to late forties. The veterans were the ones she had to win over first, she thought. They would be less concerned about her being a woman and more interested in her skill set. The younger guys would have more ego on the line.

Will made introductions. She shook hands with everyone and did her best to remember names. It would take a little longer to get to know personalities, but she had time.

The surveying team would arrive within the hour. Will suggested which guys would help with that. She agreed and put the others to work clearing. For a second, she stared enviously at the big equipment, but knew there would be plenty of time to have her way with the tracked excavator.

The morning flew by. Nevada surfaced long enough to head to the portable outhouses, only to find one had been draped in pink ribbon. She checked inside to make sure it was free of rodents and creepy-crawlies, then used it. After washing her hands at the portable sink, she went back into the office, made a sign that said

Girls Only, taped it to the outhouse door, then went out to join the surveying team.

Will came by around noon to tell them to break for lunch. Nevada had planned to join the guys, but Will pulled her aside before she could settle in.

"Doing okay?" he asked, as they walked back to the trailer.

"Sure."

"Like what you've done with the place." He motioned to the porta potty as he spoke.

"Thanks. I like the pink."

He chuckled. They went into the trailer and got out their lunches from the small refrigerator. Will sat on the edge of his desk.

"What do you know about Jo Trellis?" he asked, as he removed a sandwich from a bag.

Nevada stared at him. "You get right to the point. I take it you're interested?"

"Could be."

Nevada thought about the question. Jo had arrived in Fool's Gold several years ago and bought the bar. She was friendly, a regular participant in girls' night out, always there when someone had a crisis. But in all the time Nevada had known her, she'd never seen Jo on a date or heard her talk about a guy.

"Jo's my friend," she began.

"I'm not interested in getting laid and moving on," Will told her. "I'm too old for that. I'd like to get to know her. She's resisting the process."

Nevada smiled. "I'm not surprised. Jo keeps to herself. She's a friend, but even I don't know anything about her past. She never talks about it."

"Any men?"

"No. There have been offers, but she always refuses."

"Know why?"

Nevada shook her head. "There are dozens of theories. Everything from Jo being a Mafia princess on the run from her father to her escaping an abusive husband. I doubt either is true."

Mayor Marsha probably knew all about Jo's past, as the good mayor seemed to know everything about everyone. Nevada had never been able to figure out how she got her information. But even if the mayor did know the truth, Nevada knew she wouldn't share it with Will.

"I don't have any dating advice when it comes to Jo," she admitted. "I guess you're on your own. I will warn you not to hurt her. She's one of us and we protect our own." Will was a good guy and she liked him, but family came first.

He nodded slowly. "I'm glad she has friends looking out for her."

"One of the advantages of a small town. Are you finding it enjoyable here, or are the walls closing in?"

"I like it. I heard there's going to be a festival soon. I'm looking forward to it."

"Don't worry. If you miss this one, there will be another one in the next couple of weeks. We're known for our festivals."

She heard someone on the steps, then the trailer door opened. She expected one of the guys to walk in, but instead Tucker stepped through the doorway.

Will glanced at his watch. "Nearly noon. Going for a personal best?"

"I was filing paperwork at city hall. Fool's Gold hasn't embraced the digital age." He looked at Nevada. "Sorry. I meant to be here on your first morning. Did Will get you settled?"

"Yes. I'm doing fine. Don't worry about it."

She managed to speak the words and act normal, but her gaze settled on the faint shadow of a bruise on his jaw.

News of Ethan hitting Tucker had spread quickly. Outside of her immediate family, no one knew the reason, which left people speculating.

Will excused himself to talk to the surveyor. For a second, Nevada thought about escaping with him, but knew she had to talk to Tucker eventually.

"I'm sorry about what happened with my brother," she said as soon as the door closed behind Will.

Tucker rubbed his jaw. "He's good. Nailed me one."

She did her best to remind herself that there was no reason to get embarrassed. Her brother had been looking out for her and there was nothing bad in that. It was just the idea of them fighting in public that made her squirm. And everyone knowing why.

"He shouldn't have hit you."

"If the situation had been reversed, I would have done the same."

She rolled her eyes. "Because you couldn't simply have a conversation? I'm not sorry he defended me, but there were a lot better ways to do it."

"I don't agree with that, but okay." He crossed to the small refrigerator and pulled out a bottle of water.

"Ethan did say something interesting," he told her, before pausing to drink.

Panic exploded, making her chest tighten. She waited, hoping it wasn't anything hideous. Like, "Nevada never got over you," or, "It's kind of funny how she was so in love with you and you only had eyes for Cat." Not that Ethan would know any of that, but still.

Tucker lowered the bottle and looked at her. "He said it was your first time."

Involuntary reactions were a bitch, she thought grimly as she felt color flare on her cheeks. She ignored the sensation, grabbed her sandwich and held it up like a pitiful protective shield.

"Don't flatter yourself," she hedged. "I had a boyfriend in high school."

Tucker studied her for a second, relief battling with concern. "You sure?"

"It's something I would remember." She took a bite of her sandwich and forced herself to chew. After she swallowed, she managed a faint laugh. "Don't sweat it. You were not my first time."

"Good. Because that would have made a difference."

"You were pretty drunk. I don't think that kind of information would have helped."

"Probably not." He shook his head. "So we're done talking about this?"

"You're the one who brought it up. But, yes, we can be done."

"Friends?"

"Of course. Always."

She'd never thought of herself as Tucker's friend. She was the girl he hadn't noticed, despite her love for him.

He was the one who got away. But a friend? Maybe it was something to try. After all, they were going to be working together and she wasn't stupid enough to fall for him a second time.

AFTER LUNCH NEVADA went outside and checked on the surveying team. A hundred acres was a lot to deal with, so they worked on a grid. Her attention kept drifting to where the guys were using the real equipment to clear.

A timber company had already been through to take out the biggest trees. The heaviest growth was being left intact. The walking path would weave through it.

One of the guys—she thought his name was Brad— walked up to her, holding one hand in the other.

"Cut myself," he said. "Do you have any bandages in your truck?"

"Sure, but there's a first-aid kit in the office."

He shook his head. "Using that means filling out paperwork."

She hesitated. The last thing anyone wanted was more paperwork, so if the cut was small, she would go along with his request. Later, she would talk to Will and find out if she'd made the right call, or if the guys were trying to get her in trouble. After all, she was new to the team, not to mention female.

She hurried to her truck and pulled open the passenger door. As she reached for the glove box, she saw something move on the bench seat.

A snake was coiled up on the driver's seat.

Nevada managed to keep from jumping, more out of self-protection than bravery. She studied the dark brown color, the light stripes along the side and knew it was a garter snake. Harmless, and not too old, judging by the length.

Several facts clicked into place. The test wasn't about breaking the rules, it was about cojones. She would bet money Brad hadn't been cut at all. The guys had simply wanted to get her to open her truck door and see the snake.

The creatures weren't her favorite, but she'd grown up with three brothers and, to borrow from the Texans, this wasn't her first rodeo.

Drawing in a deep breath, she reached across the seat and grabbed the snake. From what she remembered, it would bite. It wasn't considered poisonous to humans, but she grabbed it by the back of the neck to avoid getting punctured.

The poor thing practically whimpered as it recoiled and tried to squirm away. Its body wrapped around her arm, then let go as quickly. She straightened and stepped away from her truck. When she turned, she saw her whole team standing behind her.

"One of you missing your girlfriend?" she asked.

The guys exchanged glances, then started to laugh.

She walked to the edge of the thicker growth and let the snake go.

"How long did it take you to catch it?" she asked.

"Nearly all morning," Brad told her. "We thought you'd scream."

"Sorry to disappoint you."

One of the older guys grinned. "We're not disappointed at all."

"Glad to hear it. Now, let's get to work."

FRIDAY AFTERNOON Nevada found herself walking through Fool's Gold with Tucker. She'd gone with him to file more paperwork and now they were heading back to his truck to return to the job site.

"So when's the next festival?" he asked. "I keep hearing about them."

"Next weekend, although there's plenty going on tomorrow. The Fool's Gold cheerleaders are back from camp and will be showing off everything they've learned. That's always fun."

"The town has cheerleaders?"

"They're from the high school. We do like to celebrate here, so any excuse will do."

"I've heard that."

They turned a corner and walked toward the parking lot.

"You enjoying yourself at work?"

She nodded, aware of him walking close to her. The days were still warm, so she was in a T-shirt. Every now and then her bare arm brushed against his. She told herself not to notice, that the whispers of heat had nothing to do with the man and everything to do with…

She sighed. She would have to come up with some handy excuses to trot out when she needed them.

Working with Tucker was both easier and harder than she'd thought it would be. He was a fair boss, who trusted his team to get the work done. That was the good part. He was also a hunky guy with whom she shared relatively close office space. In the trailer, as here on the narrow sidewalks, it was difficult not to be aware of him.

"I thought the guys might put a bigger snake in my

truck, but I guess I passed the test." She glanced at him. "Unless you told them to back off."

"Nope. You want the job, you have to be able to handle yourself with the guys. I figured you'd hit me harder than Ethan if you found out I was going behind your back."

"Good. Because that's true."

He grinned. "You'd have to catch me first."

A group of teenage girls walked toward them. Both she and Tucker moved to the right, stepping into the doorway of a clothing boutique to let the girls pass. The space was small and she found herself crowded up against him, her butt pressing against his hip.

She told herself to ignore the heat and the way her hand bumped his.

"Hey, Nevada."

It took her a second to realize one of the girls was Melissa. "Ah, hi. What's going on?"

"We're getting ice cream." Melissa looked past her to Tucker and raised her eyebrows.

"This is my new boss. Tucker Janack, Melissa Sutton. She's my niece."

Melissa grinned. "Sort of. I guess explaining our relationship would be too complicated." Melissa waved and hurried after her friends. "Nice to meet you."

"That's one of Ethan's girls, right?" Tucker said as they started walking again.

"Yes."

"I saw her picture when Ethan and I had lunch."

They'd reached the truck. He held open the passenger door for her.

"Explain that to me," she said, not yet climbing in.

"How can he punch you and then the two of you have lunch?"

"We'd worked through everything. Why not have lunch and catch up?"

"Men are very strange."

He laughed.

She stepped into the truck, but her boot slipped on the metal by the door. She started to fall forward. Even as she put out a hand to brace herself, Tucker wrapped an arm around her waist and pulled her back.

For the second time in as many minutes, she found herself pressed against him in a tight space.

Her body enjoyed the moment, getting all tingly and aware. She knew this was potentially dangerous, not to mention foolish, so she told herself to act as if nothing had happened and everything was fine.

"I'm good," she said.

"I don't want my newest employee getting hurt on the job and suing the company," he told her gruffly as he released her.

"I wouldn't do that."

She went to climb into the truck, only to find herself shifting toward him instead. She wasn't sure if she was the one doing the turning, or if he was helping. Either way, she was suddenly facing him, their bodies still close, his dark eyes staring into hers.

Without wanting to, she found herself moving back through time. Instead of being in a Fool's Gold parking lot, she was standing in the living room of a Hollywood Hills mansion.

She'd only gone to the party because it was a chance to spend time with Tucker again. Even if Cat was the one to ask her. She'd known the evening would be miserable, but she couldn't help herself.

Standing in a sea of people she didn't know, she realized she should have stayed back at the dorm. Despite all the celebrities circling around, she only had eyes for Tucker and he could only see Cat.

Tucker followed her around like a puppy, his tongue practically hanging out. Even with Nevada's inexperience, she knew he was putting it all on the line. While Cat seemed to like him, her gaze lacked the desperate need Tucker had in his.

"Do I know you?"

Nevada looked at the tall, movie-star-handsome guy walking toward her, only to realize he *was* a movie star. His summer blockbuster had made millions and he'd been on the cover of *People* magazine.

"I don't think so," she said, wishing she could get half as fluttery at the sight of him as she did when she saw Tucker.

"You could," he said. "Get to know me."

He was obviously drunk and maybe a little high, if his dilated pupils were anything to go by.

"No, thanks."

"I can change your mind."

He'd grabbed her arm then, tugging her toward the back of the house. She pulled away and was about to use the tricks her brothers had taught her when Tucker appeared at her side.

"Not so fast," he'd said easily, removing the other man's hand from her arm. "This one's with me."

"Oh, sorry, man. I didn't know."

The other guy took off. Tucker pulled Nevada against him.

"I can see you're not to be trusted on your own," he told her. "You'll get eaten alive in a crowd like this. Stick close, kid. I'll get you out of here in one piece."

Then he'd kissed her. A light, friendly kiss that had probably meant nothing to him but had rocked her world. She'd wanted to pull him close so she could kiss him again.

Then Cat had strolled up and it was as if Nevada didn't exist. Tucker had physically stayed in place, but she'd seen the change come over him. In his world, there was only Cat and not Cat. There was no middle ground. No chance for anyone else to matter.

"Nevada?"

She jerked herself back to the present and found that she was pressing against Tucker. His expression was curious.

"You okay?"

"Fine," she said as she quickly turned and climbed into the truck.

He went around and got in on the other side. "Ready to go back?"

She knew he meant to the job site, so she nodded. But what she was thinking was, no, she wasn't going back. She was never going to be in that position again. Wanting someone she could never have had been one of the worst experiences in her life.

CHAPTER FIVE

MONDAY MORNING, Nevada saw a car and a small SUV on the side of the road. She was on her way to the job site, north of town, and there wasn't usually much traffic. Two women stood beside the car. Nevada pulled over to see if she could help.

As she got out of her truck, she recognized the tall, pretty blonde as Heidi Simpson, the goat girl. Heidi and her grandfather had recently moved to the area and purchased the Castle Ranch, just west of the job site. Years before, the ranch had been a viable business, with cattle and horses. She remembered going out to the ranch as a kid for pony rides.

The owner had died and the place had been abandoned until Heidi and her grandfather had bought it. Instead of raising cattle, Heidi had goats and was making artisanal cheese.

"Hi," Nevada called as she approached the women. "Everything okay?"

Heidi moved toward her, shaking her head. "We have a flat tire." She pointed to the petite redhead. "This is Annabelle Weiss."

"The new librarian," Annabelle said with a wry smile. "I just got into town yesterday and was driving around, getting to know the place. A plan that ended badly." She motioned to her left rear tire.

"I can call someone from town to come help," Nevada said, pulling her cell phone out of her pocket.

"No service," Heidi said. "We're hit-and-miss out at the ranch, too. But I have a landline, so I was going to take Annabelle there. Do you have the name of someone we should contact?"

"Sure. There are a couple of good garages. Donna's teenage son is always looking for an excuse to drive the tow truck, so I'd say call her. He'll be here in a flash."

"Donna?" Annabelle asked with a frown. "Donna, as in..."

Nevada laughed. "Something for you to get used to here in Fool's Gold. We are a town of women. For years there weren't enough men, so a lot of the traditionally male jobs are held by women. The police chief is a woman, as is the fire chief, most of the sheriff's department and nearly everyone on the city council." She held out her hand. "Nevada Hendrix."

Heidi sighed. "Sorry. I should have introduced you. I'm a little scattered. Some of the wild cows got into the goat pen this morning and scared us all."

"Wild cows?" Nevada asked.

"The cows that seemed to come with the land. They're feral, assuming cows can be. They've been living on their own for years, breeding. The herd is a pretty decent size. I think they're trying to influence the goats to rebel and go live with them."

Nevada looked at Annabelle, who raised her eyebrows. "You're concerned about goat corruption?"

Heidi laughed. "When you put it like that, it sounds pretty silly. But I swear, every time the cows show up, the goats act weird."

"Maybe they're territorial," Annabelle offered. "Maybe they don't like sharing."

"I hadn't thought of that. I've never had to deal with wild cows before."

Nevada grinned. "You should find yourself a handsome cowboy to take care of the problem. You'd have to import him, because we don't have any around here, but that could be fun."

"Maybe." Heidi sounded doubtful. She shrugged and looked at Annabelle. "Okay, let's go to the ranch and you can make your call." She turned to Nevada. "Thanks for stopping."

"You're welcome. It's what we do here."

"I know. One of the reasons I'm happy my grandfather and I settled in the area. People are very friendly. And they're cheese eaters, which is good for business."

"Nice to meet you," Annabelle told her.

"Let me know if I can do anything to help you get settled," Nevada offered.

"I will."

They started to head toward their cars when a large truck pulled up next to them. Nevada recognized Charlie, a tall woman with short-cropped hair. Charlie stuck her head out the window.

"Interesting place to call a meeting," she yelled, then saw the tire. "No way. Do not tell me none of you are capable of dealing with that."

"Fire department," Nevada murmured as Charlie pulled over and parked in front of the string of vehicles.

"She's going to yell at us for sure," Heidi whispered back.

Charlie got out of her truck and stalked over. She

was nearly five-ten, and looked as if she could wrestle all of them into submission at once. Her features were pretty enough, but she never wore any makeup and her clothes were nothing more than practical. Even Nevada, who generally preferred jeans and a T-shirt to anything fancy, managed to put on lip gloss every now and then. She had a feeling Charlie would rather have a root canal.

"It's a flat tire," Charlie announced.

Nevada pointed to the other women. "Annabelle Weiss, the new town librarian, and Heidi Simpson. Heidi and her grandfather bought the Castle Ranch."

"Goat girl," Charlie said. "I've heard of you. Great cheese."

"Thank you."

"This is Chantal Dixon."

Charlie glared at Nevada. "You did not just say that name."

Nevada held in a grin. "But it's so pretty."

"Don't make me hurt you." She turned to the other two women. "Call me Charlie and we'll get along fine."

"Why don't you like your name?" Heidi asked.

"Do I look like a Chantal? My mother had delusions of grandeur when it came to me." She paused. "She hoped I would be petite and delicate like her. But I take after my dad. Thank God." She walked toward the car. "This seems simple enough."

"We were just going to call a tow truck to help," Annabelle murmured. The librarian barely came up to Charlie's shoulder.

Charlie shook her head. "It's a flat tire, ladies, not the end of the world."

They all looked at each other.

"I'm pretty good with repairing a barn," Heidi admitted.

"Not helpful if you want to drive." Charlie turned to Nevada. "You have to know what to do. You have three brothers."

"My three brothers are the reason I never had to worry about my car," Nevada told her cheerfully, then laughed as Charlie's frown turned into a scowl. "Yes, I could have learned how to change a tire. I chose not to. If it helps, I'm great with a backhoe."

"You're giving women a bad reputation," Charlie muttered. "I swear, I need to hold some classes in how to be self-sufficient. You probably can't fix a leaky faucet, either."

"I can do that," Nevada said. "I'm much better with home repair than cars."

"Not helpful right now."

Nevada leaned toward Annabelle and Heidi. "She's not usually so crabby."

"Yes, I am," Charlie snapped as she went to the trunk and popped it open. "At least you have a spare. All right, you three. We're going to do this together. I'll talk you through it."

"I'm already late for work," Nevada said, inching toward her car. "So, I'm going to pass."

Charlie shook her head. "Don't even think about it. You're all going to learn something today."

"The guys at the construction site put a snake in my truck and I was fine with it. Does that count?"

"Was it poisonous?"

"No."

"Then it doesn't count. Come on. Gather 'round." She held up a tool in the shape of an X. "Anyone know what this is?"

Jo FINISHED LOADING the vodka bottles, then flattened the box and folded it into the recycling bin behind the bar. It was a warm, sunny afternoon, the kind of day when nearly anyone would rather be outside than stuck in a bar. Anyone but her. She left the bright blue sky behind and ducked back into the restful quiet of her business.

Everything was going well, she thought happily. A steady flow of customers kept her bank balance healthy. She saved a little each month, putting it aside for emergencies, retirement, whatever. She had a cat whom she adored and plenty of friends. A good life, she thought with only a small quiver of guilt.

She'd heard that people who were really successful sometimes felt like impostors. They worried that they would be told that their good fortune was all a mistake—that they weren't talented, or they didn't get the promotion. Sometimes she felt like that. Not about her job, but about her life.

She'd never thought she would be this at peace. This happy. She hadn't expected to find a warm, welcoming community, to have friends, a nice home. The truth was she didn't deserve it, but there didn't seem to be any way to give it back.

She walked back to the kitchen, where Marisol, her part-time cook, scooped avocados into a bowl for fresh guacamole.

"Got everything?" Jo asked.

The tiny fiftysomething woman smiled at her. "You

always ask and I always tell you all is well. The suppliers are good people. They deliver when they say."

"I like to be sure."

"You like to keep control." Marisol wrinkled her nose. "You need a man."

"So you've been telling me for years."

"I'm still right." She switched to Spanish, probably telling Jo she was shriveling up inside and that all her problems could be solved by the love of a good man.

"You're hardly an unbiased source," Jo muttered. "You got married at, what? Twelve."

"Sixteen. Nearly forty years and we already have eight grandchildren. You should be so lucky."

"I should, but I'm not. You enjoy your blessings. I'm fine."

"Fine is not happy."

Fine was good enough, Jo thought, heading back into the bar. Fine was plenty. Fine was safe and allowed her to sleep. If she had much more happiness in her life, she would worry that some balancing force would want to punish her to keep things even. Better to stay safe.

She carefully wrote the happy hour special of the day on the chalkboard and turned on the television. In the lull between lunch and happy hour, she enjoyed quiet. But soon customers would start to arrive, and they enjoyed the various shows.

The front door opened and a man stepped in. Jo recognized Will Falk and didn't know if she was pleased or annoyed.

"How's it going?" he asked as he moved toward her, his stride uneven.

"Good." She set a napkin on the bar. "What can I get you?"

"I came by to see if I could help put the toys together."

"Already done. We had two kids in at lunch today and they had a great time."

"I'm glad to hear it." He slid onto a barstool. "I'll take a beer. What you have on tap. Want to join me?"

"I don't drink while I'm working."

"I'm not that much work."

She gave him a slight smile. "Sorry, no."

He was a nice enough guy. Probably decent, the kind of man who enjoyed sports, a home-cooked meal and twice-a-week sex. She'd learned to make quick but accurate judgments about people. She would guess he didn't cheat at cards or on women, that he had plenty of friends and a strong moral code.

He wasn't anyone she could get involved with. She'd yet to meet someone she could, but Will was definitely out of the question.

She put the tall glass of beer in front of him and started toward the other end of the bar.

"Is it the limp?"

The question stopped her in her tracks. She turned slowly, then returned to stand in front of him.

"No."

He shrugged. "Some women don't like it. They're into perfect."

"That's not me. I don't find perfect appealing."

"Okay. Then what is it?"

He was attractive, she thought. Normal. Lately her

friends had been falling for normal, nice guys. She envied them.

"What happened?" she asked, ignoring his question.

"Construction accident. Fell off the side of a bridge. Nearly broke every bone in my body. Took a long time to get better."

She sensed there was more to the story. He must have spent weeks or months in the hospital, hundreds of hours in physical therapy.

"Do you have a lot of pain now?"

"I know when it's going to rain, but I'm okay." He gave her a slow, sexy smile. "Want to see my scars?"

She found herself wanting to say yes. To tease him back, to let her guard down for a few minutes. To remember what it was to be like everyone else.

"Maybe another time."

"I'm here for a couple of years. I have plenty of time."

"But then you'll go to a different project?"

He nodded. "Nature of the business. I've seen most of the world. Travel is exciting."

"I prefer staying in one place," she said, admitting a truth before she could stop herself. "It took a lot of looking to find this town."

"What do you like about it?"

"The people. They're very warm. As is the climate. It's a great location."

What she didn't tell him was that here she was allowed to pretend it all was real. That she was just like everyone else, that her past had never happened. Here she was simply Jo, the owner of Jo's Bar.

"So, show me," he said. "I'm the new guy. Don't I at least deserve a tour?"

She looked at him. For once, she was tempted to give in and flirt. To touch and be touched. It had been years since she'd been with a man. Years since she'd allowed herself to be that vulnerable. Last time the consequences had destroyed people. Because of her great need to love and be loved, a man had died.

"I can't," she said abruptly. "It's not about you—it's not personal. I'm sorry, but that's how it has to be."

Will nodded slowly, then got up from the stool. He tossed a ten on the bar.

"The drink's on the house," she said stiffly.

"No, thanks. I only accept drinks from my friends."

With that he left. She watched him limp out. When the door closed behind him, her stomach lurched and she wondered if she was going to throw up.

She'd hurt him, she knew that. Just as painful, she'd hurt herself. But she didn't have a choice. She couldn't take a chance. This time, there would be too much to lose.

"I LOVE THIS TOWN," Tucker said, as he closed the email. "They've approved our permits ahead of schedule." He looked across the small trailer toward Nevada. "Did you have anything to do with it?"

"While I'd love to take credit, no. I've told you. Everyone is very excited about the project. You're bringing jobs and tourists to the area. Where's the bad?"

Her words made sense, but the ease with which everything was moving forward made him a little apprehensive. Every job he'd ever been on had problems. He preferred them to be up-front, so he could deal with them and move on.

"Don't worry," she told him.

"Worrying makes me good at my job." He stood and crossed to the coffeepot. "Want some?" he said, holding up the full pot.

"Sure."

She rose and carried her mug toward him. He moved toward her. She moved left, he moved right, which meant they went in the same direction and nearly bumped. She backed up with comical speed.

"Sorry," she murmured.

"You're a little jumpy."

"I'm not." She sounded more defensive than indignant.

"It's a small trailer. We're going to bump into each other."

"I'm aware of that and it's not a problem."

"You're acting like it's a problem."

Defensiveness turned into annoyance. "You're reading too much into the situation," she snapped.

"Am I?"

Her chin rose. "You are." She held out her mug. "Could I have my coffee, please?"

"I think you're attracted to me and you don't know how to handle it."

She opened her mouth, then closed it. "Are you insane?"

"I've never been evaluated by a professional, but I'm thinking no."

"This is all about what happened before. We agreed to let that go."

He filled her mug, set the pot back in place, then leaned against the corner of Will's desk. Teasing her was more fun than he'd expected.

"I'm not the one who brought it up."

"You were thinking about it."

"I wasn't. But you have been. A lot."

Color stained her cheeks. "Not in the way you think. You're trying to prove something. Well, you can't. I'm over you and—"

She stopped talking and pressed her lips together.

"Over me?"

"Shut up," she demanded.

"Over me?"

"I swear, Tucker, I'll pull an Ethan on you."

"This is getting more interesting by the minute." He liked where their conversation was going. "You're saying that you were attracted to me before."

She set down her mug and folded her arms across her chest. Her brown eyes snapped with irritation. "I slept with you. What did you think?"

"I am pretty irresistible."

"Not today."

"You're still attracted to me."

She rolled her eyes. "What is with you? We work together. It's a long-term project. Why are you trying to be difficult?"

"It comes naturally to me."

"I'm not attracted to you."

He winked. "It's okay. You can tell me. I'll keep your secret. You want me."

"Only so I can back the car over you."

He was curious about how much of her indignation

was real and how much was self-protection. She was wary around him, something he wouldn't have expected. Did she feel the chemistry between them, too?

He did his best to remind himself that they were working together and this was a complication neither of them needed. Still, Nevada was smart, funny, sexy and willing to go toe-to-toe with him. No way he could ignore that.

"GO AHEAD," HE SAID SOFTLY. "Kiss me. Come on, get it out of your system and you'll be able to concentrate."

"I can concentrate just fine," Nevada told him, her teeth gritted. "Your ego is the size of Mars."

"I have big hands, too."

She groaned. "Go away."

"Chicken."

"I'm not chicken, I'm sensible."

Hanging on to self-control was proving more of a challenge than Nevada would have thought. For reasons she couldn't explain Tucker pushed buttons she didn't even know she had. As much as she wanted to hit him really, really hard in the stomach, she wanted to kiss him just as much. Maybe more.

Even more inexplicably, she hadn't been thinking about kissing him until he'd mentioned it. Now the idea filled her brain, making her toes curl and her insides quiver with anticipation. Talk about crazy.

He made a clucking sound.

"Stop it!" she demanded.

"Make me."

There was something to be said for a man who knew how to play, she thought, grabbing on to his shoulders, raising herself onto her toes and leaning in. Something good. Something that—

Her lips touched his. In that split second of contact, she felt as if she'd been transported out of the temperature-controlled trailer and drop-kicked into Mississippi in August. There was heat everywhere. Intense, muggy heat—the kind that clung to your skin and didn't let go for three days.

The air felt heavy, just like her body. Her blood was thick, but still moving quickly, carrying need to every part of her.

She drew back and stared at him. His dark eyes were unreadable.

"Is that all you've got?" he asked softly.

"No."

She leaned in again and tilted her head slightly. Her mouth settled on his. The heat came again and she found herself wanting to rip off her clothes. Not only to cool her body, but so Tucker could touch her.

She felt tingly and ached in the most interesting places. She wanted to wrap her arms around him, to pull him hard against her. She wanted to run her fingers up and down his chest, to dip lower and find out if he was feeling what she was feeling.

Instead she kept still, not moving her mouth, not trying to deepen the contact. Her intent had been to give him the kiss he would never forget. Only she couldn't. She was too afraid of how she would react.

She straightened, pulling away, aware he would probably tease her again. This time she didn't know how she was going to defend herself, because kissing him wasn't an option. Not when a simple, platonic peck had left her trembling. What would happen if he made any effort at all?

"Happy?" she asked, turning away and walking back to her desk.

"Very."

She drew in a breath and told herself to stay strong. "It's all about you and your ego, isn't it?" she asked, facing him.

He looked bemused and a little stunned. "It was back then. Now it's different."

They stared at each other. She didn't ask why, because she was as afraid of the answer as she was of kissing him again. If he'd felt it, too, if he'd been on the verge of losing control, then they were in big trouble. Better not to risk it by going there at all.

Last time…

No, she told herself firmly. There had been too much remembering. She wasn't going to do that anymore.

"We need to go over the blasting schedule," she said, randomly pulling a piece of paper off her desk and hoping it was relevant. "It requires coordination with several agencies, including the Fool's Gold Fire Department. I'm happy to coordinate with them, if you want."

"Sure. That would be great."

"It's my first time," she said, then held in a groan. "I mean, I've never been on-site with blasting before."

"It'll rock your world."

Despite feeling uncomfortable and awkward and more than a little scared, she laughed. "I'm not sure I need my world rocked."

"Try it. You might like it."

His gaze was steady, his expression open. She wanted to walk over and kiss him again. She wanted to know how much more she could feel in his arms, figure out what else he could do to her body.

Except that would be beyond stupid. Job first, fantasies second, she told herself as she dropped into her chair and turned her attention to her computer. But instead of the report on the screen, what she saw was the fireworks she'd experienced and the black cloud of impending doom should she ever give in.

The problem wasn't Tucker. The problem was her. She hadn't been able to resist him ten years ago and back then he hadn't even been trying. What was she supposed to do if he decided he wanted to do more than play?

The man was leaving in a year, she reminded herself. More important, he'd made it clear he wasn't interested in ever settling down. For her, home was everything. He'd already broken her heart once. Did she really need a second lesson from the likes of Tucker Janack? Logically, he was a bad choice. She wondered how long she would have to keep telling herself that before she would start to believe.

CHAPTER SIX

AFTER A LONG WEEK at the construction site, Nevada was more than ready to spend a quiet evening not thinking about Tucker. Since "the kiss," he'd been invading her thoughts way more than was reasonable. So, when her mother had invited her over for a family dinner, it had seemed to be the perfect escape.

She arrived around six, as requested, and met Dakota, Finn and Hannah coming from the opposite direction.

"Who's my best girl?" Nevada asked, taking the baby from her sister and hugging her tight.

"Na-na-na," Hannah squealed in delight as she waved her pudgy arms.

"Nevada. That's right. Who's a smart girl?" She swung Hannah in her arms, then grinned at her sister and soon-to-be brother-in-law. "Hi, you two. How are things?"

"Great." Finn put his arm around Dakota. "She's growing, as you can see. Crawling everywhere. Starting to try to walk."

He sounded happy and proud, Nevada thought, pleased her sister had found such a great guy.

Just a few months before, Finn had come to town to rescue his twin brothers from a reality show—*True Love or Fool's Gold*. The "boys" had actually been twenty-one and more than capable of making their own decisions, but Finn hadn't seen it that way.

Dakota had assumed she wouldn't find a forever kind of love and had already contacted an adoption agency. While falling for Finn, she'd received word she'd been approved to adopt Hannah, then six months old. The situation had only gotten more complicated when Dakota became pregnant. It had been a busy few months.

Now Finn had relocated to Fool's Gold, bought a local air cargo and tour company and they were planning a wedding.

"You two set the date yet?" Nevada asked as the three of them walked toward the front door.

Dakota looked at Finn, then back at Nevada. "No. We're still talking."

Finn pushed open the door and they stepped into bedlam.

The rest of the family was already there, along with a big golden retriever–Labrador mix named Fluffy, who did her best to greet everyone by knocking them off their feet and licking them into submission.

"We seem to be the last to arrive," Nevada told Hannah as the baby looked around and laughed when she saw all the people she loved.

Ethan and his wife, Liz, had their three kids with them. Kent and his son, Reese, were attempting to corral an uncooperative Fluffy, while Montana, Nevada's other triplet sister, offered advice. Her fiancé, Simon, stood quietly on the sidelines, as he always did. But these days he looked much happier and more relaxed. Tucker was chatting with Denise and—

Nevada stiffened as she visually backtracked. Tucker?

"You're here!" Denise patted Tucker on the arm and hurried toward the door. "There you are, Hannah. Come to Nana, my darling girl."

Hannah held out her arms as her grandmother approached, and the child went easily into Denise's embrace. Nevada stepped back, not so much to get out of the way as to regroup.

"Finn, have you met Tucker?" Denise asked. "He's an old friend of Ethan's and now Nevada works for him. His company is the one building the resort and casino outside of town."

The two men shook hands.

"What is he doing here?" Nevada asked her mother, whispering so the question wouldn't be overheard.

"He's alone in town. I thought he would enjoy a family meal."

"You told Ethan I slept with Tucker so Ethan would beat him up."

Her mother didn't look the least bit guilty. "I had to do something. Now he's been warned and we can move on."

That was just like her mother, Nevada thought, telling herself she shouldn't be surprised.

"What are you? A member of the Mafia? Did it occur to you I would find this awkward?" she asked.

"How could you? You work with him."

Right. Because they didn't have a personal relationship now—all kissing aside.

"Fine," Nevada said with a sigh.

"I'm glad you're all right with this, because I put you next to him at the table."

Denise took Hannah into the kitchen. Nevada stood there, not sure if she should follow or duck upstairs and hide. Before she could decide, Tucker walked over with a glass of wine and handed it to her.

"I'd forgotten what it was like to be around your family," he admitted.

"It's been a long time."

"Not since that summer Ethan and I went to cycling camp with Josh Golden. We were sixteen."

That made her all of ten. She hadn't noticed him back then. He'd just been one of her brother's boring friends.

"We're louder now," she told him.

"And bigger. I can't get over Ethan's family."

She looked at the teenagers, who were laughing about something together. "I like that they stay in the room with us instead of disappearing into the family room to play with the Wii Mom bought them."

"Both Montana and Dakota are engaged."

"Uh-huh. Simon's a surgeon and Finn is a pilot. Cargo and private tours. That kind of thing. He's from Alaska."

"We did a job there."

"Is there anywhere you haven't done a job?"

"Not really." He glanced around the room. "I never had anything like this to come home to. My mom died when I was a baby. Dad hired a nanny and took both of us with him."

"I can't imagine living without my family. They're everything to me."

Tucker rubbed his jaw. "Your brother sure looks out for you."

"You deserved it."

He surprised her by laughing. "You're right. I did. Have I apologized?"

"Yes, and you don't have to again."

Ethan walked over and joined them. "Everything all right here?"

"Stop fighting my battles," she told him. "I can do it myself."

"Sometimes a guy has to step in and take care of his own. Tucker gets that."

Tucker nodded.

Ethan asked if Tucker planned to watch the preseason football games this Sunday. While the guys talked football, Nevada thought about where Tucker might usually spend the afternoon. He'd always been on his own—odd man out. He wasn't just dealing with a new school every couple of years, but a new country and a new culture, not to mention language barriers. She couldn't imagine what it would be like not to have roots.

"Be careful," Ethan was saying. "There are a million single women in town."

"You're exaggerating." Tucker sipped his wine. "I'm not worried."

Nevada grinned. "You should be. Until recently, we've had a man shortage. The ladies will be all over you. A strong, rich, construction guy." She blinked her eyes several times.

Tucker laughed. "I can handle myself."

Nevada turned to her brother. "Just think. In a couple of weeks, you'll get to say, 'I told you so.'"

"I'm looking forward to it." Ethan laughed.

Tucker shifted uneasily. "It can't be that bad."

"Keep telling yourself that," Nevada said, before heading to the kitchen to help her mom.

"I KNOW THE WAY HOME," she said four hours later, after a huge dinner.

"I'm not walking you home," Tucker told her. "You're walking me. If what you and Ethan said is true, I need the protection."

"Oh, please. I think you can handle a few love-starved women."

"Not at the same time." He leaned toward her and lowered his voice. "I've never been into the group thing. After the first five or six times, it's not all that fun."

"You're not impressing me with stories like that."

"What kind of stories do impress you?"

"Move across time like Kyle Reese in the first *Terminator* movie. That will get my attention."

"I'll work on it."

The night was warm and clear, stars dotting the sky. There were still plenty of people walking around, so nothing about walking next to Tucker should have felt intimate. Still, she was aware of him close to her, of the breadth of his shoulders and the sound of his voice.

"Your family is great," he said. "Your mom really has it together."

"She's good at managing a crowd."

"She's been alone a long time. Does she date?"

"She started this year. I can't believe my dad's been

gone over ten years. That's a long time for her to be by herself." She glanced at Tucker. "Your dad never re-married."

"True, but he wasn't alone. He's a big believer in the concept of a girl in every port. Or in his case, a woman at every job site. The man's made a fool of himself over more women than I can count."

"Does that bother you?"

Tucker shrugged. "I don't get the volume. He never takes a break. But he loves to keep them coming. He's pushing sixty and acting like he's seventeen. Like I said, he's acting the fool. But love does that."

"Love doesn't make people foolish."

"It can."

She knew who he was thinking about. "Only if you pick crazy artists."

"She didn't change my opinion."

They rounded a corner and Nevada realized they were on her block. "I thought I was walking you home."

"I'll hide in the shadows," he said.

They crossed the street and walked toward her front door.

Lights were on in both apartments, but there weren't any sounds.

"Whoever invented headphones deserves to be made a saint," she said. "Both my tenants are college guys. They don't make a move without listening to some-thing, but I don't have to hear it."

"Lucky you."

They were standing by her porch. The moon had barely cleared the horizon and she could see it over Tucker's shoulder. One would think a big white object hanging in the sky would capture her attention, but all she seemed to see was the man in front of her.

"Thanks for walking me home," she said, prepared to turn and go inside. Quickly, she thought. Because if she didn't, she was in danger of wanting what wasn't sensible.

"You're welcome."

His gaze was intense, seeking something in her face. She stared back, not sure what he was thinking or how best to protect herself. Actually she knew how. The truth was she didn't want to.

He cupped her jaw with one hand and put the other on her waist, then kissed her.

She'd seen the kiss coming, could have stepped away. But she didn't and then his mouth pressed against hers and nothing else mattered.

The heat was back, all sticky and sweet, and when it engulfed her, she surrendered. She wrapped her arms around his neck and leaned in, letting herself fall into the madness of bad judgment and great kissing.

He claimed her lips with a confidence that made her tremble. She was aware of nothing but the man holding her and the way his touch made her feel.

He shifted his hands so they were both at her waist, then swept his tongue against her bottom lip. She parted instinctively, welcoming his gentle invasion.

He tasted faintly of the brandy they'd had after dinner. Each stroke aroused her until she lost what little will she'd had left. When he pulled her closer, she went willingly, letting her body press against his.

Her breasts found comfort against his chest. Her belly nestled against the hardness of his erection. He drew back enough to kiss his way down her jaw to her neck. He nipped at her earlobe, before licking the sensitive skin below. Goose bumps broke out on her arms.

Then they were kissing again, his tongue teasing and exciting her. She moved her hands up and down his back. Her breasts ached, wanting their share of his attention. Between her legs, she felt the first erotic ache of swollen flesh, hungry to be claimed.

Somewhere in the distance she heard a car engine and crickets. Unwelcome awareness forced her to acknowledge the reality of standing on her front porch, kissing the man she worked for.

Inviting him in would be the easy choice, she thought, aware his eyes were bright with wanting. *This* time he would be choosing her, not taking what was offered. But having sex with Tucker was a long way to go to prove something, and she was tired of having regrets in her life.

"I really like my job," she said quietly, then had to clear her throat. "I don't want to screw that up by sleeping with the boss."

Tucker nodded once, then swore under his breath. She recognized the frustration and told herself at least this hadn't been a party for one.

"Nevada," he began.

She cut him off with a shake of her head. "That time before? It wasn't all you messing up. I knew you were in love with Cat. She told me it was over, and I wanted to believe her. But I knew it would take you a long time to get over her."

"Don't. It wasn't your fault and it wasn't mine. Cat believed in manipulation as a form of entertainment. We were just ordinary mortals. We didn't stand a chance."

She wondered if that was true. "She was so beautiful."

"She was a drug," he said flatly. "And I was her fool. I thought losing her would kill me, but it was the best thing that ever happened to me."

Nevada wasn't sure how things had ended with Cat and decided she didn't need to know.

"About tonight," she began.

He cupped her face in his hands. "I get it. We work together. We will for a while. I'm only on-site for a year. So we'll pretend it never happened." His mouth curved into a wicked smile. "Until I'm leaving. That's going to be a hell of a weekend."

His words made her insides melt. "You're assuming I'll still be interested."

"You will be," he said confidently, then kissed her lightly. He dropped his hands and stepped back.

"If I change my mind?"

"I'll convince you otherwise."

Something to look forward to, she thought, waving at him. She went inside, still caught up in the kisses and the past. Tucker was a complication. But one she could handle, she thought. Now that there were rules in place, it would be easier at work. She wouldn't be thinking about him all the time.

She climbed the stairs to her apartment and unlocked the door. When she opened it, she reached to the right and flipped on the lights.

They came on, but instead of seeing her familiar

living room, she saw another place and time. Cat stand-ing in the doorway of her dorm room.

"It's over," the other woman had said, her dark eyes bright with mischief. "Tucker and I. It's done. I know you're in love with him. He needs you tonight, Nevada. You should go to him."

Being around Cat was like looking at the sun. It was difficult to see anything else, to focus. The rest of the world blurred.

It took Nevada a second to process what she was say-ing. Embarrassment poured through her as she franti-cally wondered who else had guessed her secret. Did Tucker know? Did he pity her? Because that would be the worst.

"I don't understand," she whispered.

Cat grabbed her arms and shook her. "He needs you. Go to him. He's at home right now."

"I…"

Before she could say anything else, Cat was gone, leaving a trail of exotic perfume fading at the door.

Nevada spent the next twenty minutes trying to fig-ure out what to do. Go to Tucker? Could she? He loved Cat. He couldn't see anyone or anything else. But if they'd broken up, then he was available. And hurting.

In the end, her heart had won the battle. She'd grabbed her car keys and fled down the stairs to the parking lot by her door. Sooner than she would have thought possible, she was at Tucker's door, knocking.

He opened it almost immediately, as if he'd been waiting for her. But when he saw her, the expectation on his face faded to disappointment.

"I thought you were Cat," he said, his words slurred.

"I heard what happened." She followed him inside. "She left me."

He collapsed on the sofa, rested his elbows on his knees and dropped his head into his hands.

"She left me," he repeated, as if he couldn't believe the words.

Nevada had never been to his place before. She knew where he lived, as she had picked him up here a couple of times, but she hadn't gotten past the parking lot.

Now she quickly took in the leather sofas, the carved tables. The room was elegant. More *GQ* than bachelor pad. The artwork looked original and expensive. There was a metal sculpture in the corner, and she had a feeling it had been done by Cat.

In fact, the whole apartment screamed Cat's name. Not just in the pale gray walls or the textured drapes, but in the stack of books in French and Italian. The *London Times* resting on the coffee table.

Jealousy twisted Nevada's stomach. Had the other woman lived here? She didn't want to believe it was true, but couldn't ignore the evidence. If Cat wasn't here permanently, she had spent enough time to leave her mark.

"I can't do this," Tucker muttered.

Nevada crossed to the sofa and sat next to him.

"I can't live without her." He turned to stare at Nevada, his eyes bloodshot. "She's my world. Without her..." Pain tightened his features. "I never want to feel this way again. Love blows. But I couldn't help myself, you know? Not with her."

"It's okay," she told him, tentatively touching his

shoulder. "I know it hurts now, but you'll find some-one else."

"No. Never. There's only her."

His pain ripped at Nevada, leaving her desperately wanting to fix him. She ignored her own ache, hear-ing the man she loved declare his feelings for someone else.

"There isn't." She put her hand on his face and turned him toward her. "There isn't just her." She drew in a breath, dug deep for courage and blurted, "There's me."

His brows drew together in confusion.

"I love you," she said quickly, before she lost her nerve. "I have for a long time. Cat doesn't care about you. She can't care about anyone. But I do care, Tucker. So much."

She kissed him, her mouth bumping his awkwardly.

He didn't respond. He didn't pull away, but he didn't kiss her back. Instead he sat there, immobile. She ig-nored the humiliation, the voice screaming at her to run while she still had some pride left.

"Tucker, please," she whispered against his lips, then grabbed his hand and placed it on her breast.

She'd never done anything like that before in her life. Part of it was that she'd never had sex before. While she'd dated in high school, the farthest she'd ever gone had been a boy lightly stroking her breast over clothes.

But this was different. This was Tucker and he was her world. As much as he thought he loved Cat, Nevada knew she loved him more. Her love was great, bigger and stronger. It would survive anything.

Suddenly he started kissing her back. His hand

closed over her breast, squeezing so hard it hurt. His tongue pushed into her mouth as he shoved up her shirt and fumbled with her bra.

He never got it unfastened. Instead he pulled her breast out of the cup and rubbed the nipple.

Everything was so strange, she thought, trying to figure out what to pay attention to. He tasted and smelled of Scotch, which wasn't exactly what she was used to. And while the hand on her breast no longer hurt, she didn't have time to decide if she enjoyed it or not. Because just when she thought she might have felt a tingle, he was grabbing her around the waist and sliding her down on the sofa. His hands moved between them.

She felt fingers on her belly, then her jeans and panties were being lowered. He pushed one pant leg off, taking her sandal with it, but left the other on.

It was everything she wanted and it was happening too fast. A voice in her head whispered she hadn't imagined it like this. Not on a sofa with him drunk and her...

"Tucker, I..."

Even as she tried to figure out what she wanted to say, he shifted back on the sofa and bent between her legs, pressing his mouth against her intimately. Before she could figure out what was happening, he was kissing her *down there!*

She'd read about it, had heard friends talk about it, but nothing had prepared her for the deep, slow kiss. His lips were so soft and, when he moved his tongue like that, back and forth, she thought she was going to die.

It was perfect, she thought, sinking back on the sofa and giving herself up to an unfamiliar tingling surging through her. Better than perfect. This had to prove that Tucker cared about her. He couldn't do this to her if he didn't love her.

He licked her over and over, making her squirm. She felt tense and aware, not sure what was supposed to happen next. Something beckoned and she knew she wanted more. She parted her legs as much as she could and did her best to hold in her whimpers of pleasure.

He straightened and looked into her eyes. "I want you," he breathed. "Do you want me, too?"

"Yes," she breathed, "more than anything."

She felt a rush of longing, of need, and drew him close. He moved toward her, positioning himself between her legs.

His first thrust took her by surprise. She went from arousal to uncomfortable in a second and had to bite her lip to keep from crying out.

He continued moving in and out, slowly at first and then faster. Nevada had just started to feel the first tendrils of pleasure again when he cried out, "It's always been you, Cat. Only you. God, yes. Just like that."

She was too stunned, too broken to say anything back.

He didn't even know who she was.

That thought tumbled over and over in her mind, cutting her with each repetition. She lay still as he pushed into her a couple more times, then stilled with a groan.

When he was done, he pulled out. She gritted her teeth against the unfamiliar sensation. He shifted away and stood, then fastened his jeans. She lay there a second, waiting for him to realize what had happened. Despite everything, she wanted him to make it okay.

He gave her a lopsided smile. "Be right back," he promised, then walked toward the bathroom.

Nevada lay there, one pant leg on, one off, tears beginning to leak into her hair. Finally she got up and dressed.

All her hopes and dreams and love crashed in around her and she sat back down on the sofa, sobbing into her hands. Everything she'd imagined was gone—broken by reality. Tucker didn't care about her in a romantic way. He never had. He was in love with Cat. To him, she was nothing more than his friend's little sister. She'd misread kindness as affection and had built a fantasy out of nothing more substantial than sand.

Still fighting tears, she got up and went back to her dorm. After spending an hour in the shower, she still felt awful. Worse, she felt stupid. She'd been a fool and she had no one else to blame.

She'd spent a long night lying awake, wallowing in self-pity, wondering how long it was going to take until she would get over her first love.

The next morning, she'd gone to class just as if nothing had happened. She'd talked to her friends, had fake-laughed at all the right places, had acted as if she was fine.

It hadn't helped.

Two days later, Cat had called.

"Was it wonderful?" the other woman asked.

"What?"

"Your night with Tucker. You were in love with him so I wanted you to have him."

Nevada pressed her fingers against her temple. "I don't understand. You said you broke up with him."

"That's what I told him, too. He wouldn't have slept with you otherwise. It was my gift to you, Nevada. We're friends. That's what friends do."

Everything about that night returned to her. How drunk he'd been, how he hadn't even known it was her. At least, not at the end.

"Does he even remember what happened?" she asked, hating herself for wanting to know.

"Bits and pieces." Cat laughed. "He was pretty hungover when I talked to him. He confessed all, expecting me to be angry. I wasn't, of course. Having you with him was my idea. And now he's grateful I'm taking him back."

"You are?"

"Yes. I told you. I gave you your night with him. So, tell me everything. Was it wonderful?"

Nevada shook her head and returned to the present. To the living room she'd remodeled and decorated herself. To the life she'd made.

Ten years ago she'd hung up on Cat and had never spoken to her again. Never spoken to Tucker, either. She'd managed to move on with her life, to heal. But she'd never forgotten that night. The humiliation of it. She would have told anyone who asked that she was over Tucker Janack. Now she had the chance to prove to herself that she wasn't lying.

DENISE HENDRIX SAT in the family room, the morning paper spread out on the coffee table in front of her, knowing she was flirting with disaster. At her age, skipping her yoga class wasn't something she could afford to do. She was at risk of getting creaky or worse, and there were all those scary commercials about bone loss and hip replacements.

But the thought of spending an hour trying to perfect downward dog wasn't appealing. Nor were any of her usual activities. She felt restless and on edge. It was like being a kid and knowing Christmas was only a few days away. Anticipation made focusing on anything impossible. The difference now was she didn't know what she was waiting for.

Her children were all happy and successful. Her friends were healthy, her investments sound. She'd had the furnace checked for the winter, the gutters cleaned and there was plenty of food in the refrigerator. So, what was she waiting for? She needed to get on with her life.

The doorbell rang, saving her from further introspection. While she was excellent at understanding everyone else's lives, she'd never been very good at ruminating over her own. She preferred to be going and doing. A good thing, considering she'd raised six children.

She walked through the living room, toward the front door, and pulled it open. Only to find herself staring at a man she hadn't spoken to in more than thirty-five years.

To the day, she thought, realizing the source of the restlessness. This was the anniversary of the last time she'd seen Max.

Max Thurman had been her first love, her first lover, her first everything. She'd thought she would love him forever, until she'd met Ralph Hendrix. The two men couldn't have been more different. Max had always been wild. He rode a motorcycle, was a troublemaker. Ralph had been responsible, with plans to go into his father's business.

She'd impulsively accepted a date with Ralph during one of her frequent fights with Max. She'd expected to be bored but had instead been charmed.

Max had left town a few weeks later. No one had known where he'd gone. About a year ago he'd reappeared. She'd carefully stayed out of his way, not sure how she felt about her old boyfriend returning to the scene of the crime.

He looked good, she thought absently. His blond hair had gone gray, but it suited him. The blue eyes were as piercing as she remembered, the smile as easy, the body as muscled.

"Hello, Max."

"Denise."

She stepped back to invite him in.

As he walked past her, she felt a remembered thrill, as if all that time hadn't passed. It was kind of comforting to know she could be as foolish now as she had been at nineteen.

They faced each other.

"It's been a while," she said. "How are you?"

"Good. I moved back last year."

"So I heard."

"I've seen you around town a time or two."

She nodded, then looked away. "I've avoided you."

"I noticed. I figured you needed time."

She laughed. "It's been thirty-five years. How much more time were you going to give me?"

He smiled and it was just like it had been back then. Her knees went weak and her heart fluttered.

"Until today," he told her.

She didn't know what he wanted or what he expected, but none of that mattered. This was Max. Her Max.

"Ralph died nearly eleven years ago," she said.

"I know. I'm sorry."

"I loved him very much. We had a wonderful life together and he gave me six beautiful children."

Max nodded slowly. "I saw what was happening. After your first date with him. That's why I left. I knew I couldn't compete with him. I could have seduced you back into my bed, but I couldn't have kept you there. I didn't deserve you back then."

They stared at each other.

"Now that we have that out of the way," she said, "what happens now?"

"I thought we could start with a cup of coffee. We have a lot of catching up to do."

CHAPTER SEVEN

TUCKER STOOD AT THE SIDE of the dirt road, looking stunned. He held a casserole dish in his hands.

Nevada sighed. "This is where you tell me you can handle it yourself. Isn't that what you said? That a few single women couldn't frighten you?"

"They're everywhere."

A slight exaggeration, she thought, amused. "Only three."

"In one morning."

She knew it wasn't just the food. He'd also had two invitations to dinner and one request for a coffee date.

"I warned you and you didn't want to listen."

"I was wrong." He turned to her. "What do I do?"

She smiled. "Am I correct in assuming you're not interested in a liaison with one of the lovely ladies in town?"

"No. I'm not. But I also don't want them pissed at me. You have to help."

"Technically, I don't."

Maybe it was wrong to enjoy watching him squirm, but she was willing to live with the guilt.

"Face it, Tucker. The town has something of a man shortage and you're a man."

A man who knew how to kiss, she thought, then pushed the memories of the other night out of her head.

It had been a whole lot easier not to think about Tucker when she didn't have to see him every day. And when the last memory of their time together had been so awful. Now she knew what it was like to kiss him when he was sober and just as interested as she was.

"You have to make them stop," he told her.

"What will you give me if I do?"

The question was automatic, honed from being one of six siblings. Before he could say anything, she held up her hands.

"Never mind. Don't answer that. I'll help you because I'm a nice person and it will make my mother proud. There's no other reason. Come on."

She started walking to her truck.

"Where are we going?"

"Into town."

They were there in less than fifteen minutes. She parked by the lake and turned off the engine.

"We're going to walk through town and you're going to pretend you're completely into me. By the time we get back here, word will have spread and your problem will be solved."

"I can do that."

She was grateful he didn't press her on why she was helping. Sure, some of it really was about her mother. But while she'd enjoyed watching Tucker squirm, she didn't actually like those other women coming on to him.

She and Tucker might have agreed they were going to be all business, all the time, but that didn't make her any less aware of him.

"We'll hit the grocery store, then Morgan's Books.

After that we'll do a quick walk down Frank Lane and you'll be untouchable."

"I owe you," he said as he got out of her truck.

In more ways than he knew, she thought.

They started toward the center of town. When they reached the corner and stopped for the light, Tucker grabbed her hand.

It took her a second to remember this was part of a plan, and her idea. While her brain was busy processing the information, her body was stirring as heat sparked and her girl parts woke up.

No way, she told herself. There was no more reacting to Tucker. But lecturing didn't help much, not when he laced his fingers with hers and squeezed.

They walked through the grocery store. She made what she hoped was sparkling conversation, all the while trying not to notice how their shoulders brushed and the way he smiled at her.

Back on the street she was relieved to see Pia and Raoul walking toward them, the former football player pushing a double stroller.

"Hi," she said eagerly, pulling her hand free of Tucker's and hurrying to meet her friends. "You're out."

"Finally," Pia said. "We thought it was time to introduce the girls to their hometown. Plus, they're starting work on the Fall Festival today and I want to check on things. Then there's the whole artist series, with a surprise guest. And it's time to check the inventory for the Halloween decorations, if you can believe it."

Nevada introduced Tucker. The two men shook hands. He surprised her by peeking in at the twins.

"They're beautiful," he said.

Pia nodded. "I can't take the credit, so I'm comfortable saying I agree with you. Plus, they're both really good. I've been reading tons of nightmare stories online about colic and sleepless nights. We're lucky. What are you two up to?"

"I'm protecting Tucker from the single women in town."

Tucker glanced at her. "Did you have to share that?"

Nevada grinned at him. "I'm sorry. Was it a secret?"

Raoul shook his head. "Don't let your pride get in the way. Women in this town are determined." He put his arm around Pia. "Look how you stalked me."

"I did not. You were the one begging me to marry you. I took pity on you."

"Keep saying that and maybe one day it will be true."

Nevada knew they had unexpectedly fallen in love with each other while Pia was pregnant with her friend's embryos.

"If it gets bad, you can hang out with us," Pia said, leaning into Raoul.

"Thanks."

They left the young family and continued their stroll through town.

At the corner by Morgan's Bookstore, Nevada was about to say they could stop for fudge before going in when Tucker surprised her by pulling her toward him.

"What?" she asked.

Instead of answering, he bent down and kissed her.

The feel of his mouth was delicious and her already alert body sent up a cheer. Aware they were in the middle of town where everyone could see, she wanted to draw back. But she couldn't. Something about his touch made it impossible to move, impossible to do anything but lose herself in the sensation of his lips against hers.

He wrapped his arms around her so they were touching from shoulder to thigh. The intimate embrace made her want to hug him back and the last of her resistance faded. Just when she was about to part her lips so they could deepen the kiss, he stepped away.

She blinked in the bright sunlight.

"What the hell was that?" she demanded.

He grinned and took her hand again. "Just doing what you said. Making them believe I'm into you."

Oh, right. The plan to protect him.

"I, ah, fine." She cleared her throat. "You did well."

He winked. "I liked it, too."

So much for the "work only" rules. So much for just being friends. The truth was Tucker Janack got to her. He always had, and she had a bad feeling he always would. The trick was going to be figuring out how to manage her reaction to him and stay sane at the same time.

AFTER A COUPLE OF DAYS of dodging Tucker, doing her job and wanting nothing more than to escape the daunting sexual tension she felt every time she was around the man, Nevada was relieved when she got a call from Montana. She and Dakota were calling a triplet meeting. They agreed on a time and suggested meeting at their mom's house.

Nevada arrived early. It had been a great excuse to leave the job site. She was hoping that after her sisters talked about whatever their issue was, she could ask for a little advice on how to clear her head when it came to Tucker. She didn't have any ideas of her own.

Focusing on the past and hating him wasn't really an option. It had been ten years ago, she'd been as much to blame as he was and she preferred to look forward rather than back. Plus, she really did love her job and wanted to keep working with him. Having him wear a gorilla mask every day would help, but she wasn't sure how to ask for that.

She walked up to the front of the house, knocked once as she always did and pushed the door open.

"It's me," she called. "Am I the first one here?"

There wasn't an answer. She heard a noise from the kitchen and moved down the hall, wondering what the discussion was about. Maybe Montana was pregnant. That would be fun. Simon was a great guy. Maybe they were announcing their engagement. That would mean both her sisters were happy in love.

Good for them, she thought, telling herself not to get into a funk about it. She would find her own guy eventually. She had to stay positive.

Lost in her own thoughts, she barely noticed that the odd sound was repeated again. Even as she registered that it was more a moan than a word, she walked into the kitchen to find her mother with Max Thurman.

Naked.

On the kitchen table.

Having sex.

It was one of those moments that slowed time. She felt as if she were underwater, unable to move quickly, or even breathe. The image burned itself onto her brain. She shrieked and covered her eyes, but it was too late.

"Nevada!"

"I'm sorry," Nevada yelled and ran away as fast as she could. She made it outside, where she stood in the center of the lawn, trying to catch her breath.

"No, no, no!"

Closing her eyes didn't help, nor did humming. Whatever she did, she could still see them doing it.

"What's going on?"

She saw her sisters hurrying toward her and she ran in the other direction. They chased her down the street.

"Stop it!" Montana yelled. "Dakota's pregnant. She can't run after you."

That brought Nevada to a stop, but she couldn't face them.

"Oh, God, it's horrible. I'm going to need therapy for the rest of my life."

Her sisters surrounded her, looking worried.

"What happened?" Dakota asked, grabbing her arm. "Are you sick?"

Nevada pointed back at the house. "In there. On the table."

Montana went pale. "Did something happen to Mom?"

Nevada waved her hands. "She's fine. I can't. Don't make me say it."

She thought of kittens and chocolate and boats. She wondered if there were aliens on Mars, then gave in to the inevitable and allowed the theme from "It's a Small World" to fill her brain, but even that didn't help.

Dakota shook her. "Will you please tell us what's going on?"

"I saw Mom having sex with Max. On the kitchen

table." She shrieked the words, then covered her face again. "I can't get it out of my head."

She dropped her hands and saw her sisters looking at each other. Montana's mouth began to twitch.

"It's not funny," Nevada insisted. "We've had breakfast at that table. Decorated cookies, done our homework there. How can I ever face her again?"

"I think that's more her problem than yours," Dakota told her. "Wow—I can't believe Mom was having sex with Max. I guess he is the guy in the tattoo."

Their mother had the name Max tattooed on her hip.

"I'm having more trouble with the Max part than the Mom part," Montana admitted. "He's my boss. This could be complicated."

"I can never go back," Nevada moaned. "I grew up in that house. I love that house. I can never go in there again. Or talk to my mother."

"You'll recover," Dakota told her, sounding much too calm and way too amused.

"You don't actually know that. You're guessing."

"I'm a professional. Trust me. You'll be fine."

"I wonder if electroshock therapy would work," Nevada muttered, thinking whatever pain was involved would be worth it. Not that she didn't love her mom and want her to be happy, but did she have to do it on the kitchen table?

"They're old. Shouldn't they be worried about their joints and stuff?" she asked. "Wouldn't a bed be better? It wouldn't have been so shocking in a bed."

"I think it's impressive," Montana announced. "When was the last time you had sex on the kitchen table?"

"I can't remember the last time I had sex." Nevada sighed. She was simply going to have to accept she was emotionally scarred.

She started toward the center of town. Her sisters fell into step beside her.

"Do you think a latte will help me forget more than ice cream?" she asked.

"How about a mocha Frappuccino?" Dakota patted her on the shoulder. "The best of both worlds."

"Perfect."

"It's really very sweet," Dakota began.

Nevada stopped her with a look. "Don't go there. You're not the one who saw it. Until you've stared into the eyes of your mother having sex on the kitchen table, you don't get an opinion. Got that?"

"You bet."

"I'll bet Max has a great butt," Montana said conversationally. "Not that I want to think about it too much, but he takes care of himself."

Dakota grinned. "I'm sure he does."

"I hate you both," Nevada muttered.

They hugged her. "You can't hate us," Montana said, kissing her cheek. "We have your DNA."

"I want it back."

Her sisters laughed and reluctantly she joined in. She'd always known there were ups and downs with having a big family. Pluses and minuses. This was a really big minus she was going to have to get over.

She linked arms with her sisters. "All right. Enough of my emotional trauma. What did you two want to talk to me about?"

Her sisters came to a halt, forcing her to stop walking as well. They faced her, their expressions a combination of concern and something that if she didn't know better she would say was guilt.

"What?" she demanded. "Don't play games with me. I've had a tough day."

Although, on the bright side, seeing her mother having sex put her problems with Tucker in perspective.

"We're planning a wedding," Dakota said.

"Yours. I know." Nevada glanced at Montana. "Unless you and Simon have made it official. Just a tip here—we all know you're in love and planning to get married, so what's with the guy not coughing up the ring?"

Montana laughed and held up her left hand. A giant diamond sparkled in the morning light.

Nevada shrieked and grabbed her. "The guy has taste. You gotta love that."

The three of them hugged.

When they'd started walking again, Dakota drew in a breath.

"We've been talking.…" She trailed off.

Nevada frowned. Dakota always knew what to say. "What?" she demanded.

"We were thinking we would really like a double wedding, but then we thought you'd feel bad, so we decided not to, but it makes financial sense, but if it's mean or you're hurt or don't want us to, we won't."

Dakota got the words out in a rush, then stood there, twisting her hands together.

"We love you," Montana added.

"I know that," Nevada told her, stunned by the words. A double wedding. Sure. They were engaged and sisters and Dakota was pregnant so getting married made sense. As for them doing it at the same time, the three of them had shared nearly all their milestones. Why not a wedding?

Except she would be left out, what with not even dating, let alone being serious about someone.

"I think it's a great idea," she said, smiling, hoping she sounded excited and happy. "Do you have any dates picked out?"

"We were talking about Thanksgiving weekend," Dakota said. "Mom thinks Ford will be home for the holidays."

Ford was the youngest of their brothers, although still older than them. He was in the navy and stationed overseas.

"You'll want Ford here," she said firmly. "I think Thanksgiving weekend is a great time."

They both studied her, as if searching for the truth. Nevada held in a sigh. What was she supposed to say? That she felt lonely and abandoned? That while she was thrilled her sisters had found happiness, she wanted a little of that for herself? Well, she did. But wanting something wouldn't make it happen and there was no way she was going to stand in the way of her sisters' weddings.

"You'd better decide pretty soon," she said. "There aren't a lot of places that can hold the whole family and half the town." She smiled at them both. "I'm sure. This is the right thing for you to do."

"Thank you," Dakota whispered.

"I'm the superior triplet," Nevada told her. "I don't know why you were worried. Now, you two run off and plan your wedding. I'm going to find something with equal parts sugar and fat to clear my head."

She left her sisters talking about whatever it was prospective brides talked about and hurried toward the closest Starbucks. Once there she got a mocha Frappuccino with whipped cream and told herself that her sisters getting married was a good thing. They deserved to be happy and in love. The fact that she deserved it, too, was something she would wrestle with another time.

SATURDAY AFTERNOON, still reeling from the embedded memory of her mother's escapades and slightly off-balance from her sisters' announcement, Nevada found herself with nothing to do and nowhere to go. She wandered into Jo's Bar thinking she might find some of her friends there. Heidi, Charlie and Annabelle were at a table in the middle and they waved her over.

"We're escaping the happiness of the Fall Festival," Charlie announced, pushing a bowl of chips toward Nevada. "I love the festivals, but all those children." She shuddered.

Heidi laughed. "Not a kid person?"

"Individually they're fine, but as a group? I don't think so. Did you read *Lord of the Flies?*"

Annabelle tilted her head. "It's not about children," she began. "It's an allegory for—"

Charlie groaned. "You really are a librarian."

"Because I would lie about that?"

They laughed.

Nevada relaxed for the first time in days. Here she

could escape the complications of her life and just hang. Was that why men liked bars?

She studied the three women at the table. Heidi was casually dressed in jeans and a T-shirt, as suited her goat-girl status. Her long blond hair hung in a thick braid. She had a fresh, clean kind of pretty. Annabelle, on the other hand, was a petite redhead who favored delicate prints and wore dresses with puffed sleeves. A little fussy for Nevada's taste, but they suited her. Charlie was at the other end of the spectrum. Nevada had always considered herself pretty casual, but compared to Charlie, she practically wore couture. Charlie's off-duty uniform consisted of cargo pants and a big, open shirt over a tank top. Her short-cropped hair looked as if she'd cut it herself because it was easier than going to a salon.

Jo walked over to the table. "You drinking today?" she asked Nevada.

"No. I'll have a Diet Coke." She glanced at her friends. "Want to split nachos? These chips have put me in the mood."

Annabelle groaned. "I love nachos. And they love my thighs. Sure, I'll share."

Heidi and Charlie both nodded.

Jo looked at Heidi. "Want me to use some of that cheese you brought me?"

"Sure." Heidi smiled. "I'm bringing samples to all the businesses in town. To get some interest going. With a big ranch comes a big mortgage."

"I'm not sure I want to know how the dry cleaner is going to use cheese," Charlie muttered.

"You never use the dry cleaner," Nevada reminded her.

Charlie grinned. "A point of pride with me."

Jo looked at Nevada. "Is it true? Was your mom really going at it with Max Thurman on the kitchen table?"

Nevada winced. "Which of my sisters told you?"

"Both of them."

So typical. No one kept secrets in this town.

"I have to say," Jo continued, "I've always liked your mom, but now I have complete respect for her. She's raised six kids, survived the death of her husband and now this. I hope I'm just like her when I'm her age." She winked. "You have a great gene pool. I hope you're grateful."

"Yes, but oddly traumatized by the sight of my mother having sex."

Jo laughed, then returned to the bar.

"Did you really see Denise like that?" Charlie asked. Her voice was more "you go, girl" than shocked.

"Why is everyone taking her side?"

"Because I don't have it in me to have sex on a kitchen table," Heidi admitted. "Wouldn't it be cold and uncomfortable?"

"It depends on the surface," Annabelle said. "Glass could be freezing, but wood isn't...." She cleared her throat. "Theoretically, of course."

Charlie raised her eyebrows. "Someone has a past."

Jo returned with the soda, then went back to the bar.

"How are things out at the ranch?" Nevada asked Heidi.

"Good. We've nearly finished repairing the barn. The goats are great. The cheese takes time to produce, so what I'm selling now I made before we moved here. Next year we'll do much better with the cheese. Until that happens, cash is going to be tight. We're thinking of boarding a few horses. Do you think there's a market for that?"

"I'm looking for a place to put my horse," Charlie said.

The three of them stared at her.

"You have a horse?" Nevada asked, trying to imagine Charlie riding.

"Sure. I like horses, I like being outside."

"I've never seen you on a horse."

"I board him at a place about thirty miles from here. I'd like to get him closer. I'm not the only one. Morgan just bought his granddaughter a pony and they're keeping it in the same place."

Heidi grinned. "Thanks for telling me. The barn is ready to go. Seriously, why don't you come by and look it over?"

"I will."

They set a time for the following afternoon.

Jo arrived with the nachos. Conversation shifted to the Fall Festival and what was going on in town.

"I got the paperwork on the blasting permits," Charlie told Nevada.

"Good. Are you going to be our fire department representative?"

Charlie grabbed a chip covered in cheese. "I'll be there, keeping you in line."

"I don't plan to cross the line, believe me. We want everything to go smoothly."

"Oh, look." Annabelle shifted in her seat and pointed toward the door.

Nevada turned around and saw Will walking in. He crossed to the bar and waited for Jo to notice him.

"They were fighting in the alley the other night," the librarian said. "Well, not fighting exactly, but having a heated discussion." She lowered her voice. "He really wants to go out with her and she keeps telling him no. I'm not sure why. He's cute and he seems nice."

"He is," Nevada said absently, watching as Jo shook her head, ignoring whatever it was Will was saying. "I work with him. He's a sweetie."

"I don't get it," Charlie said. "There aren't that many good guys out there. If someone like him is interested, she should go for it."

Nevada glanced at the tall woman. Charlie sounded almost wistful.

"Jo's been burned," Heidi told them. "She has the look. Trust me. Some guy broke her heart and she doesn't want to go there again."

"No one knows for sure," Charlie said. "With Jo, it's all unsubstantiated rumors."

A few minutes later, Will left. Jo checked on their table.

"How are you four doing?" she asked.

"What's up with the guy?" Charlie asked, delicate as always.

Nevada thought Jo would say it was none of their business, but instead she shrugged. "He's interested, I'm not. End of story."

"You know he's a great guy, right?" Nevada said, then held up her hands. "Sorry. I can't help it. I work with him."

"Then you want what's best for him," Jo told her. "That's not me."

She walked away, leaving them all staring after her.

Annabelle reached for a chip. "I love this town. It's better than TV."

"YOU COULDN'T DRIVE?" Tucker called, pushing off the truck and walking toward the man stepping off the private jet that had just landed at the Fool's Gold airport.

Nevada hung back, not sure why Tucker had asked her to come with him to pick up his father. Tucker crossed the tarmac and the two men shook hands, then embraced.

They were about the same height, with similar dark hair and easy smiles. Nevada shifted from foot to foot, then moved toward the two of them.

"Mr. Janack," she said, holding out her hand.

"Elliot, please," he said. "Good to see you again, Nevada. You keeping my son in line?"

"Doing my best."

They climbed into Tucker's large truck. She took the rear seat. Elliot angled toward her.

"I'm glad you're on the team," he told her. "Having someone local is a big asset. I remember when we were working in South America and I pissed off one of the local farmers. He cut off my water supply until I apologized and bought designer handbags for his eight daughters." Elliot chuckled. "I don't want to make that mistake again."

"You'll be pleased to know our town council isn't that hard to work with."

"Good to hear." Elliot faced front again. "Are we on schedule?" he asked his son.

Tucker brought him up to date on the clearing, explained about the permits for water and sewer and told him when they would start the blasting. By the time they arrived at the job site, Elliot knew as much as any of them.

After Tucker parked, Nevada got out of the truck.

She expected to tell Elliot goodbye and go back to work. Instead the older man motioned for her to stay with him.

"Tucker has to make a few calls," he said as his son walked toward the trailer. "Show me around."

It sounded a lot more like an order than a request, but she was okay with that. The teams were doing great work and she was proud to show it off.

She pointed to the various clearing sites and explained how they were saving the largest-growth trees.

"People like that," Elliot said. "It's good for the environment and not much more work for us. A win. How do you like working with Tucker?"

"He's a good boss," she said, not sure what information he wanted. She would bet a lot of money that Elliot didn't know about her past with Tucker, so the question was probably general rather than specific.

"He's going to be taking over for me in a year or so."

"I didn't know that."

Elliot smiled at her. "He claims I'm not ready to retire, but I could start cutting back. He calls this project his last test. His chance to prove he has what it takes."

"That's a lot on the line," she murmured. While she'd known Tucker was taking on more and more responsibility, she hadn't thought of him running the multibillion-dollar company. "He'll do well."

"I agree."

"So, he'll be located where the headquarters are, right?"

"Yes. Chicago. I'm thinking of spending part of the year in the Caribbean."

He said something about buying a sailboat, but she wasn't listening. Tucker was leaving. She'd always known he would—that this job was temporary. But now she understood that this project was simply a stepping-stone to something bigger. Running the family firm. Of course he would want to do that. It wasn't as if she'd expected him to stay in Fool's Gold.

Location wasn't exactly the biggest problem, she admitted to herself. It was Tucker's attitude about relationships. Being in love didn't mean being a fool, no matter what he thought. Not that they had a relationship, other than friendship. She knew better than to fall for him again.

One of the guys hurried toward her. "Sorry to interrupt, boss," he said, nodding at Elliot. "We have a problem."

She raised her eyebrows, waiting for details.

"Goats," he told her. "We have goats."

CHAPTER EIGHT

"THIS IS A FIRST FOR ME," Tucker admitted, leading two goats down the road. He'd had to deal with wildlife before, but not goats. At least they were friendly enough.

"Poor Heidi," Nevada said, hanging on to her own two goats. "I think she assumed the fencing was secure. I know she's going to blame this one on the cows."

"She has cows, too?"

"Sort of. They're feral."

Tucker chuckled. "Feral cows? Is that possible?"

"According to her, it is. They came with the ranch, but they've been running wild for years. The old man who used to own the Castle Ranch died a long time ago. I barely remember when he lived there. It was abandoned close to twenty years."

And he'd been worried that building a hotel and casino in Fool's Gold would be boring.

"You know those cows," he said with a chuckle. "They can cause all kinds of trouble. Skipping class, smoking behind the gym."

She grinned at him. "Is this where I remind you you're dealing with goats on your job site? Don't mock the cows. They may come after you."

He laughed. "I can handle feral cows."

"You say that now. I noticed your dad didn't volunteer to return them to Heidi."

"He's more of a hotel guy. Too many years behind a desk."

"Ever since you started heading the big projects, I'll guess," she said.

He nodded. After his disastrous relationship with Cat had ended, he'd thrown himself into his work. Within a year, he'd been managing a ten-story building in Thailand. The following year he'd built a bridge in India. His father had started spending more time in the office.

"I don't think I could live like that," she said. "Going from place to place. I like having a home."

"Moving around is all I've known."

He glanced at her. Sunlight illuminated the various shades of blond in her hair. Her profile was perfect, her mouth full.

He looked away, not wanting to stray too far down that path. It was tempting but dangerous. Better to think about the day, the bright blue sky, the trees, the rhythmic clip-clop of the goats.

"Tell me about Fool's Gold," he said.

She smiled. "I'm not sure we have that long. It has a distinguished history."

"I'm sure. No pirates or scoundrels here."

"Maybe a few, although I am a direct descendant of one of the founding families. The first people to live here were *your* relatives, though. The Máa-zib tribe."

"Strong female warriors who used men for sex, then abandoned them. Something you can respect."

"*Appreciate* might be a better word." Humor danced in her eyes. "They left or died out. History isn't clear on that. In the eighteen hundreds, a young woman named

Ciara O'Farrell was on her way to an arranged marriage to a very wealthy older man. She fled her ship in San Francisco to look for gold and make her own fortune so she would never be at the mercy of a man."

"This place does something to women," he said. "I need to warn my guys."

"They can take care of themselves. Do you want to hear the story or not?"

"I do. Tell away."

"The captain of the ship, Ronan Kane, pursued Ciara."

"Ronan, like the guy who built my hotel?"

"It wasn't a hotel back then. He came after her and they fell in love and found gold. He built her a beautiful mansion to show his love to the entire world." She looked at him. "That's your hotel."

"Okay. I like that. Drama, a chase, a happy ending."

"We're so pleased you approve of our history."

"Is there still gold in the mountains?"

"Probably, but no one is looking for it. Kids sometimes go panning for gold. It's been years since anyone discovered anything."

"Maybe Heidi could train the goats to sniff out gold."

"I'll mention that to her."

They rounded a corner and saw an old farmhouse up ahead. It had been built in the thirties, he would guess. The roof wasn't in bad shape, but the whole place needed painting. He wondered if any of the original woodwork remained. He appreciated craftsmanship in any form.

A woman ran out the open gate and hurried toward them.

"Heidi," he guessed.

"Looking for her goats."

"Maybe I should get a goat."

Nevada laughed. "Start with something small. Like a fish. If you can keep that alive, we'll talk."

"You wound me."

"I'm sorry," Heidi called as she approached. "It's all my fault. I wasn't paying attention and I left the gate open."

"Not to worry," Nevada told her. "They found their way to the construction site and scared the guys. I enjoyed seeing that happen."

Heidi gave her a sad smile. "We were distracted by some bad news." The smile faded. "A friend of my grandfather's told us he's sick. He needs surgery and medicine and doesn't have insurance. It's a terrible situation." She took the lead ropes. "Thanks for bringing them back."

"You're welcome." Nevada touched her arm. "What can I do to help with your friend?"

Tucker noticed the phrasing. Not "Can I do anything?" but "What can I do?" There was a difference. An assumption of getting involved. Another small-town characteristic?

"Nothing right now, but I'll let you know if that changes."

"Please do. You're one of us now, and we take care of our own."

Heidi's blue eyes filled with tears. "Thank you," she said, and hugged Nevada. Then she turned back to the ranch, leading the goats.

"That was nice," Tucker said when they'd started back to the construction site.

"I meant it. If she needs help, we'll be there for her. We can do a fundraiser or check with the local hospital to see if they can give the guy a break on the cost." She frowned. "I'll go back later today and explain all that. Maybe talk to the mayor."

"Why would the mayor get involved?"

"That's the beauty of a small town. Or, at least, Fool's Gold. If anyone tries to mess with Heidi or her grandfather, he or she is going to be messing with the whole town."

"You should put out a warning sign."

"We prefer the thrill of the surprise."

The Gold Rush Ski Lodge and Resort sat up on the mountain at just over four thousand feet. There was plenty of snow in the winter for skiers and snowboarders, and the cold weather was also a great excuse for those who simply wished to look good sitting around the fireplace. The elegant resort was home to Fool's Gold's only five-star restaurant and had a monthly "chef in residence" dinner that brought in people from as far away as New York and Japan. It was the kind of place where anyone who enjoyed food looked forward to going for dinner. That meant Nevada should be thrilled to be there. Except she wasn't.

The invitation had come when her mother left a message on her voice mail. "Family dinner at seven. You'll be meeting Max."

As Nevada had already seen Max naked, she wasn't sure an introduction was necessary at this point. Nor was it especially welcome. What was she supposed to say? Where was she supposed to look? There were dozens of potential pitfalls and she wasn't confident in her ability to avoid them all. Not that staying home was an option.

She'd briefly thought about bringing Tucker with her as a distraction, but if she asked him she'd have to explain why she needed him, and she didn't want to have to relive the moment by talking about it. Instead, she deliberately arrived a few minutes late, hoping the crowd of her brothers and sisters, their families and significant others would shield her.

She saw Simon, Montana's fiancé, in the lobby, talking on his cell phone. His expression was intense, so she hung back until he'd ended the call, then crossed to him.

"Hi, Simon."

He tucked the phone into his suit jacket pocket, then smiled and took both her hands. "Nevada. How are you?"

After kissing her cheek, he tucked her arm in the crook of his elbow and led her toward the private dining room off the lobby.

She came to a stop, forcing him to do the same. "I need to ask you a medical question."

He faced her, his gray-green eyes meeting hers. "Of course. How can I help?"

Simon was possibly the most handsome man Nevada had ever seen. There was a beauty to his face that made him slightly separate from others who were merely good-looking or attractive. But that was only half the picture. The other half was a set of burn scars that savaged half of his features.

He was both beauty and beast—outwardly. From what Nevada knew of him, on the inside he was a gifted healer who sacrificed all for his patients and loved her sister with a devotion that would cause the happiest of women a slight case of envy.

"Is there some way to erase a specific memory?" she asked. "Hypnosis or maybe some kind of electronic probe in my frontal lobe?"

The perfect side of his mouth twitched slightly.

"This isn't funny," she added, knowing she sounded defensive.

"It's a little funny."

"Fine." She sighed. "Be amused, but I still want an answer."

"What do you know about your frontal lobe?" he asked.

"Not much."

"Trust me. It's not a place you want to go messing around in." He kissed her cheek again. "Your mother is an amazing, vital woman. You should be happy for her."

"I am. I just didn't want to *see* her 'vital' side. She's my mother. It's not natural."

He chuckled. "I'm sorry. I can't help. For what it's worth, the memory will fade with time."

"That's not worth very much."

"It's the best I have."

"And here I thought you were a gifted doctor."

He was still laughing when they walked into the dining room.

She stood in the doorway, watching Simon walk to Montana, then took in the rest of her family. Kent with his son, and Ethan with Liz. Their kids laughing and talking. Dakota with Finn, who held Hannah. Nevada braced herself for the rush of memories and allowed her gaze to sweep over her mother and the tall, well-dressed man next to her.

Here it is, she thought, trying not to wince. The memory slammed into her, making her want to cover her eyes and shriek. Instead she grabbed a glass of champagne from the table by the door and sucked about half of it down in a single gulp. To quote that dead German guy, that which didn't kill her would make her stronger.

She made the rounds, greeting her siblings, her nieces and nephews, spouses and fiancés, then finally, when there was nothing else to do, walked toward her mother and Max.

Denise saw her coming and whispered something to Max, before meeting Nevada in the center of the room by the elegantly set table.

"How are you?" Denise asked, frowning slightly. "I wasn't sure if I should call or come by."

"I'm fine, Mom."

"That's not what I heard."

Nevada drew in a breath. "I'm glad you and Max are happy. Really. It's great. Don't take this wrong, but I never, ever want to walk in on the two of you having sex again. Especially on the kitchen table."

Denise grinned. "Weren't you even a little impressed?"

"No. You're my mother. I ate cereal at that table. It was too twisted for me."

"I know. I'm sorry. I'll make sure the door is locked when we...you know, do it."

Nevada winced. "Please don't say 'do it,' I beg you. Let's call it *armadillo*. You'll lock the doors when you armadillo and then no one will surprise you. How's that?"

Her mother laughed, then hugged her. "I can't wait for you to have children of your own."

"I don't see that happening in the near future, but, sure."

"Are we okay?"

Nevada nodded. "We're fine."

"Good. Now, come meet Max." Her mother drew her toward the man. "You're really going to like him. He's great."

"I'm sure he is. And, hey, what a butt."

Denise started to laugh. Nevada joined in and decided that maybe it was going to be all right after all.

AFTER DINNER, Nevada drove home, but found herself too restless to stay inside. She changed into jeans and tennis shoes, then grabbed her keys and a hoodie and went outside. It was nearly ten and the sky was clear. She could practically touch the stars as she walked. There was a bit of nip in the air, so she shrugged into the hoodie, but didn't bother zipping it.

They were nearing the end of September. One morning she would wake up and the leaves would all be changed. Then winter would come and the mountains would be blanketed in white. For the most part Fool's

Gold only got a small portion of the snow that was dumped higher up, but there could be enough to slow construction. She made a mental note to go over the schedule to make sure there were contingencies and allowances for bad weather.

Once she reached the center of town, she paused, not sure which way to go. Jo's Bar was always an option, but on Friday and Saturday night it was more a date place than a girl hangout. Good for Jo's business, but not so fun for single women who were restless.

"How was dinner?"

She turned and saw Tucker walking toward her. "Hi. It was good. I got through it without shrieking."

He grinned. "I'm sure that pleased everyone. You and your mom okay?"

"We were always fine. I wasn't mad at her, I was just freaked a little. And don't tell me to get over it. Would you want to walk in on your dad having sex with some woman?"

"It depends on the woman."

She shoved his arm. "You're lying. It would send you screaming into the night just as much as it did me."

He raised both eyebrows. "You saw my dad having sex? When?"

"Stop it. You know what I mean."

"Yes, I do. Come on. Let's go back to my hotel. I'll buy you a drink and you can tell me all about it."

"The sex or the dinner?" she asked.

"The dinner."

She nodded her agreement, even as a voice in her head warned her against the plan. Hanging out with Tucker socially was trouble. They couldn't seem to be alone together without some kind of physical reaction, at least on her part. Did she really want to take the chance?

Then he grabbed her hand and pulled her along, and she found herself going because backing out would make too big a deal out of it—and maybe, just maybe, she wanted something to happen, because he was Tucker and she'd never completely gotten him out of her system.

She drew in a deep breath, grateful one could think long thoughts without getting winded.

"What did you do tonight?" she asked.

"Got an early dinner, then saw a movie."

"Still liking the town?"

"Sure. Everyone is friendly. They all know who I am, which is a little scary, but I'm dealing."

She grinned. "Any more encounters with the ladies?"

"No. You are excellent protection. Which is why I'm paying for the drinks."

The bar at Ronan's Folly was only about half-full. Tucker led them to a small booth in the back corner. They both ordered cognac and leaned back against the leather bench seats.

"Did everyone like Max?" he asked.

She nodded. "He's Montana's boss, so it's not as if he was a stranger. He's basically a good guy. From what I can figure out, he knew my mom when she was a teenager and it was a pretty hot romance. Then she met my dad and she knew he was the one. So Max left town."

"He didn't fight for the girl?"

"I guess he knew he was going to lose. Dakota's talked to Mom about it. She said Max knew he wasn't ready to settle down. And Mom wanted a husband and a family."

"It's been a long time since your dad died. I'm glad she's found someone."

"Me, too. As long as I don't have to be a witness to the hot monkey sex."

The cognac arrived. She took a sip and felt the liquid burn its way down her throat.

"Come upstairs with me."

The words and the request both caught her off guard. She looked at Tucker, but couldn't figure out what to say. Her hands started shaking, so she tucked them under the table.

"Tucker, I…"

She pressed her lips together, mostly to keep herself from blurting out an agreement. She knew what going upstairs meant. That they would touch and give and take and make love. That she would feel his hard body against hers, his hands pleasing her. She wanted to know what he would be like inside of her, this time, when she was ready and hungry.

His dark eyes were bright with passion. She was sure hers were the same.

"I want you," he murmured, then lightly touched the side of her face.

His fingers were warm. She was already melting inside. Imagine what would happen if she gave in.

"I really like my job," she whispered.

"This has nothing to do with that."

She knew what he meant—that giving in or refusing

wouldn't affect her employment. Tucker wasn't going to fire her for saying no. But making love with him would change everything.

He leaned in to kiss her. She met him more than halfway and anticipated a deep, sensual, passionate kiss. Instead he barely touched his mouth to hers. The light brush of sensitive skin against her own trembling mouth aroused her more than nearly anything else she could imagine. The restraint and the promise weakened her resolve.

Her breasts ached for his touch. Between her thighs, she was already swollen. Just trying not to think about how it would feel to have him touch her made the image even more clear.

Give in, she thought. She wanted to.

"I can't," she whispered, against his mouth, then slid out of the booth. "I can't."

She stood beside the table, frustrated, near tears and yet determined. "This has to stay strictly business."

"It's already too late," he told her.

Maybe, but for now she could pretend. She opened her mouth, then closed it, turned and fled the bar. She made it all the way home without once looking back, without admitting that she hoped he would follow her. He didn't. When she reached her house, she went upstairs alone and faced a very cold, very empty bed.

TUCKER DIDN'T LIKE to lose. Not in business and not in his personal life. He'd spent a hellishly long night wanting what he couldn't have. He was pissed off and didn't care that all the reasons against it made sense, that Nevada had made the right decision.

What had started out being driven by having something to prove had turned into something else. Something more important. That didn't ease the ache or the hunger. Sometimes, life was a bitch.

He stalked back to the trailer, thinking coffee would help his mood. When he arrived he faced not only an empty pot but a well-dressed, white-haired woman sitting in the chair beside his desk.

"Mr. Janack," she said, coming to her feet. "I'm Mayor Marsha Tilson."

"Mayor Tilson." He held out his hand.

They shook. "Call me Mayor Marsha," she said. "Nearly everyone does."

"All right, Mayor Marsha. How can I help you?"

"I wanted to talk about the project out here. What you're doing and how it's going."

Visiting local officials rarely brought good news, he thought. He crossed to the coffeepot and replaced the used filter and grounds. After flipping the switch to start, he faced the older woman.

"We're still on schedule. Of course it's been all of a month, so that could change by this afternoon. We're current on all our permits. We'll start excavating to put in the sewer and water pipes within a week or two."

He leaned against the trailer's counter and crossed his arms over his chest. Now it was her turn.

She stood and moved closer. Her light blue suit and fussy blouse were out of place in the construction trailer. The strange thing was, *she* wasn't out of place. He'd met people like her—those who belonged anywhere. It was an important gift, especially in a politician.

"The town is very happy with your work," she told him. "You pay attention to local regulations and you don't cut corners. Your employees are respectful." She smiled. "They're also generous tippers."

He raised an eyebrow. "An interesting fact to keep track of."

"This is my town. I care about what happens here, and very little happens that I don't know about."

He wondered if she was going to take him to task for trying to sleep with Nevada. Although if she were a man instead of a grandmother, she would be congratulating him on his good taste and wishing him luck.

"We appreciate what the resort will bring to Fool's Gold," she continued. "Business, jobs, tourists. There will be complications, of course. Something this big will have a settling-in period. We'll get through it—we always do."

He sensed there was more and waited.

"Your company won't be running the resort."

She wasn't asking, but he answered anyway. "No."

"But you do have a say in who is hired. Janack Construction is part owner."

"We'll have input. Why? Do you have a nephew you want me to recommend?"

She smiled. "No. But I would like to be consulted when the upper-level management decisions are made. People have to fit in, respect the town. I'm not interested in an us-versus-them mentality."

On the surface she looked like the kind of old lady who got her hair done once a week, baked cookies and clucked her tongue at "young people today." But he could tell those assumptions were wrong.

"You're pretty tough, aren't you?"

"When the situation calls for it," she admitted. "Will you do as I ask?"

"Sure. But in return I want to know why Jo Trellis keeps blowing off Will. He's only trying to get to know her."

"You're assuming I have that information."

"I'm not wrong."

The mayor shook her head. "No, you're not. There is a reason."

"Are you going to tell me what it is?"

She picked up her purse and walked toward the door. "No. It's not my secret to share."

"So, there's a secret."

"Everyone has secrets, Mr. Janack. Even you."

CHAPTER NINE

MAX LEANED IN and kissed Denise on the mouth. They were lying in bed, where they spent a good part of their time together. She found it kind of nice to know that, even at her age, the hormones were alive and well. Being around Max made her feel all tingly and happy.

"My kids really liked you," she said, staring into his blue eyes and smiling.

"Did they have a choice?"

She laughed. "They could have been difficult, not that I expected them to be. You'd already won over Montana. She loves her job."

"She's great to have around. She's responsible and inventive. A combination that's hard to find. Nevada avoided looking at me all evening."

"Can you blame her?"

"No. We really need to start locking the doors."

"I agree." She snuggled close, her legs tangling with his.

She'd spent the first few years after Ralph's death wondering how she was going to survive. Even though her kids were grown, she'd kept busy. Recently, she'd thought it would be nice to start dating again. She'd hoped to find someone who interested her. She'd never thought she would be lucky enough to fall so completely for a man as amazing as Max.

"I never stopped thinking about you," he told her. "Wondering how you were, what you were doing."

"I thought about you, too." She had, fleetingly. After all, she'd been taking care of Ralph and their six kids. There hadn't been a lot of time for speculation.

"Not the same," he told her lightly. "You were married to someone else."

"You never married?"

He shook his head. "Didn't want to. There were women," he added.

She smiled. "Dozens. Hundreds."

"At least."

He kissed her.

She felt a twinge and pushed the jealousy away. She had no right. She'd been off being happy and she should want the same for Max. Thirty-five years was a long time.

"I wanted to come back when I first heard about Ralph," he admitted. "But I knew that would be a mistake."

"You're right. It would have been. I wasn't ready. I grieved for him for a long time. Plus with the kids…"

He kissed her again. "I wasn't ready, either. I knew I had to change, to be the man you deserved. Grow up, I guess. But it's different now. I can be that guy."

She traced the shape of his jaw, then rested her hand on his bare shoulder. "You were always that guy."

"No, but I had potential. I love you, Denise. I want to marry you."

She heard the words, followed by a rushing sound. The room tilted, then seemed to spin out of control. All she could think about was when she'd married Ralph.

How proud he'd been when the minister had introduced them as Mr. and Mrs. Hendrix. How she'd known then she would love him forever.

"No," she said involuntarily, sitting up and pulling the sheet with her. She scrambled out of the bed, wrapping the sheet around her. "I'm sorry. But no." Her breath came in short gasps as her lungs constricted.

She stared at him, strong and handsome and naked in her bed. In her bedroom. What had she been thinking?

"I'm sorry," she repeated, giving in to the panic.

Max got to his feet and came around the bed. "What's wrong? Why are you crying?"

She touched her face and was surprised to feel tears. "You're a good person. No, a wonderful person. But this would be all wrong." She knew she wasn't making any sense, but couldn't stop herself from speaking.

"Getting married would ruin everything," she said, backing away from him. "There's more to a relationship than great sex. More to marriage. Haven't you figured that out by now? We're having fun. Just two people having fun."

He looked concerned rather than angry. "Are you feeling all right?"

"No."

She ran into the bathroom and closed the door. "I'm not feeling very well," she yelled to him, through the door. "I think you should go."

"Denise, you're not making any sense. We have to talk about this."

"We don't. Please, just go away."

She sank onto the floor and started to cry. Guilt

attacked her as she realized she'd betrayed the man she truly loved. She'd cheated on Ralph. She'd allowed herself to believe she could be with someone else.

She heard noises from the bedroom, followed by silence. Seconds later, the front door closed. Max was gone.

She pulled her knees up to her chest and wrapped her arms around her legs. She was cold. And alone.

NEVADA WATCHED all the equipment being off-loaded.

"Makes your heart beat a little faster, doesn't it?" Charlie asked.

The fire department engineer stood next to her, at the job site.

Nevada grinned. "Oh, yeah. I can't wait to try it all out."

"Tell me about it. I don't technically have to be here, but I couldn't help coming to watch. How's the surveying going?"

"Great." Nevada shoved her hands into her back pockets. "We still use tripods for housing construction and remodels. It's fast and cheap. Here we're using GPS. We can get within an eighth of an inch using a satellite twenty thousand miles away. You gotta love technology."

"If only those satellites could put out fires," Charlie said, watching a track loader being moved off to the side. "That one is going to be fun to ride. No wonder the guys want to keep it to themselves."

They weren't the only ones watching the equipment arrive. Several members of Nevada's team were standing together, supposedly to help should something happen. Nevada caught a couple of them eyeing Charlie with a fair degree of interest.

"I think a few of my guys are going to ask for your number," she told her friend.

"Don't bother giving it to them." Charlie didn't even glance toward the cluster of men. "I'm not interested."

"You sure? Some of them are pretty nice and a few are cute."

"Let me guess. None of them are both cute *and* nice."

Nevada grinned. "I can think of one or two who meet that criteria."

"Doesn't matter. I'm not very successful at relationships. It's easier to avoid them. So let's talk about something more fun. The permits for the explosives have been approved. You can go ahead and order the dynamite."

"I get all quivery at the thought."

"You should. It's going to be a hell of a day." Charlie's phone beeped. "I can't believe you got a cell tower out here."

"It was delivered last week. Janack Construction has friends in high places."

"So I've heard. Let me take this, then we can go into town and have lunch."

They were meeting Annabelle and Heidi at Jo's Bar for a quick meal. Something they'd started doing weekly ever since the incident with the flat tire.

While Charlie talked on the phone, Nevada went back to the trailer to grab her car keys. She walked up the stairs and opened the door, only to breathe a sigh of relief when she discovered Tucker wasn't th

She wasn't exactly avoiding him, but she'd been staying out of his way ever since that night at his hotel. When he'd told her he wanted her and she'd turned him down.

She didn't regret her decision. She sighed. Perhaps she regretted it a little, but she knew she'd made the right choice. Getting involved with Tucker was a complication she didn't need. Better to focus on what was important rather than what felt good. Although being with Tucker felt really, really good.

She set her hard hat on her desk, then picked up her purse and met Charlie outside.

Twenty minutes later they were sitting in Jo's Bar with Annabelle and Heidi. They'd gone girly and had all ordered salads, with a plate of fries for the table.

"Don't let me have more than three," Annabelle was saying. "I don't have the advantage of being tall like all of you. Every extra pound shows at my size."

"Next she'll complain about being too rich, too," Charlie grumbled, sipping her iced tea.

Annabelle didn't look the least bit intimidated. "You try being the size of a flea and we'll see how you like it."

"You try being taller than ninety percent of the male population."

"At least you can kick their butts if they annoy you," the librarian said with a smile.

Charlie grinned back. "You got that right."

The women laughed.

Nevada joined in, pleased to be with her new friends. Recently her social life had gotten a little stagnant. She mostly hung out with her sisters. As they were moving in a different direction than her—getting married and, in Dakota's case, starting a family—it was good that she'd branched out. Being the last single triplet was going to mean her sisters wouldn't have as much time for hanging out.

Reality intrudes, she thought, happy for them but a little sad for herself. While change could be good, it wasn't always easy or comfortable.

Jo walked over with their salads and fries.

"How's it going?" Annabelle asked. "I saw Will here the other day. He's such a cutie."

"We're not going out," Jo said flatly. "I don't care what anyone says. I'm not dating him."

The four of them exchanged a look. Nevada found herself feeling badly for her coworker.

"You know he's a nice guy," she said quietly. "On the job site all the guys respect him, but they like him, too."

Instead of looking relieved, Jo scowled. "You think I don't know he's nice? Did it occur to you that his niceness is the problem? I'm not going to get involved with him just to screw up everything."

She slapped the plates on the table, then stalked away.

Nevada looked at Charlie. They'd known Jo the longest. Charlie had shown up in Fool's Gold about the same time Jo had.

"Not a clue," Charlie said, reaching for a French fry "Sounds like she's dealing with something from t' past."

"We all are." Annabelle gazed longingly at the ing she'd ordered on the side, then ignored i' speared a piece of lettuce. "Relationships with men are never easy. If I were to make a list of all the mistakes I've made and line them up, I could reach China."

Heidi looked intrigued. "Any you want to share?"

Annabelle shook her head. "Let's just say I wasn't always the quiet librarian I am now. I used to be…different."

"Men can be real bastards," Heidi said with a sigh.

"You got that right," Charlie muttered, taking another French fry.

Nevada thought about how her heart had been broken in a single night. While she would lay part of the blame at Tucker's feet, she knew she had some culpability, too.

"Relationships are never easy," she admitted.

"No, but your boss is yummy," Heidi said with a grin. "Please tell me being around him makes you tingle. I can't remember the last time I felt a tingle."

"We work together." Nevada knew she sounded prim but was afraid they would guess how he tempted her.

"You don't have to grab the merchandise, but you have to be looking." Heidi raised her eyebrows. "Have you seen his butt?"

"He does have a good butt," Charlie told her. "I hate nearly all men and even I've noticed that."

Annabelle nodded. "I agree. Your brother Ethan is pretty hot, too. I say that in a respectful way. He's married and obviously crazy in love with his wife." She sighed. "Despite everything, I find myself wanting to find the right guy. Still."

"Not me," Charlie grumbled. "There is no right guy."

"You can't really believe that," Heidi told her. "While

I'm not interested in someone for myself, I can understand the longing. I used to feel that way. Until I had my hopes and dreams crushed." She speared some of her salad on her fork. "Now I live with my grandfather and raise goats. Who says life doesn't have a sense of humor?"

"There are still great guys out there," Nevada said. "Both my sisters are happy and in love."

"True," Heidi admitted.

"Annoying." Charlie rolled her eyes. "Your sisters got lucky. I'll admit that. There are—" She paused. "Is that your mom?"

Nevada turned and saw her mother standing in the center of the bar. When Denise spotted Nevada, she hurried over.

"I'm sorry to bother you," she began.

Nevada was already on her feet. Her mother's face was pale, her eyes red. It was obvious she was upset and had been crying.

Nevada grabbed her hand and pulled her away from the table. "What's wrong? What happened? Is someone hurt?" A million possibilities, each one worse than the one before, passed through her mind.

"It's not that." Tears filled her mother's eyes. "I wanted to let you know, I'm selling the house and moving out of town."

Nevada stared at her. There was no way she'd heard that correctly. "What are you talking about? What are you saying?"

"I have to leave right away."

"Why?"

"Max wants to marry me."

"I SHOULD HAVE BEEN an orphan," Nevada announced.

Tucker looked up from his computer, her words pulling him away from the schedule he'd been revising. "You love your family."

"Most of the time, but every now and then I think it would be nice to go it alone." She glanced at him. "My mother is threatening to sell the house and move."

"Why?"

"She's hysterical. Max wants to marry her. I'm guessing she doesn't want to marry him, although getting her to talk in complete sentences that make sense is tough. All she keeps saying is that she has to leave Fool's Gold and she's never coming back. I'm meeting my sisters at the house later. We're going to try to get this cleared up."

Too much information, he thought, trying to figure out which problem he should address first.

"She doesn't want to move," he told her. "This is her town." He frowned. "I thought she liked Max."

"Me, too. They're crazy about each other. We had that family dinner to meet him and we all thought he was great. Even me."

He guessed the "even me" part was more about Nevada's having seen the man naked and having sex than her being unwilling to accept her mother's new boyfriend.

"I thought all women wanted to get married."

"Cliché much?" she asked sharply, then slapped her hands on the desk. "Sorry. I'm snippy. This just isn't like my mom and it's weird to have her unsettled. Whenever something happened when we were kids, she was a rock. Dad died and she was crushed, but she kept moving forward. So to fall apart like this because Max declares his love and wants to marry her doesn't make any sense."

"You're talking to her in the morning. You'll get it straightened out then."

"I hope so. Sometimes relationships are complicated."

"Agreed." The main reason he avoided them.

"Look at Jo and Will."

"Do I have to?" he asked. "I work with Will and we don't talk about personal stuff."

"Such guys. Talking about it helps."

"How?"

"You can work out your issues."

"If you don't get involved with anyone, you don't have issues in the first place."

She narrowed her gaze. "That's like saying you're never going to eat again because you don't want to risk food poisoning. Or is it Cat you're trying to avoid?"

"I don't need to avoid Cat. She's out of my life."

Nevada wheeled her chair around so she was staring at him. "Are you saying you haven't been in a serious relationship since Cat?"

"No. Would you want to be with anyone after her?"

"But she wasn't a regular person. She was more like a…" She paused, as if searching for the word.

"Drug," he said flatly. "She took over my head and tried to suck the life out of me. No way I want to do that again."

At the risk of getting too in touch with his feminine side, with Cat he'd lost who he was. He'd been her slave—emotionally and physically, which proved love made people into idiots. He'd been lucky to escape.

"That wasn't love, it was obsession," Nevada told him. "There's a difference."

"Maybe, but I'm not willing to take the chance."

"A mature relationship would be totally different."

He shook his head. "Your mother was in a mature relationship and look what happened there. Max wants to marry her and she wants to move out of town. Trust me, friendship and sex. That's plenty." Now it was his turn to look at her. "Do you want more than that?"

"That's not the point," she told him. "To say you're not interested in falling in love—that's just sad."

"I believe in love itself," he told her. "People love each other. But romantically, there are more pitfalls than it's worth."

He was sharing his opinion, but he was also warning her. While he wanted her, the rules needed to be clear. If she was expecting more, he wasn't the guy for her.

Something he hadn't fully considered, he realized. Both her sisters were engaged. Dakota was pregnant, had a kid she'd adopted. Talk about the dream of the white picket fence.

"You're like them," he said slowly, still getting hold of the truth and not liking it. "Your sisters."

"I don't know what you mean, but of course I'm like them. We're identical. We have the exact same DNA."

He swore quietly. What had, until this second, been a game he'd wanted to win had just gotten a whole lot more serious.

"What?" she asked. "What's wrong?"

Disappointed didn't begin to describe the reality of knowing he could never have her. Nevada was all sass and temptation. Smart, funny and skilled with a backhoe. Did it get any better than that?

He'd imagined them in bed, naked, hungry. He'd wanted to know what it felt like to please her, to have her screaming his name. Sure, that was a lot of male ego, but he didn't think wanting to please her was a hanging offense. But now, everything was different.

"I'm not that guy," he said flatly.

She shrugged her shoulders. "What guy?"

"The white picket fence guy—Finn, Simon. I'm the guy who doesn't get involved. I did that once and I'm not going back. It's hell."

She rolled her eyes. "You're a little dramatic today. What you felt for Cat wasn't love. It was…" Her eyes widened. "Oh. You're not talking generalities. You're talking about us. Not that there is an us."

"There's an us."

"Okay."

She shifted in her seat. "I wasn't expecting you to marry me just because we slept together. Not that we've done that, either."

"We were going to."

Color flared on her cheeks. "I hadn't decided."

He had and he'd been confident in his ability to convince her it was a good idea. Not anymore, he thought grimly. He liked her and respected her enough not to play games.

"You were right to say our work relationship had to come first," he told her. "That we shouldn't get personally involved. I was wrong to push. This project is important to me and you're a key member of my team. I won't forget that again."

An emotion chased across her face. He couldn't read it, nor could he guess. Relief made the most sense. Assuming his disappointment was more about his own ego than it was about her.

"Okay, then," she murmured, then glanced at her watch. "I'm supposed to meet my sisters to strategize about our meeting with Mom. I'll pass on the coffee."

"Sure."

She collected her keys and purse, then left.

He watched her go, wondering if she really had to be somewhere or if she was trying to get away from him. In the end, he knew it didn't matter. From time to time he might be a bastard, just like every other guy on the planet, but he was determined to do the right thing when it came to Nevada.

By THE NEXT MORNING Nevada had nearly convinced herself that Tucker was smart to insist they return to a "business only" relationship. The decision was sensible and easier in the long run. If she was a tiny bit annoyed that he didn't find her irresistible, well, that was something she would have to get over. If she was sad that there wouldn't be any more amazing kisses, that was a fact she would deal with over time. It wasn't as if she'd fallen for him or anything.

She walked up to the front porch of her mom's house. The door opened before she reached it. Dakota and Montana were waiting for her.

"How is she?" Nevada asked.

"Still hysterical and insisting she's moving." Dakota

sighed. "And we've only been here for about three minutes. This isn't going to be a fun conversation."

"None of us thought it would be."

Nevada followed her sisters into the kitchen, where they found their mother frantically scrubbing an already clean sink.

"I don't want to talk about it," Denise announced when she turned toward them, her sponge dripping on the floor. "You can't change my mind. I'm not marrying Max."

The sisters looked at each other, then back at her.

Dakota spoke first. "It's okay, Mom. None of us were telling you to marry Max."

Denise returned her attention to the sink. After rinsing it, she attacked the counters. "Good, because I'm not going to. I was married to your father. He was my husband, and that's not going to change."

"I don't understand," Nevada admitted. "Why are you acting as if we're all insisting you accept Max's proposal? Why does anything have to change?"

"He won't understand," Denise said, moving to the cooktop and removing burners. "He'll be upset."

"Max?" Montana asked.

"Yes. I don't want that."

"You think he'll be happier with you moving out of town?" Dakota asked softly.

Denise dropped the sponge and seemed to crumple in on herself. She returned to the sink, peeled off her purple gloves, then started to cry.

"I can't do this," she sobbed. "I'm too old to fall in love again. Or re-in love."

Her daughters moved in and surrounded her. Nevada

wasn't sure if she was being especially stupid today, because she didn't understand the crisis.

"I know what you're thinking," Denise said between wiping her face and blowing her nose on a tissue she'd pulled out of her jeans pocket. "That I'm not being a very good role model. That I always said to be strong and stand up to your problems. You think I don't want to be like that? Sometimes it's hard, but I had to say those things because that's what mothers do."

"Okay, you've moved from upset to talking crazy," Nevada told her, taking her hand and leading her into the family room. She set her mother on the sofa, then settled next to her. Dakota took the other side, while Montana sat on the coffee table, facing her.

"Mom, you're wrong," Nevada told her. "You don't have to move away from where you live because a man proposed."

Denise's eyes filled with more tears. "What am I supposed to say?"

"I'd start with the truth," Dakota told her. "That you care about him but you don't want to get married. You want to keep seeing him, right?"

Denise nodded.

"Say that. If he doesn't appreciate your honesty, then let *him* move."

"Hey," Montana snapped. "My boss, my job."

"Sorry."

Nevada rubbed her mother's arm. "Dakota's right. Just because he proposes doesn't mean you have to say yes. And refusing doesn't mean everything is over.

Maybe he thinks you're the one who wants to be married. You do seem like the type."

Denise sniffed. "Traditional? I always have been. But this is different. I do love Max, but I don't want to get married again. I promised myself that when Ralph died. I love Ralph and I love Max. Max will always be my first love. I want Ralph to always be my husband."

"So, tell him," Montana said. "I know Max cares about you, Mom. He doesn't want to upset you. What you're describing is wonderful. You want each of the men you loved to have a special place. That's great. I think Nevada's right. He was proposing as much for you as for himself. Do you really think he would risk losing you over an engagement?"

"Maybe not," Denise said slowly. "I just panicked."

"Makes sense," Dakota told her. "Talk to Max. Explain how you feel. I suspect what he wants is your love."

"All right. You have a point. He's never been especially interested in following the rules. Maybe that's what surprised me so much." She sniffed again, then smiled. "You are wonderful daughters. I don't say that enough."

"You could stitch something on a pillow," Montana offered.

Denise laughed, then hugged each of them. "Thank you for rescuing me," she said.

"You've rescued us each bunches of times," Nevada reminded her. "We're happy to help."

"Thank you. All right. Enough of my crisis. I'll talk to Max later and if he reacts badly, I'll have another breakdown. But for now I'm fine." She smiled. "I don't suppose any of you wants to share something that will distract me from worrying."

Dakota and Montana glanced at each other.

"We could talk about the wedding," Dakota offered. "We've picked the date."

Denise's breath caught. "You have? When?"

"New Year's Eve," Montana said with a grin. "It's a Saturday, which is perfect. I don't know why, but the Gold Rush Ski Lodge and Resort had a recent cancellation on their main ballroom, so it's available."

Denise bounced on the sofa. "It is? Did you reserve it?"

Dakota and Montana both laughed.

"We did," Dakota admitted. "Right away. It's so perfect. We went to see it a couple of days ago and it's beautiful. We're thinking night with lots of twinkle lights."

Nevada forced herself to smile and nod, as if she were thrilled with the news. Not that she wasn't happy for her sisters. Of course she wanted them both to have the perfect wedding. But somehow knowing they were getting married on the same day made her feel kind of funny inside. As if somehow she'd missed out on something big.

Montana turned to her. "Are you okay with this?"

"Sure," Nevada said. "It sounds perfect. You're really lucky to have a cancellation only a few months out. You'll be able to have a big dinner and dancing. It's going to be so much fun."

Dakota studied her for a second, as if making sure

she was telling the truth. Nevada held her gaze, willing herself to look as normal and happy as possible.

"It's fine," she promised.

Dakota nodded, because when had Nevada ever lied to her sister before?

NEVADA RETURNED to the construction site in the early afternoon. She'd filed permits with the city, confirmed the blast dates and stopped by to see her nephew Reese and his exuberant dog, Fluffy, but nothing seemed to lift her mood. She wasn't upset or sad or even confused. She was restless. It felt as if something important was about to happen. Or maybe that was wishful thinking on her part.

She was supposed to spend the afternoon doing paperwork, one of her least favorite things. Maybe she should put it off and go dig out tree stumps with big equipment. That always made her feel better.

She walked into the trailer, intent on grabbing her hard hat and heading out. Tucker was inside, pulling something from one of the file cabinets.

"Hey," he said absently, paying more attention to the papers in his hand than her. "Everything okay with your mom?"

His dark good looks caught her off guard. As if she'd just this second realized how masculine he looked with his strong jaw and broad shoulders. He wore the usual construction uniform—jeans, work boots and a long-sleeved shirt. Not elegant clothes, but the look suited him.

Her gaze roamed over him, settling on his mouth. The mouth that knew exactly what to do to hers. The mouth that made her feel desire and wanting for the first time in forever.

Suddenly she knew why she was restless and what would make her feel better. Unfortunately, Tucker had just changed all the rules.

Fine, she told herself, walking toward him. She would change them back.

He glanced up as she approached. She didn't give him time to figure out her plan. As she got closer, she pulled the paper from his fingers and dropped it to the floor, then put her hands on his shoulders, raised herself onto her toes and kissed him.

She moved her mouth against his, at the same time sliding her hands down his back and shifting her body close enough to press against him. There was a split second when he didn't react, when she knew he could pull away, leaving her feeling more than a little stupid. A consequence she would accept if she had to, she thought.

He stiffened. She felt the stillness in his body, the indecision, then he groaned and surged against her, wrapping his arms around her and pushing his tongue into her mouth.

Passion exploded. His hands were everywhere, her hips, her back, her breasts. He cupped her curves, then rubbed his thumbs against her already tight nipples. She moaned as ribbons of need twisted through her. Heat and dampness surged between her legs.

She cupped his face in her hands, kissing him back, circling his tongue with hers. They danced and moved, the fire everywhere. She rubbed her palms against his chest before starting to unbutton his shirt. He pulled her long-sleeved T-shirt off, then unfastened her bra in a matter of seconds. Before she could register what he'd done, his mouth closed around her right nipple.

The combination of warmth, dampness and lips was nearly too much. Her thighs began to tremble. He moved to her other breast, sucking deeply, rhythmically. The pulling sensation shot down to her belly, then lower, making that most feminine part of her ache with longing.

He drew back and walked to the door, where he turned the lock. From there he crossed to Will's desk and began tearing open drawers.

"Where are they?" he muttered. He swore, pulled open another drawer. "Yes!"

He held up a condom.

"Fascinating office supplies," she said as she pulled off her boots.

"He keeps them around for the guys, more as a joke than anything else."

"I've always liked Will."

She finished with her boots and socks. Tucker headed back toward her, pulling off his shirt as he went.

She gave herself a second to enjoy the view—the sculpted muscles and narrow waist, the erection jutting against his jeans. Then he was undoing the button on her pants and pulling down the zipper. She found herself a whole lot less interested in how things looked rather than in how things felt.

He wrapped one arm around her and pressed his mouth to hers. As he kissed her into a quivering mass, he slipped one hand between her bikini panties and her hip, then moved his hand slowly, oh so slowly around. At last he eased his fingers between her thighs.

She'd been wet and swollen since the first kiss. Now she held in a groan as he explored her, sliding his fingers against slick flesh, finding that one spot and circling it slowly before brushing over it.

Heat burned down to her toes. She had to stop kissing him, had to stop even breathing so she could focus on the brush of his fingers. Back and forth, over and over. The trembling in her legs increased. She could barely stay standing.

In a matter of seconds, she was inches from coming. She gritted her teeth, then pushed him back.

"Naked," she demanded. "Now."

He obliged by pushing down his jeans and boxers. She pulled off her clothes, then shifted onto the table behind her. He put on the condom, then joined her.

She reached between them, guiding him inside of her. He was thick and long and filled her until she gasped with the pleasure of it. Every nerve ending cheered. Deep inside, she felt the tension start to increase again.

"This isn't going to go well," he groaned, pulling out and thrusting in again. "Dammit, Nevada."

Despite the building tension, despite the threatening release, she laughed. "It's not my fault."

"Sure it is. You feel too good."

He pumped in again. At the same time he cupped her breasts in his hands. His forefinger and thumb caressed her nipples. The sensations were amazing, perfect. Just enough.

"Go for it," she told him, wrapping her legs around his hips. "Just go for it."

He hesitated for a second. She pulled him in with her thighs and he sank in as far as he could.

"Like that," she breathed.

He took her at her word and moved faster, deeper. She gave herself up to the rhythm and over to the man. He dropped his hands to the desk for leverage. Again and again he filled her, stroking her so deliciously that she let her head fall back and rode the inevitable wave.

Her orgasm hit with the subtlety of a freight train. One second she was enjoying the ride, the next every muscle contracted and released. She clung to him, crying out her pleasure. More, she thought frantically. More and more and more.

He kept going. Thrusting, filling, carrying her on until the last of her contractions eased and she could breathe again. Then he groaned her name, pushed in one more time and was still.

She could feel the frantic beating of his heart and knew hers pounded just as hard. Their breath came in pants. Muscles spasmed. From outside, she heard the low rumble of heavy equipment.

She looked up and met his bemused expression.

"I thought we weren't going to do that," he told her.

"We weren't."

"That was the best not doing it I've ever had."

She laughed. "Me, too."

She supposed the awkward bits would come later—when she'd had a chance to think about what they'd done and wallow in the consequences. But for now there was only the hum of satisfaction and a pleasant relaxed sensation.

He kissed her once, then withdrew. They dressed, handing each other items of clothing. As she reached for her boots, he grabbed her and kissed her again. She went into his arms. Somewhere outside a vehicle pulled up close to the trailer.

Tucker swore and glanced toward the sound. "Rain check?" he asked.

She nodded.

They finished dressing, then unlocked the trailer door. She opened it and stepped outside.

A long, black limo had parked by the trailer. The driver got out and walked around to the rear passenger door.

Tucker moved next to her. "Someone from town?" he asked.

"Fool's Gold isn't much of a limo place," she said, curious as to who would arrive with so much fanfare.

The first thing she saw was a black leather boot with a thin high heel. Next she saw a slender, jean-covered leg, then a woman emerged.

She was of medium height, with layered dark hair. Large sunglasses covered much of her face, but Nevada recognized her all the same. There was no way she could forget the high cheekbones, the full mouth, the perfection that was unmistakable.

Caterina Stoicasescu had come to Fool's Gold.

CHAPTER TEN

NEVADA FOUND IT DIFFICULT to breathe, let alone speak. Fortunately, no conversation was needed. She could simply stand there, staring, blinking, probably looking like an idiot.

Cat, wearing a white wool coat over a dark red sweater, pulled off her sunglasses.

"I see you're both surprised," she said, then laughed, the light, tinkling sound exactly as Nevada remembered. "Good. That's what I wanted. When I accepted the invitation, I insisted no one be told. Pia promised. I've known for nearly a month I would be surprising you both!"

Bright sunshine illuminated her face. The harsh light should have been unkind. Instead of adding shadows or lines, it simply played across the perfection of her face, making her look exactly as she had ten years ago.

Nevada knew the other woman had to be in her mid to late thirties. She might even be forty—but she couldn't tell. If anything, Cat had gotten more stunning with age.

Cat hurried toward them. As she approached, Nevada inhaled the scent of her perfume and knew that, yes, this really was happening. She'd just thrown herself at Tucker, only to have the one woman who'd obsessed him show up. Talk about crappy timing.

"How I've missed you both," Cat said, throwing herself at Nevada and hugging her tightly. The other woman was strong, probably from her years of working with metal. She kissed Nevada on both cheeks, then turned to Tucker.

"You've thought of me often," she announced, before embracing him.

Nevada didn't want to watch, but she couldn't turn away. Tucker looked as stunned as she felt. It was probably like being swept up in a tornado. You could see it coming, but before you could get out of the way, it was there, sucking you up in its grasp.

Cat hugged him just as tightly, then stepped back and linked arms with Nevada. "Isn't this a wonderful surprise? When I received the invitation, I nearly threw it out. I get asked to so many places. The fame." She sighed. "Sometimes it's a burden. But then I recognized the name. Fool's Gold." She squeezed Nevada's arm. "You talked about this place, about growing up here. So I simply had to come."

Nevada cleared her throat. "I don't understand." That was more polite than what she was really thinking. Something along the lines of "Why the hell are you here?"

"There's an artist festival. I don't remember the details. That is why I have a staff." She smiled again. "Not to worry. I won't let them keep me too busy. I want us to spend time together. To get to know each other again."

The irony didn't escape Nevada. Cat had returned to both her and Tucker's lives and Nevada only had herself to blame. Why couldn't she be like other people and want to escape where she'd grown up?

Cat released her and turned to Tucker. "I thought we could spend some time together, too. It's been so long."

This time Nevada managed to turn away. She told herself she was studying the job site, getting an idea of what was going on with her crew. But it was a lie. Instead she was doing her best not to get lost in the past.

She knew what would happen. Despite his claims of being over Cat, there was no way Tucker could resist her. She was too beautiful, larger than life. Tucker was a regular guy—mortal. What hope did he have against someone like Caterina Stoicasescu?

Nevada took a step away and felt a slight ache in her hips and thighs. A reminder of their lovemaking a few minutes ago. Talk about feeling stupid, she thought glumly. How long would it take for her to feel the way she did in college? Always out of place, on the fringes, looking in and wanting what she could never have. Telling herself she was a mature adult now didn't help very much.

"I'm busy," Tucker said flatly, pulling away from Cat.

Instead of looking insulted, Cat simply smiled. "Not too busy for an old friend." She turned to Nevada. "Have dinner with me tonight. Both of you. It will be like it was before."

Nevada would rather have a root canal. "I can't."

"Of course you can. You must. Otherwise you'll break my heart. I've so been looking forward to seeing you again." Cat stared at Nevada intently. "You have to believe me."

All those years of being told to be polite by her

mother came back to bite Nevada in the butt. She found herself verbally stumbling over a believable lie.

"I, ah, I…" She sighed. "Fine. Dinner. It'll be great." *Hell* was a better word, she told herself. "But for now, I need to run."

Then she did just that. She turned her back and raced to her truck, thankful that her keys were in her jeans pocket. Seconds later she was on the dirt road leading to the highway, leaving the danger of Cat behind.

TUCKER WATCHED THE DIRT kicked up by Nevada's truck as she sped away. He couldn't blame her for getting gone while the getting was good, but now he was stuck with Cat.

She didn't seem concerned by Nevada's abrupt departure. Instead she leaned into him and smiled.

"Come with me to the hotel," she said, taking his hand in hers and tugging him toward her limo. "I want to know all you've been doing since we last saw each other. It's been what? Four years? Five?"

"Ten," he said, finding himself going along with her.

"That long? Time moves so quickly for me."

She motioned for him to go first, then slid in beside him. The driver shut the door. Seconds later they were following the path Nevada's truck had taken, albeit at a slower pace.

In the smooth leather seat, Cat angled toward him. "Tell me everything. You're still working for your father?"

He nodded cautiously.

"You always liked building things. I know the feeling of creating something beautiful from nothing. To have that piece stand alone, pure."

He wasn't sure bridges and buildings qualified as pure, but okay.

"How long are you in town?" he asked.

"I'm not sure. I'll know when it's time to leave." She gazed at him. "Still handsome."

He had to consciously keep from moving away from her. After all this time, he could still remember the first time he'd met her. She'd asked Janack Construction to build the installation for her latest piece and his dad had sent him to deliver the bid in person. He'd been a kid just out of college and she'd been unlike anyone he'd ever met before.

She'd been working on a metal piece about fourteen feet high when he'd walked into her studio. He remembered the sun pouring in the windows, the sparks from the welding and the sound of her laughter. She'd been laughing as she worked.

She'd climbed down the scaffolding to meet him. He'd taken one look at her and been lost. They'd introduced themselves, then she'd kissed him. They'd become lovers that afternoon, and she'd moved into his condo that night.

Being with Cat had consumed him. He'd blown off work, ignored his friends, spent every dime he had taking her places and buying her presents. Nothing had mattered but Cat. He'd been a junkie and she'd been his drug. Eventually he'd realized he needed to break free or he would be lost forever, but leaving her had been harder than he had thought. Each time he tried, she called him back and he'd been unable to resist.

Now, in the car, she reached out as if she were going to touch his face. He grabbed her wrist and lowered her arm to her side.

"Where are you staying?" he asked.

"At a hotel up on the mountain."

"The Gold Rush Ski Lodge and Resort," he said, relieved they weren't at the same hotel. He was in town. A safe distance from Cat.

It wasn't that he didn't trust her, he thought. It was that he didn't trust himself. There were too many memories.

"Travel is exhausting," she said, leaning back in her seat. "The public is so demanding. You remember what it was like. There is never any rest. Always something to be doing. The French government has commissioned a piece and I'm at a loss. There is so much beauty there already. What can I give them that shows my brilliance and yet pleases them."

"You worry about what your audience thinks?" he asked. That was new.

She lowered her sunglasses so he could see the startling green of her eyes. The way the corners crinkled in amusement. "No, but sometimes I pretend I do."

"That's the Cat I know," he said before he could stop himself.

"Did you think I'd change?" She looked out the window. "I spent the summer in South America. In the rain forest. The native people there are at one with nature. I learned so much from them—spiritually. I had thought perhaps butterflies for inspiration. Did you know there are butterflies who fly thousands of miles every year?

They migrate. I was impressed, but they didn't inspire me as much as I had hoped."

She turned back to him. "You've been following my career?"

"It's hard not to read about you," he said, dodging the question. Honestly, he did his best to avoid all things Cat.

"I imagine it is. So much of my life is interesting to the press. You can't know what it's like to want to be like everyone else. To be normal. To walk to a grocery store without being hounded every step."

"You want to go to a grocery store? Why?"

She smiled. "Perhaps not a grocery store, but you know what I mean. Being so famous and talented is difficult."

"Your life is pain."

She sighed and leaned against him. "I knew you would understand."

Obviously the irony of his statement had been lost on her. Not surprising. But what *was* different was that the feel of her weight against him wasn't distracting. He had no urge to put his arm around her or pull her close. Sure, she was beautiful, but so what?

He sat there, inhaling the familiar perfume and carefully probing his heart. The cliché that the opposite of love wasn't hate but indifference suddenly made sense. He didn't want Cat. He wasn't interested in her. She was someone he used to know. Given the choice between getting naked with Nevada and the woman next to him, the decision was easy. Making love with Nevada had been pure pleasure with a big dose of fun. Mostly because he liked her.

That was it, he realized. He liked Nevada. She was someone he enjoyed talking to and spending time with. He'd never liked Cat. He'd been infatuated with Cat, nearly possessed by his desperation to be with her. But liking her hadn't ever been part of their story.

He felt like Scrooge at the end of *A Christmas Carol,* when the old man found out he hadn't missed Christmas at all. That he still had time to redeem himself.

Of course now he wasn't alone with Cat. He would want to make sure that he still felt the same when it was just the two of them. But breathing just got a whole lot easier.

"What are you so happy about?" she asked, looking up at him.

"I'm a happy guy."

They arrived at the hotel. One of the bellmen stepped up quickly to open the door and Cat slid out.

Although Tucker was right behind her and saw what happened, he couldn't have explained it. As soon as Cat straightened and smiled, people came running. Two more bellmen appeared and pushed each other in an attempt to be the one to escort her into the hotel. Three members of the staff rushed toward Cat and welcomed her. A small, frightened little man with round glasses and pale, trembling hands joined the group.

"Ms. Stoicasescu, Ms. Stoicasescu, how are you? Are you feeling all right? Did the journey tire you?"

Cat smiled at the hotel staff, chose the arm of the tallest, youngest bellman and sniffed at the little man.

"Herbert, is my suite arranged? I'm exhausted."

"Of course," the little man said, nearly bowing as

she walked by. "I have seen to everything." The man glanced at Tucker. "Are you Mr. Janack?" he asked.

Tucker nodded.

"I'm Herbert, Ms. Stoicasescu's assistant. She told me that she's looking forward to you joining her for dinner this evening. Along with Ms. Hendrix. I've made reservations."

Tucker thought about pointing out that Fool's Gold wasn't a reservation kind of town but figured the poor guy was dealing with enough.

"I have plans for tonight," Tucker said with a drawl, enjoying his newfound sense of being his own man.

"But you're expected." Herbert sounded both afraid and horrified.

"Cat'll have to learn to live with the disappointment," he said and flagged a cab.

"But, Mr. Janack…"

Tucker ignored the little man, climbed into the back of the cab and started whistling.

"TELL ME WHY WE'RE HERE," Dakota said, following Nevada down a hallway at the Gold Rush Ski Lodge and Resort.

"You're here because you love me," Nevada told her. "I'm scared to be with Cat by myself."

"Why?" Montana asked. "She's a brilliant, world-famous artist. She must be fascinating."

"You'd think she was," Nevada said with a sigh. "And in some ways she is. But in others…not so much."

She didn't have a better answer to why they were there, because she couldn't figure out what *she* was doing there. One second she'd been back at her house, thinking that she needed wine and a bubble bath. The next the phone had rung, it had been Cat saying she desperately wanted to see Nevada, and that it would be a "girls only" evening. Nevada had tried to refuse, but she'd found herself saying yes, compelled by a force she couldn't explain or, apparently, ignore.

"Cat is like nature. You can try to go on about your day, as if nothing is happening, but she wins in the end," Nevada told them.

"That sounds intimidating," Montana admitted.

Dakota studied the names next to the various doors. They were by the main ballroom, but in a hallway that was new to them all.

"What am I looking for?" Dakota asked.

"The private dining room."

They separated, walking in different directions down the long hallway. The thick carpeting muffled their steps.

"Here it is," Montana called. "The private dining room." She pointed to the sign on the wall by a double door. "That's really what it says."

Nevada and Dakota joined her.

"Do we knock or just go in?" Dakota asked in a whisper.

"I haven't a clue," Nevada admitted, then decided to compromise. She knocked once and pushed the door open, doing her best not to remember that the last time she'd done that, she'd ended up seeing her mother naked and having sex on the kitchen table.

This time, however, the surprises were all good. The dining room was spacious, with a table set for four in the center and sofas lining the walls. There was a bar,

French doors leading to a private garden and piped-in music.

Two servers, both good-looking guys in their twenties, smiled at them.

"Ladies," the taller, blond one said. "Ms. Stoicas-escu will join you shortly. She said to welcome you."

He held out a tray with four glasses of champagne on it.

Dakota whimpered. "This is so unfair." She turned to the server. "I'm pregnant and can't have alcohol. Is there another choice?"

"Of course."

He offered Montana and Nevada champagne, then put down the tray and led Dakota to the bar, where he showed her an assortment of juices and soda. The second server approached with a tray of appetizers.

"Ladies."

Montana took a prosciutto-wrapped melon ball while Nevada picked up a miniquiche.

"Delicious," Montana said after she'd chewed and swallowed.

Nevada nodded, still eating her quiche. Cat might be a pain, but she knew how to throw a party.

Fifteen minutes later both Nevada and Montana were on their second glass of champagne and the three of them had made a serious dent in the appetizers. Just when Nevada had nearly forgotten why they were there, the doors opened and Cat swept into the room.

She'd changed into white wool trousers and a white fine-gauge sweater that slipped off one perfect shoulder. Her hair was loose and wavy, her makeup fresh, her diamond-and-pearl earrings large enough to be equal in value to the GDP of a small third world country. She looked like the kind of person who traveled with her own personal spotlight.

"You came," she said with such delight that Nevada felt guilty for trying to refuse.

Cat walked toward her, hands outstretched. Nevada put down her champagne, then awkwardly took the other woman's hands in hers.

Cat beamed. "Did I tell you how much I've missed you? I have. Desperately."

She sounded so sincere, Nevada found herself wanting to apologize for their long separation. Cat stepped close and hugged Nevada again, her arms holding her close for a second longer than Nevada expected. When Cat moved back, she turned to Nevada's sisters.

"I'm delighted you're joining me tonight. Thank you so much for coming."

Dakota and Montana exchanged a look.

"Thank you for asking us," Dakota said.

Nevada introduced her sisters.

"Triplets," Cat said, clapping her hands together. "That must have been fun growing up." She took a glass of champagne and sipped. "Did Nevada tell you who I am?" She smiled. "Some people don't know who I am at first. Then when they do find out, they feel silly for not recognizing me. I think it's easier to just say it all up front. No confusion."

The statements were amazingly self-absorbed, Nevada thought. Yet with Cat saying them, they seemed exactly right.

"Are you hungry?" Cat asked. "Can we talk before dinner? Would you mind?"

"Um, sure," Montana said. "That would be fine. We've been eating the appetizers. They're really good."

"I'm so glad."

Cat walked toward the sofas against the wall, then paused and furrowed her pale brow. "Oh, if only two of the sofas faced each other," she said, sounding disappointed.

Instantly the servers leapt into action, pulling one sofa around so it was across from the other with only a slender table in between.

"How perfect." She blessed the young men with a smile.

The four of them settled on the couches. Cat insisted Nevada sit next to her, then sipped her champagne and studied the triplets.

"I see differences," she said. "In the light, there are minor shifts in structure and color." She touched Nevada's chin and turned her head slightly. "Maybe a hint in the profile. I've never been one to sculpt people, but there is something very special about the three of you."

She dropped her hand. "I'm entering my feminine period."

The words sounded more like an announcement than a moment of casual conversation. Nevada blinked, not sure what they were supposed to say to that.

Dakota recovered first. "How nice."

Cat beamed. "Yes, it is. Until now, I've considered my inspiration to be either male or androgynous. But the earth is female and we all come from her. Dust to dust, as they say in the Bible. Now I see the possibilities of female energy. I would love to sculpt you three together."

She closed her eyes and swayed slightly. "Yes, I can see it. So beautiful and perfect. Larger than life, of course. Your three bodies draped across each other."

Montana choked. "Bodies?"

"Mmm." Cat opened her eyes. "Naked. That would be best."

Dakota's eyes widened. "I don't think so, but thanks for asking."

"What she said," Montana added quickly.

Cat turned to Nevada. "Then maybe just you."

Nevada managed to swallow the mouthful of champagne before she spoke. "I'm busy that day."

Cat only smiled.

She waved away the tray the server brought by. "If I remember correctly, the three of you grew up in this town. Is that right?"

"Yes," Nevada said, surprised she would recall anything that specific.

"It's charming. I can see why you like it here. Sometimes I think it would be nice to have a home. Restful. The familiar heals us, don't you think? Perhaps I should talk to a real estate agent. Do you know one?"

She directed the question to Montana, who nodded frantically. "Um, sure."

Nevada did her best not to choke or run screaming into the night.

Cat nodded. "I travel constantly, driven by forces I can't control. Searching for my next inspiration. Once I know what I'm doing, I work fanatically. It's exhausting."

Nevada had seen Cat work. The hours were grueling, as was the physical task of moving sheets of metal into place. While she sometimes had men helping her with the heaviest pieces, she handled most of it herself.

"Are you close?" Cat asked her. "You and your sisters?"

"Yes. We've always been close."

"When our brothers finally went to college, we still shared a room," Montana told her. "We didn't want to be apart. By the time we went to college, we were ready to be in different schools. Being separate was hard, but good for us."

Cat leaned forward, as if interested. "No matter what, you'll have each other. That's a true gift. I don't have many friends. I'm not a very good friend myself. Some of it is my schedule. Some of it is how I work. I give myself over to whatever I'm doing. I can be unavailable for weeks at a time. My brilliance is demanding."

She turned to Nevada, tears in her eyes. "Sometimes I get so lonely."

Nevada instinctively touched her arm. "I'm sure you do."

Cat drew in a shaky breath. "I should probably cut myself off from people. It's not right to let them believe I'm like them. I can never be like them. But they're drawn to me." She turned to Dakota. "I'm very transcendent."

Nevada drew back her hand and didn't know if she should burst out laughing or simply run for the door.

EVENTUALLY THEY MOVED to the table and dinner was served.

Cat focused on Dakota and Montana, asking questions

as if she were sincerely interested, then managed to switch the conversation back to herself. Nevada thought it was quite the trick. Even though she did her best to figure out how Cat did it, the other woman was too practiced.

"Do you have pictures of your daughter?" Cat asked.

Dakota pulled out her phone and pushed a few buttons.

"She's a jewel. You're so lucky. A baby on the way and this little angel."

"I'm very grateful," Dakota said.

"I would make beautiful babies." Cat handed back the phone and turned to Montana. "I couldn't help but notice your diamond ring."

Montana held out her left hand and laughed. "I know it's kind of big, but Simon was insistent."

"The perfect man," Cat told her.

"He is," Nevada said. "He's exactly who Montana needed and she certainly saved him."

"No one for you?" Cat asked her.

"No."

She thought about the time she and Tucker had spent in the trailer that afternoon, but told herself not to read too much into it. So far Cat hadn't mentioned him, but that didn't mean anything. For all Nevada knew, Tucker was upstairs waiting in Cat's bed.

The thought and the visual that went with it stabbed her in the stomach. She took a deep breath and told herself to get through the evening. She would deal with the Cat–Tucker issue later.

"I don't have anyone, either," Cat said. "There are men, of course. Everywhere. But no one is special. I'm beginning to think I'm chasing a rainbow. I'll never find my pot of gold."

She picked up her glass of wine. "When Nevada and I met in Los Angeles we had so much fun together. I remember that Hollywood party we went to. Do you?"

"Yes." She glanced at her sisters. "I was completely out of my element. There were plenty of famous people and I kept expecting someone to ask me what I thought I was doing there."

Cat smiled at her. "You were charming. It's hard for me to trust people, but I trusted you right away. You were a good friend and I never forgot that."

Nevada found herself oddly touched by the admission, even as she wasn't completely sure she believed it. Who was the real Caterina Stoicasescu? The proud, narcissistic artist who did her best to suck all the oxygen from the room, or the beautiful, slightly tragic woman who lived her life very much alone?

CHAPTER ELEVEN

THE DOOR TO THE BAR opened and two couples walked in. Jo scowled at them. The place was already crowded. Could they go somewhere else?

She shook her head and knew she was in real trouble when she complained about too many customers. Seriously, she had a problem and she was going to have to fix it. Knowing how was a detail she hadn't worked out. But, as usual, the source could be traced back to a man.

Everyone blamed Eve for the whole being thrown out of Eden thing; but Jo preferred to think Adam had some culpability. The man could have said no. But no one ever talked about that. If his friends had said to go jump off a cliff, would he have done that, too? Although, since technically Adam and Eve were the first two humans, according to the Bible, Adam wouldn't have had any friends.

A lovely mental distraction, she thought as she dropped ice into the stainless steel container, put on the top, then shook the martini into submission. But it didn't get to the heart of the matter, which was Will.

One of the many problems with him was that she couldn't make up her mind. She knew what she *should* do. That was easy. Avoid him and say no when she couldn't. It was a philosophy that had worked for her for years. Yet, when she was around Will, she found herself wondering what it would be like to give in. Just the one time. Except it wouldn't be one time and then there would be all kinds of trouble.

The truth was men were bad for her. Or she was bad for men. Or both. Smarter to stay alone. Safer. She loved her life here—did she really want to risk screwing that up?

She mixed drinks, took orders and directed her weekend staff. Around eleven, the front door opened again. She felt it rather than heard it, then without even turning around, she knew.

Will.

She told herself that he'd probably come by to tell her that he was done playing games. That she'd had her chance and he was finished. While that would make her sad, it would be for the best. She drew in a breath and turned around.

Will was standing at the far end of the bar. Their eyes locked. He looked good, she thought, telling her heart to stop pounding so hard. Really good.

Still watching her, he crossed the line no customer crossed and stepped behind the bar. Purposefully, he moved toward her, intent dark in his eyes.

"This is bullshit," he told her, then grabbed her upper arms, pulled her close and kissed her.

She felt the contact all the way down to her toes. Long-dormant nerve endings raised their heads and gave a little giggle. Her lungs stopped working, as did her brain. There was only the warm, sexy feel of Will's mouth on hers.

In the back of her mind she was aware of the bar

going completely silent. In all the years Jo had lived in Fool's Gold no one had ever seen her with a man. And for good reason—she hadn't been on a date, let alone kissed anyone.

He drew back. "Go ahead," he said. "Yell at me."

A second later, conversation resumed around them. She was sure it was mostly forced, as people tried to listen without listening.

"I don't yell," she told him, then walked toward the storeroom.

He followed.

When they were inside, she flipped on the lights then closed the door, giving them a little more privacy. He moved toward her, but she held up her hand to stop him.

"Wait."

"No." He sounded firm and his expression was determined. "I'm not going anywhere, Jo. I'm not that kind of guy. I like you. I'm just asking for the chance for you to like me, too."

He spoke as if he meant it, which was damned unfair. How was she supposed to resist a line like that? Except it wasn't a line, which made the whole thing worse. And amazing.

"You are going somewhere," she reminded him. "When the resort is done, you're leaving."

He swore under his breath. "Sure. That's years away. You'll be tired of me by then. If not, we'll figure something out. I can learn to deal blackjack."

His easy discussion of the future floored her. How could he say those things, imply that this was more than just a night of sex?

He stared into her eyes. "I'm not that guy."

The implication being she was worried about "that guy." She wondered what he'd heard. Which of the various rumors had been shared with him. There were so many and everyone had his or her favorites.

He thought she was worried about him leaving. That she was afraid of falling in love and being abandoned. If only he knew the truth. His leaving wasn't her problem. He wasn't her problem. The trouble went much deeper than that.

"No one hit me," she told him flatly. "In case that's what you were thinking."

His mouth twisted. "Good to know. Now I don't have to hunt the bastard down and beat the shit out of him."

She was pretty sure he meant it. That he was the kind of man who protected what was his. A good man. Someone she in no way deserved.

"I don't want forever," she told him. "I'm only interested in right now."

"I can do now."

Maybe, but he wasn't looking for a fling, she thought with a certainty she couldn't explain. He wanted more than a night. She wasn't sure she could promise that, but she also wasn't sure she could resist what he offered.

She thought about what it would feel like to be with him, to have him hold her, and she ached. Some of the longing was about sex, but most of it was about connecting in a way she hadn't allowed herself in years.

"I have a cat," she told him.

"Everyone has a flaw."

She smiled. "He's a pretty cool cat. You're going to

like him." She pulled her keys out of her jeans pocket and handed them over, then gave him her address. "I'll be done here in about an hour."

He took the keys, then leaned in and lightly kissed her.

"You can trust me," he whispered, before he straightened and walked out.

Trusting him wasn't the problem, she thought, watching him go. The real question was whether or not he could trust her.

NEVADA WANTED to spend the weekend avoiding Tucker. She wasn't sure she could explain the logic to him, but it made sense to her, and that was what mattered. Not that it was an issue, because he was nowhere to be seen. That was very annoying. Shouldn't he have come looking for her? After all, they'd had sex in the trailer. Conventional wisdom required a conversation after that. On a different topic, shouldn't he want to know how things were going with Cat?

Or was that where he was? With Cat, in her bed, restarting his obsessive relationship with the other woman.

Even though she didn't want to think about the two of them together, Nevada kept getting herself worked up over the possibility. She tried to put her energy to good use by cleaning her place and taking long walks in town. By Sunday afternoon, she was ready to jump out of her skin.

She was on the verge of going for a long run, a truly desperate measure considering she rarely exercised and never ran anywhere, when someone knocked on her door.

Tucker, she thought in relief. Having him to yell at would make her feel much better. Then he could tell her he was sorry and they could figure out what they were going to do with Cat.

She crossed to her door, pulled it open and stared at the Devil herself.

"Am I interrupting?" Cat asked, strolling inside. "Those boys downstairs are delicious. I met them both."

"Cody and Ryan?"

"Yes." Cat walked through the living room. "Oh, this place is wonderful. I want to live here."

Words to cause Nevada's insides to turn to ice. She shook that off and dealt with the more pressing problem.

"Cody and Ryan are in college."

"I know."

"They both started young because they're really smart, so even though they're in graduate programs, I'm not sure they're more than twenty."

Cat touched a small glass bowl on a shelf, then ran her hands over several books. "You're sweet to worry. They're adults. Let it go."

Nevada felt vaguely responsible for them. She didn't want Cat mucking around with their lives, but wasn't sure what she could do to prevent anything from happening. It wasn't as if either of the guys would listen. Cat was irresistible.

Even dressed casually in jeans, low boots and a dark purple sweater, she radiated an energy that was difficult to describe and impossible to ignore. There was something about the way she moved, as if she were so new to this world that every part of it was an exciting discovery.

Cat put down the book she'd been holding.

"What are you doing now?" she asked. "Whatever it is, you can do it later. Come on. I want to see your town." She held out her hand, as if expecting Nevada to take it.

"Um, sure. I can show you around." Nevada collected keys and her cell phone, then stuck a few dollars in her pocket.

They went out onto the street.

"What would you like to see first?"

"Whatever matters most to you. What places are special?"

Not your typical stroll, Nevada thought, heading for the park.

The day was sunny but cool. Children played by the lake, feeding the ducks. Parents watched from the benches. To the south, several young boys played soccer. To the north, by the trees, couples cuddled on blankets.

"The first known residents of the area were the women of the Máa-zib tribe," Nevada said.

Cat nodded. "I've read about them. A very powerful and artistic group of women. They were known for their intricate work with gold."

"I didn't know that," Nevada said.

"I've seen several pieces in different museums." She linked arms with Nevada. "The Gold Museum, otherwise known as El Museo del Oro in Bogotá, Colombia, has a large exhibit. I could spend hours there. You should come with me to see it."

"I'm busy with work now, but thanks for asking."

Cat smiled. "Always so shy. I remember that, too. From what I can tell, life has been kind to you. So why do you resist new experiences?"

Nevada pulled free and stepped back. "That's not true. I like new things."

Cat raised her perfect eyebrows. "Do you? Give me an example?"

"I have a new job."

"In the town where you've always lived, working for someone you've known for years. You are like a little bird, afraid to leave the nest."

"You don't know me well enough to make that kind of judgment."

"Am I wrong?"

Nevada raised her chin. "Yes. You are."

She spoke defiantly, but with a worrisome suspicion that Cat might be right. She'd never been especially adventurous. Not that everyone had to be. Maybe she should change that.

"I like my life," she added. "I like having my family around me and keeping the same friends. You're always on the go. Are you running to something or from something? What are you afraid you'll find if you settle in one place?"

Cat leaned back her head and laughed, then linked arms with Nevada again.

"This is what I've missed. You stand up to me. No one does that."

"Because you're so transcendent?" Nevada asked, only a little sarcastically.

"That and fear."

"At least you're honest."

"I can be when it suits me. What about you? Are you honest?"

"Mostly."

"Are you with Tucker?"

Of all the questions for Cat to ask, she thought, doing her best to keep her worry from showing. If she said yes, she would not only be overstating what was going on but she might be challenging Cat. Nevada didn't think that was a competition she could win. If she said no, Cat might decide to go after Tucker again. Either way, Nevada lost.

But if he was so easily persuaded to return to a disastrous relationship, then he wasn't anyone she wanted to be with.

Cat stopped and faced her. "It wasn't supposed to be a difficult question."

"I know. It's complicated."

"The best things in life are simple." Cat stared into her eyes. "Like your love of this town and the life-style it gives you. You're right, I am running all the time. Running to find inspiration. Running because if I stop I don't know what I'll find. Running because the going, the back and forth, keeps me from admitting that I'm alone."

For the first time since meeting Cat ten years ago, Nevada knew the other woman was speaking from the heart.

"I'm sorry," she whispered.

Cat squeezed her arm. "I'm a world-famous artist who is extremely wealthy. I'll be fine."

Nevada smiled, because that was expected. Inside she wondered if Cat had ever been fine or if all the bravado was an act.

"Now," her friend said, "show me the rest. There must be a town square and I insist on seeing it. Then we'll go to Starbucks and order a drink that comes with whipped cream."

Nevada nodded. "That sounds perfect."

Tucker had endured the incessant whistling for the entire morning. But when Will came back after lunch, still making the noise, Tucker turned on him.

"Enough. You're happy. We get it."

Will grinned. "Someone's not getting any. Too bad. Life is a whole lot nicer when there's a woman around."

"Jo?"

Will shrugged. "I'm not the type to kiss and tell."

"Sure you are. It has to be Jo. Things must be going well." Not that he begrudged his friend some happiness. If Jo was his type, then good for him. "Just give me a break on the whistling."

"I'll do my best." Will leaned back in his chair and propped his feet on his desk. "I'm starting to really like this town. It's a nice place to settle down."

"What would you know about that?"

"More than you. I grew up in one place, at least for the first fifteen years of my life. There were good things about it. Friends."

Tucker knew enough about Will's past to guess that

the bad had come very close to outweighing anything positive.

"You sure you want to be talking like that after a single weekend with Jo?"

"I'm not making any decisions right now. I'm considering my possibilities."

"What are the possibilities of you doing work?"

Will laughed and straightened, slamming his boots against the floor of the trailer. "Talk nice to me and they're pretty decent."

Tucker went over the timetable for the week. Work-wise, they were right on schedule. With a project this big, there were bound to be delays. They were built into the project costs and projections. His goal was to make sure he didn't need to use them.

From outside he heard a couple of guys arguing. Before he'd even made it to the door, the sound of a female voice cut through. By the time he got outside, both men were shuffling their feet, looking sheepish.

"I thought so," Nevada told them. "This isn't going to happen again, is it?"

The men shook their heads and walked away.

"Want to tell me what happened?" he asked.

Nevada glanced at him. "Nope. All taken care of. That's why you pay me the big bucks."

He hadn't seen her in a few days. Not since Cat had arrived. Or more importantly, not since their wild and satisfying encounter in the trailer.

That she hadn't wanted to talk about, he realized. Isn't that what women did? Talk about it after the fact? Endlessly?

"Everything else okay?" he asked, aware there were several guys within earshot.

"Of course."

"I was gone this weekend. With Josh. We went on a hundred-mile bike ride." His legs were still protesting the unusual activity. "I probably should have said something." He cleared his throat. "In case you needed to talk to me about work."

"Thanks for the news flash." She seemed amused by his statement. "I stayed in town. With Cat."

"On purpose?"

"It was fine. She's different."

"I'll say."

He wanted to tell her that he was over Cat. That she didn't matter to him, but he still hadn't been alone with her and couldn't be completely sure. Even if he was sure, he couldn't figure out how to get that across in such a public setting. Asking Nevada into the trailer wouldn't help because Will was in there.

"I'm going back to work now," she told him.

He nodded and returned to the trailer.

"What was that about?" Will asked.

"Some trouble with a couple of the guys. Nevada handled it."

"She's good with the men. They respect her."

"That's why I hired her."

Will snorted.

Tucker narrowed his gaze. "Are you saying there's another reason?"

"Sure, but because I'm in such a good mood we'll pretend there isn't."

DENISE KNEW she was going to throw up. Her stomach whirled and spun and flipped as if it were possessed by some gastrointestinal alien. Her palms were damp, her skin clammy. Under any other circumstance, she would have told herself she had the flu and raced home. However, she'd already been hiding for too long and the symptoms had nothing to do with being sick and everything to do with a man.

That explained why she was standing in front of Max's house. She'd left him two messages, which he hadn't returned. Her reaction to his proposal made her ashamed of herself. She felt guilty and small. It was not a happy combination. So it was time for her to do something about it.

Drawing in a breath, she rang the doorbell. It would serve her right if Max refused to speak to her, but she was hoping he had more character than she did.

It turned out she was right. He opened the door a couple of seconds later, then smiled at her.

"Thanks for coming by," he said, holding open the door.

"Aren't you going to yell at me for my immature reaction?" she asked, walking past him and moving into a bright living room.

There were several sofas, nice wood tables and pretty artwork. If she had to guess, she would say he'd used a decorator. That instantly made her wonder if the decorator had been a woman and if they'd slept together.

"You've been doing that for me," he said.

"What?"

"Yelling at yourself."

"I have been. I'm sorry. I should have come to see you sooner."

"Why? You weren't ready."

Kind words that made her want to scream. "Don't be nice. I don't deserve it." She held up her hand. "Please. Let me say what I have to say."

"All right. Do you want to sit down?"

"No. This is a standing-up kind of speech."

He nodded. "Go ahead."

Her mind went blank. She opened her mouth, then closed it. Nothing. Then the words came in a tumble.

"I'm glad you're back. I never thought I'd see you again, and here you are. It's been wonderful, rediscovering what we had. Only it's different now. Better, I think. I'm older, but you seem to be okay with that."

"Should I wait until you're done or comment as you go?"

"Wait until I'm done." She stared into his blue eyes and knew she had to tell him the truth.

"I loved Ralph so much more than I ever thought I could. He was a good man, a wonderful husband and father. I know people say that all the time, but it's really true. He loved his kids and he loved me. Sometimes he would ask me if I was sure. If I had regrets. I hated that. Hated knowing he had questions. Because he was the one. I told him I didn't have regrets, and I hope he believed me."

She twisted her fingers together. "I remember when I had the girls. It was Christmas morning and the delivery was difficult. I lost a lot of blood. For a while they weren't sure I was going to make it. I don't remember very much except Ralph holding my hand, begging me not to die. I could feel his tears on my skin and I knew I had to stay with him. Because we were a family."

She pressed her lips together. "We weren't allowed to grow old together and that is my one regret. It's been ten years and I still miss him. I still wish he were here."

"I'm not trying to come between you and Ralph," Max told her.

"I know. But when you walked into my house, I was so happy." Tears burned in her eyes. "Happier than I should have been."

"You said it yourself. Ralph's been gone over ten years. Don't you think it's okay to be happy? Do you have to spend your life grieving?"

"I know all this," she said. "I've been in therapy to help me through the stages of grief. I've been strong for my children. I'd even convinced myself that it was time for me to find someone of my own. My love for my husband will live on regardless of what I do. Nothing can take that away. But I won't get married again. I want Ralph to have been the only man I married. He deserves that."

He crossed to her, but didn't touch her. "Denise, I proposed because I thought you would be more comfortable if we were married. You're the kind of woman who gets married. But I don't need that to love you. Hell, I've loved you for nearly forty years. It's not going away. I want to be with you and you can define that however you want."

"You're not mad that I won't marry you?"

"No." He touched her face with his fingers. "Love me. Be with me."

"That's enough?"

"That's plenty."

She flung herself at him. He caught her and pulled her hard against him. Then his mouth was on hers and they were kissing and spinning. Or maybe just the room was spinning. Either way, it was perfect.

When he finally drew back, he brushed the tears from her cheeks.

"Promise me something," he said.

She nodded.

"Next time, talk to me. Don't run."

She took his hand in hers and kissed his palm. "I promise. For always, Max."

"For always, Denise."

CHAPTER TWELVE

FRIDAY, NEVADA STEPPED OUT of the bakery, the pink box she carried neatly tied with string. Yes, there were six chocolate cupcakes inside and she was pretty sure she was going to eat them all by herself. But it had been a stressful week and she deserved a sugar rush to make it all seem better.

The weird part was she didn't usually eat a lot of sugar. Nor could she point to any particular event in her week and complain. Work was going great. They were going to be blasting in a couple of weeks and she was excited about that. From what she could tell, Cat and Tucker weren't spending a lot of time together, although she kept reminding herself it wasn't her business if they were. So the need for cupcakes was inexplicable, but very powerful.

She turned the corner and nearly ran into a man carrying a pizza box. Her body registered who it was before her brain recognized him.

"Tucker."

He smiled at her. "I called you about a half hour ago, but you weren't answering."

She held up the pink box. "I had an emergency errand to run and forgot my cell phone at home."

"I thought you might be out on a hot date."

"Do three chocolate cupcakes and three coconut vanilla cupcakes count as a date?"

"It depends on what you do with them."

They seemed to be staring at each other, she thought, rooted in place by forces she couldn't name.

"I haven't seen you much this week," she murmured. "We're both on-site at the same time, but in different places."

She was out with her crew and he was in the trailer doing whatever it was potential owners of multibillion-dollar companies did.

"You've been busy with Cat," he reminded her.

"She's taking up a lot of my free time. Have you spent any time with her?"

"Not since the day she arrived." He sounded pleased as he spoke, as if this were good news.

"She's still really beautiful."

He shrugged. "Not interested. I'm done with her. It was over years ago."

"Oh."

Suddenly her shoulders didn't seem as tight and the evening was a little brighter.

He held up the pizza box. "I'll show you mine if you'll show me yours."

She laughed. "Sounds good. Let's go back to my place. I have wine waiting."

"Wine and cupcakes. Talk about a party. You're my kind of girl."

Twenty minutes later they were sitting at her kitchen table, pizza on plates, wine in glasses.

"How's your mom doing?" he asked between bites.

"Good. She and Max have worked things out.

Apparently he proposed because he thought that's what she wanted and she freaked out. They've talked everything over and are in a committed relationship that won't end in marriage." Nevada shook her head. "While I'm thrilled that she's happy, I never thought this was anything close to a conversation I would be having with my mother."

"You are part of a classic American family."

She laughed. "I'm not sure about that." She took a bite of pizza and chewed. After she'd swallowed, she said, "You really haven't seen Cat?"

"Nope. No reason to. I'm not sure why she's in town, but it's not for me."

He sounded cheerful as he spoke. As far as Nevada could tell, there wasn't even a hint of longing for what had been.

He poured her more wine. "This is nice. I like your place. Did you remodel?"

She nodded. "I did most of the work myself. The house was built in the nineteen twenties. The traditional Victorian style didn't fly with the neighbors, but the original owner was powerful and no one told him no."

"A man after my own heart. I like being the guy no one says no to."

"You would. In this case, people came to like the house. I've loved it from the time I was a kid. Over the years it was sold and turned into a low-rent apartment building. No one took care of it. By the time I bought it, the whole place was trashed. It took me nearly three years to do all the work, but it was worth it."

She'd also squeezed every penny she could from the second mortgage she'd used to pay for the materials.

Once the remodeling was done, she'd been able to rent out the bottom two apartments. She'd paid off the second mortgage last summer and was now paying down her first. A good feeling, she thought.

"To your house," he said, raising his glass.

She touched hers to his. "Thank you."

"Want to show me the rest of it?"

There was only the third floor, which was her bedroom, the large bath and a study. She was about to say that when she realized Tucker was watching her with an interest that said he wouldn't mind his pizza getting cold. She went from hungry for food to hungry for something else in the space of a heartbeat.

He stood and walked around the table, then held out his hand. When she placed her fingers on his palm, he drew her to her feet and pulled her close.

She went willingly, wanting to feel his strong arms around her. His mouth claimed hers with a kiss that left her breathless.

He pressed his lips against her cheeks, her nose, the line of her jaw. He trailed his way to her neck, then kissed just below her ear. Goose bumps erupted as he licked the skin there. He moved lower, to her collarbone, then to the V of the long-sleeved shirt she wore. The hands at her waist reached higher.

Desire poured through her. Hunger grew. She remembered how it had been before, when he'd touched her with his skilled and patient fingers. She remembered the feel of him between her legs, filling her over and over again.

She put her right hand over his left and stepped away. Keeping hold of him, she drew him toward the stairs.

"You wanted to see the upstairs," she whispered.

"I did." He put his free hand on the railing. "Should I stop to admire the workmanship?"

She laughed. "Maybe later."

She led him into her bedroom. It was already dark outside. She flipped on the switch, which illuminated the floor lamp in the corner.

The room itself was a girly combination of soft fabrics, dozens of pillows and delicate furniture. Her queen-size bed had a carved headboard. The walls were done in pale mauve. It was a woman's retreat.

Tucker paused for a second and glanced around. "I like it. It suits you."

No one had ever said that before. Even her sisters had been surprised by her decorating choices. In her mind, this room reflected a part of her personality that she kept hidden—sometimes even from herself.

Tucker toed off his boots, then walked toward her. "Tell me there's a big claw-foot tub in the bathroom."

She smiled. "There is."

"You're my kind of girl."

They moved into the bathroom. While he got the bath temperature right, she lit candles. As water poured into the tub, he crossed to her. He kissed her, his tongue plunging inside and circling hers. His hands roamed her body.

Everywhere he touched grew more and more sensitized. A stroke of his fingers across her hip had her squirming toward home. Fingers down her arm had her wanting more. When his hands finally settled on her breasts, she had to consciously keep from begging.

He brushed against her tight nipples. Tension

surged in her belly, then moved lower. She closed her lips around his tongue and sucked. The fingers at her breasts moved faster.

"Water," he murmured as he pulled back.

She released him reluctantly, knowing the disaster an overflowing tub would cause.

He turned off the taps, then unbuttoned his shirt. When he'd dropped it on the floor, he went to work on what she was wearing. Her shirt followed his. He unfastened her jeans and tugged them off along with her socks, then quickly removed her bra and panties. He paused to kiss her breasts before taking off the rest of his clothes.

She stepped into the tub first. The water was warm, lapping against her skin. He stepped in behind her and settled in. She sat in front of him, her back to him.

"Wait a minute," she complained. "This isn't going to work."

"It's going to work just fine," he whispered against her skin. "Trust me."

He pressed his lips to the skin at the nape of her neck. At the same time, he brought his hands around her body and cupped her breasts. The curves were buoyant in the water, her body more sensitized to his touch.

She closed her eyes and let herself relax against him. Tucker was strong enough to support her, she thought hazily, pleased by the feel of his large erection pressing into her back. Smart enough to know what to do next and plenty willing to take them both on a ride. Very nice qualities in a man.

He continued to stroke her breasts, paying particular

attention to her nipples. Fire licked through her, moving to all the best parts of her body, heating her, causing her to squirm slightly and want just a little bit more. As if he could read her mind, he moved one hand lower, sliding deliberately down her belly until he found his way between her thighs.

She was already swollen, excited, halfway there. He rediscovered her most sensitive spot, rubbing it with his fingers. She parted her legs and gave herself up to the experience. As he caressed her rhythmically, her breathing quickened. Pleasure grew, muscles tensed.

"Come for me."

He breathed the words in her ear. They were an unexpected jolt that caused her to open her eyes.

Through the frothy layer of bubbles, she saw his hand pleasing her. Felt what he was doing at the same time. His skin was darker than hers, tanned by his hours outdoors. His hands were large, so masculine— and what he did to her.

As she watched, her muscles clenched and she knew she was getting closer. He moved faster, drawing her further along. Involuntarily, her eyes closed as she gave herself up to the moment.

Closer, she thought, focused entirely on the movements between her legs, on the pressure building, the insistent hammering of her heart. Closer. She could see it, right there. Just out of reach. So close…

She parted her legs a little more and leaned back into him, at the same time pulsing her hips toward his hand. And then she was coming, her release rippling through her, claiming her, making her gasp and cry out.

"Like that," he breathed. "Just like that."

She shuddered once as the last of her satisfaction faded. But she didn't relax and enjoy the moment. Instead she sat up, then turned to face him.

He was grinning.

"You think you're redeemed," she said, still flushed from her orgasm.

"I know I am."

"We'll see about that."

She knelt over him, then eased herself onto his arousal. The angle was different from the last time they'd done this, but he went in just as deep. He filled her, stretching her, making her groan.

She watched his eyes dilate, felt his breath catch. Then he drew her closer and kissed her, his tongue mimicking the movements of their lovemaking.

She settled her hands on the back of the tub, bracing herself so she could continue to move up and down. Want filled her again, this time more powerful than before. She wanted, needed and was determined to have. She lost herself in the deepness of their kiss, the pushing, filling satisfaction of him inside of her. When he moved his hands to her breasts and touched her there as well, she didn't know how long she could hold out.

She wanted more, she thought desperately, nipping at his lips before pushing her tongue into his mouth. This time she wanted all of it. She went faster, deeper, the water sloshing over the edge of the tub.

More, she thought frantically, her breath coming in gasps. Up and down, each thrust finding that one place inside, rubbing it, drawing her closer.

Tucker hissed, dropping his hands to her hips. "You're killing me," he said, his voice strangled.

Their eyes locked. He was close. She could see it and feel it. But he was doing his best to hang on.

"Just a second more," she begged, still moving up and down, faster and faster until—

Her release ripped through her like a tornado. She rode him, taking everything he had, all while it seemed that she'd been flung into the universe and swirled around and around. She was vaguely aware of him coming, of his hold on her tightening, then she was looking at him again. Exposing all of herself and staring into the welcoming lightness of Tucker's soul.

LATER, AFTER THEY'D USED TOWELS to clean up the water that had poured over the side of the tub and retreated to her bedroom with wine and cupcakes, they sat next to each other on her bed.

Nevada was doing her best to act normal, as if she became some kind of sex animal all the time and it was no big deal. In truth she felt a little embarrassed by her unrestrained behavior. As if she should explain or apologize. In her head, she knew neither act was required, but for the life of her, she couldn't figure out what she was supposed to say.

Tucker handed her a chocolate cupcake, then pulled it back at the last second.

"You risk your life by playing games with a cupcake," she told him.

Instead of smiling, he became more serious, his dark eyes staring into hers.

"You are unexpected."

Before she could react to the touching words, he

kissed her. A light kiss that seemed to say something more. Something she couldn't quite decipher.

He handed her the cupcake, then poured more wine into their glasses.

"I'm staying the night."

She raised her eyebrows. "Are you asking or telling?"

"Telling."

"Figures."

But she wasn't complaining, she thought, as they shifted to lean against the headboard. Somehow this all felt right.

He reached for the remote and clicked on the TV. "Because I'm such a swell guy, I'll let you pick."

She thought about torturing him with home shopping, but decided the state of her still quivery body deserved a reward.

"The USC game should still be on," she told him.

He turned to her and smiled. "The perfect woman."

"Tell me about it."

"I DIDN'T KNOW there were this many bridal magazines," Nevada murmured, fingering the stack on the coffee table.

"Talk about a fascinating industry," Montana said. "I've decided that planning a wedding in four months is going to be a whole lot easier than taking the year all the experts suggest. There's a lot less time to agonize over every decision."

They were in their mother's family room, with Dakota sprawled on the sofa, Nevada and Montana on the floor and their mother in the wing chair.

"There are still choices to be made," Denise announced. "You two need to pick out your dresses. With the location reserved, that's the next priority."

Dakota patted her relatively tiny bump. "I don't know how huge I'm going to be. Maybe I should wait until after the baby is born. Isn't being pregnant at my own wedding a little tacky?"

"No," Montana told her. "You're going to be a beautiful bride."

Denise put down her pad of paper. "If you want to wait, you can. We can use the lodge for Montana's wedding and plan something else for you in the spring." She glanced at Nevada and raised her eyebrows. "Maybe it can be a different double wedding."

Nevada raised both her hands. "Don't even think about it. The closest relationship I have these days is with Cat."

While the statement wasn't completely true, there was no way she was discussing her confusing and apparently ongoing liaison with Tucker.

They'd had a great time the previous night. Not just the sex, she thought wistfully. The conversation had been just as fun. He made her laugh, which she liked, and when she was around him, she could be herself. Some men were intimidated by what she did for a living—especially when they saw her on a construction site. But Tucker wasn't like that.

He'd stayed the night, they'd made breakfast together, then had used her shower in a very interesting way. Then she'd had to leave to come here for the "girls only" family meeting. Leaving him had been harder than she would have thought.

"I met Cat," Denise said. "I've never known a famous artist before. She's very elegant and more friendly than I'd expected. I went and looked at a few of her pieces online. They're…" She paused, as if searching for the right word. "Large."

"Cat does enjoy making a statement." Nevada sat up and stretched her legs in front of her. "In life and in art. I can't imagine what she's finding to do in a town this small. I did see her talking with Cody the other day. I hope she doesn't take things too far with him."

"Who's Cody?" Dakota asked.

"One of the guys renting from me. He's in college. Very talented—a computer science major. I don't think he usually gets the girl. Being with Cat would be way too much for him."

"A problem every college-age guy would love," Montana said with a laugh.

True enough, Nevada thought, remembering how Tucker had been mesmerized by Cat all those years ago.

"Back to the wedding, girls," Denise said firmly. "We have decisions to make."

"Sure you don't want to make this a triple wedding?" Montana asked with a grin. "Come on, Mom. You're a grandmother. Are you really not going to marry Max?"

"I'd rather not." Denise's voice was prim. "However, if you three and the boys think I should, then I'll consider it. Or if you think it would be better for the grandchildren."

"I'm not going there," Nevada said quickly. "It's your decision, Mom."

Her sisters nodded their agreement.

Denise sighed. "I prefer to have your father be my only husband. Having said that, Max and I are in love and together."

Nevada shifted on the floor and fought against the need to cover her ears and hum.

"No details, please," Dakota inserted quickly, flipping through the bridal magazine on her lap. "Remember?"

Denise grinned. "No details. However, I will warn you that Max is going to be moving in here."

"Oh, good." Nevada relaxed a little, now that the threat of sex talk was over. "I thought you might want to move in with him and then sell this house. Which would be okay," she added quickly. "It's your house."

"No." Her mother shook her head. "It's the family home and I don't want to lose it. We have so many memories here. I want Hannah to have her first Christmas with us in this house."

"What happens to Max's place?" Dakota asked. "Doesn't someone have to be there for the dogs?"

Max lived on the same property his business occupied. K9Rx provided therapy dogs to the community.

"We have staff who stay with the dogs at night," Montana said. "Eventually Max will need to figure out what to do with the main house, but for now Simon and I are going to rent it while we decide what we want to do. Build, buy or remodel. We're not sure. So this gives us time to make the right choice."

"You have it all planned out," Nevada said, wondering when all these decisions had been made. She felt as if she'd been gone a month and the whole world had changed while she was away. But that wasn't exactly true, she told herself. She hadn't really been out of touch at all.

"Does Max work?" Dakota asked. "Except for the dogs, I mean? How does he pay for everything?"

Denise smiled smugly. "Max was in Seattle during the eighties. He met Bill Gates and bought Microsoft at the initial public offering."

Nevada blinked. That would explain a lot, she thought.

"So he's rich?" Dakota asked.

"Very."

Montana laughed. "And here I've been worried about buying dog food on sale."

"You can probably let that go," Nevada told her.

Dakota held up her magazine. "What about this?" she asked.

The wedding gown had an empire waist and long sleeves.

"It's beautiful," her mother said. "We really need to go try on dresses. This week, girls. As it is, there are going to be limitations. We don't have months and months to wait for something to be made."

"What size are samples?" Montana asked.

"Usually ten or twelve."

"Then that would work."

Montana joined her sister on the sofa and they flipped through the magazines, looking at dresses.

"We're going to have to figure out if we're having bridesmaids," Dakota said absently. "Nevada, you're going to be our mutual maid of honor, right?"

"Sure."

She'd assumed she would be part of the wedding,

although she hadn't known as what. Her chest tightened a little as she thought of her sisters both getting married while she stood by and watched.

They were both so happy, she reminded herself. They deserved this and she wanted them to have perfect weddings. But every now and then she wanted that for herself, too. A happy ending, love, children. Someone to be in her life.

Not surprisingly, her thoughts drifted to Tucker and the night she'd shared.

Not him, she thought sadly. He believed love was a trap. Convincing him otherwise was unlikely. Unfortunately, he was the first guy in a long time who had captured her interest. She would have to make sure he didn't capture her heart.

CHAPTER THIRTEEN

THE BEAUTIFUL FALL AFTERNOON brought out both residents and tourists, Nevada thought as she and Cat strolled through the center of town on Sunday afternoon. The leaves were changing, bringing bright reds and yellows to the trees, dressing up the streets. Fool's Gold was a place that celebrated every season, every holiday. Although it was several weeks before Halloween, storefronts were a mass of pumpkins and ghosts. Windows had been painted, harvest baskets stood by open doors, and at the center of town was a Thanksgiving diorama with Pilgrims and Native Americans sitting down to a turkey dinner.

The display had been around for as long as Nevada could remember. The clothes were a little tattered and the mannequin faces needed a fresh coat of paint. Still, it was traditional and, in its own way, beautiful.

"I don't know," Cat said doubtfully, eyeing the Pilgrims. "They're not inspiring."

"The town puts them up every year," Nevada told her. "It's tradition."

Cat looked at the square, turning in a circle as she took in the buildings and the open space. "I think you could do better. Fool's Gold is such a special place. I can feel the feminine energy. I'm filled with inspiration."

The temperatures were mild for early October. Mid-sixties, with plenty of blue skies. Mornings were crisp and the higher elevations were already getting frost.

Cat was dressed like everyone else, in jeans and a long-sleeved shirt. Still, she managed to look more glamorous, more perfect. Maybe it was the fur-trimmed vest, or the designer boots. Maybe it was the way her layered dark hair cascaded down her back. Maybe it was how the sun seemed to focus on her high cheekbones and wide eyes.

Cat had called a couple of hours ago and insisted they spend the afternoon together. Nevada had been hoping for a repeat with Tucker, but had agreed to meet her friend instead.

Cat turned away from the diorama and smiled at Nevada. "I feel the call of Mother Earth."

She spoke seriously, as if Nevada should understand what she was talking about.

"What is she saying?"

"To create something wonderful for this town. Let's get a latte."

They walked back toward the main street. Cat nodded and smiled to nearly everyone they passed.

"Don't you love how the mountains reach up toward the sky?" Cat asked, linking arms with her. "The silhouette as dusk approaches. The colors are magical. I don't do much with color. I've thought about painting, how that could be new for me. But what if I'm not brilliant?"

"Do you have to be?" Most people were happy to be good at something. Brilliant was a whole new level.

Cat turned to her, tears in her eyes. "It's who I am."

Nevada came to a stop. "I'm sorry. I was being flippant. I can't completely understand who you are and what you do." Talk about stupid, she thought. Cat wasn't like the ordinary mortals she shared space with. Yes, she was egotistical and self-absorbed, but she was also gifted in a way very few could understand.

"It's all right," Cat told her, sniffing delicately. "I've thought of trying to paint. I have, in private. It's just that everything I do is judged so harshly. The critics, the art world. They're ready to pounce, ready to say I've reached my pinnacle and am now in decline. I'm not ready to be finished. I live for my work—I can't stand the thought of that being taken from me."

Nevada thought about pointing out that Cat wouldn't just miss the art. She could continue to work and never let anyone see another piece. But that was silliness. For Cat the art and the fame were one and the same.

"That's one of the things I love so much about this place," Cat said with a sigh. "The people are so giving and accepting. They understand that I'm just like them."

Nevada shook her head. "You're many things, but you're not like them."

Cat smiled. "All right, but I get to be close to everyone else when I'm here. That's restful. Their support gives me energy."

She was the center of her own universe, Nevada thought, more amused than annoyed by that fact. When one had been declared a great artist by the age of fourteen, being humble was probably an impossibility.

They turned and walked through the crowd to the Starbucks. Once inside, Cat greeted several people by name. She flirted with the teenager taking her order. Nevada watched him blush and fumble with the cash register.

She couldn't imagine what it would be like to have been born with that much power over men. Sure, some found Nevada attractive and it wasn't as if she had to wear a bag over her head to avoid frightening small children, but she wasn't in Cat's league. Men didn't trip over themselves in a rush to hold open a door. No rock star had ever dedicated an album to her.

"What would you like?" Cat asked.

Nevada ordered a pumpkin spice latte to celebrate the season. Although, after the cupcakes she'd consumed this weekend, she was going to have to spend the next week being a little careful. All this stress eating was going to make her jeans tight.

Cat got the same. When their order was up, they collected their drinks and went back outside.

There were several small tables on the sidewalk. One was freed up as they approached and they sat across from each other.

The sun was warm. A few leaves fluttered to the ground by them. Cat picked up the largest and set it on the table.

"See the different colors," she said, smoothing out the leaf. "It's not just red. Look more closely. There's scarlet and crimson. Cerise, carmine and vermilion. Nature gives us perfection and we spend our lives trying to come close."

Nevada could see the different colors but couldn't have named them. She barely would have noticed the leaf at all, if Cat hadn't picked it up.

Cat dropped the leaf back on the ground and put her hands around her coffee. "Sometimes I find everything so difficult. Not just the work, but living with these gifts."

Nevada took a sip and did her best not to roll her eyes.

Cat looked at her, her green eyes stark with pain. "What I have, my talent, for lack of a better word, it separates me from everyone else. I can't give up my art and live like you do, but the price I pay for that is that there is always a wall between me and everyone else."

For the second time in about twenty minutes, Nevada felt like scum. It wasn't pleasant. She'd always been so quick to judge Cat. At times the other woman was comical, but she was also a person.

"I can see where it would be difficult," she said slowly. "You're always on display. People want to know you because of your talent and your fame. How can you know when someone is being sincere?"

Cat's whole face brightened. "Yes. I knew you'd understand. I want more, but I'm afraid of it, too. Of what I'll have to give up. That if I find love or happiness, the rest of it will be taken from me." She shrugged. "Or maybe I use that as an excuse. Relationships require effort and I can be lazy. I give everything to my work and when I'm done I want someone taking care of me. I want to be the important one."

"They say understanding the problem is half the battle."

Cat laughed. "I think they're wrong. Because I'm not that interested in changing. I like being spoiled."

Her humor faded. "But sometimes I want more. I want a connection." She leaned toward Nevada. "I came here because of you."

Nevada wasn't sure what to make of that statement. "You mean because I'd talked about my hometown?" She couldn't remember much of what she and Cat had talked about ten years ago, but it made sense that she would have mentioned Fool's Gold.

"No." Cat's eyes softened. "Although you did talk about it endlessly. I came because I remembered how much I liked you. I thought we had a connection I don't find with many people."

Nevada shifted in her seat. She had the oddest sense that this conversation was about to take an unexpected turn.

"We're friends," Nevada told her. "I think you need some friends."

Cat stared at her intently. "We can be friends if you'd like. But I was thinking of something more."

With that, she moved toward Nevada. Her head tilted and her mouth...

Nevada scrambled to her feet so quickly the chair went skidding across the sidewalk. Disbelief battled with a voice in her head saying she had to have misunderstood—that there was no way Cat had been about to kiss her.

"Nevada?"

Cat didn't look the least bit upset. If anything, amusement teased at the corners of her mouth.

"I, ah, have to go," Nevada stammered. "I have to be somewhere."

She should probably say something else. Offer a

less lame excuse. But her brain wasn't working, so she turned and took off at a run.

"IT'S NOT FUNNY," Nevada insisted, pacing the length of the trailer, which, considering how small it was, wasn't very satisfying. "It's not funny at all."

Tucker sat on the corner of his desk, watching her. He was grinning like a sheep and really starting to piss her off.

"It's a little funny," he said. "Come on. Cat coming on to you?"

She spun on her work-boot heel and glared at him. "Are you saying I'm not worthy?"

He held up both hands in a gesture of surrender. "No. Of course not. I'm saying Cat is firmly in the guy camp. Trust me. I have proof."

"I'm sure you do and I know what you're saying makes sense." She stared pacing again. "It's just I would swear..."

She shook her head. Maybe she was going crazy. Maybe she'd misunderstood. But it hadn't felt like a misunderstanding. It had felt as if Cat was going to kiss her. Right there in front of Starbucks!

After their encounter, Nevada had gone back to her apartment, only to find she was too restless to stay there. She'd phoned Montana and had been thrilled to learn that Simon had been called into emergency surgery. That made her a hideous person, because that meant someone was hurt.

Telling herself she wasn't responsible hadn't helped much, but spending the evening with her sister had. They'd packed up most of Montana's small house for the impending move to Max's place. She'd gotten home late and exhausted, and still hadn't been able to sleep.

"We were talking about her," she said, going over the material for the four thousandth time.

"It is Cat's favorite topic."

"You're not helping."

"Sorry."

He didn't look sorry. He looked like a man trying not to laugh.

"I could kill you, you know," she told him. "This is my town. They'd help hide the body."

"You'd miss me."

"Not as much as you'd think."

He crossed to her and put his hands on her shoulders. "I think Cat was just being her normal, narcissistic self. It was all about her, and somehow you read that as something else."

"Maybe." She'd been so sure at the time, though. Scared, even. "You weren't there. She keeps talking about being in her feminine phase. Maybe this is part of that."

His mouth twitched again. "Were you tempted?"

She slapped his hands away. "Did I mention I hate you?"

"Can I watch?"

"Yuck. What's wrong with you? I have a serious problem."

"A beautiful woman wants you. That *is* a problem."

She grunted in irritation, then stalked to her desk. "You're not taking this seriously."

"And you're taking it too seriously. Even if she did try to kiss you, this is Cat we're talking about. She was just being her usual attention-seeking self. It doesn't mean she's serious about wanting to have sex with you."

At last he was making sense. "I can buy that," she admitted. "I was being sympathetic. I'm sure that's all it was. Her responding to that."

"Right. And if it turns out she is serious, are you making a video?"

She picked up the folder on her desk and opened it to study the compaction report inside. "Are you talking? All I hear is a buzzing sound. It's the strangest thing."

He crossed to her, turned her and kissed her. "I'm sorry she upset you. I'm sorry you were uncomfortable."

She leaned against him. "I don't have anything against girl kissing," she whispered. "In theory. I just don't want to share in it."

"Cat was playing. She'll have moved on to something else by the time you see her again."

"I hope."

"Trust me."

When a day of moving lumber and walking the site that would be blasted didn't make Nevada feel any better, she gladly accepted an invitation to join her friends at Jo's Bar after work. Heidi had promised to call Annabelle and Charlie, and the other women were waiting when Nevada arrived—as was a very tall, very cold vodka tonic.

"You read my mind," she said, slipping into the seat they'd saved for her. "Thanks." She took a sip. "How are things with everyone?"

"Good," Heidi said with a grin. "No recent goat

escapes, which is working for me. And the feral cows are keeping their distance."

Annabelle laughed. "You're the only person I know who's frightened of cows."

"I'm not frightened. They're a bad influence."

Annabelle shook her head. "Keep telling yourself that. I'm fine, too. Loving the library, loving the town. Did you all see the leaves over the weekend? Talk about beautiful."

"Leaves catch fire," Charlie grumbled.

"Ever the romantic," Nevada teased.

Charlie eyed her over her margarita. "Your sisters are getting married."

Nevada took another drink, then sighed. "That sounds more like an accusation than a question."

"I didn't mean it to. I guess I'm surprised."

Nevada realized the other two women were looking at her with identical expressions of concern. "Uh-oh. You've been talking about this."

Heidi leaned toward her. "A little. Don't be mad. We're worried. You're a triplet."

"I kind of knew that."

"What she means," Annabelle said, "is you've always done things together and now they're getting married. We're worried."

Nevada felt a rush of affection for the three of them. "Thank you, but don't be. I'm fine. I love my sisters and I'm okay with the wedding."

She paused, admitting to herself that she felt a little left out. "Maybe it's a little strange, but I don't want anything to change."

Heidi wrinkled her nose. "I know I'm new and I shouldn't have an opinion."

"Don't let that stop you," Charlie told her.

"I like your sisters," Heidi continued. "But it seems kind of mean to have a double wedding, leaving you out. Shouldn't they have gotten married separately?"

"Yes," Jo said, coming up to the table with a huge plate of nachos. "That would have made the most sense. But they're in love and happy and people do crazy things when they're in love. Dakota and Montana love their sister and would never want to hurt her. They really want to have a double wedding. There's no way to reconcile the two."

"I'm not hurt," Nevada said. "I mean that. Sure, I feel funny about it, but I want them to have the wedding of their dreams. I'll be part of it and that's what is important."

Jo put down a stack of napkins and four small plates. "You four are going to get drunk tonight, aren't you?"

"Maybe," Charlie admitted.

"Everyone walking?" Jo asked.

When they all nodded, she said, "The next round is on the house, then."

"Someone's in a good mood," Nevada said, staring at the bartender.

Jo gave a slight smile. "Maybe. But don't press me on it or I'll rescind the offer."

With that she strolled away.

Nevada stared after her. "I guess things are going well with Will. He's been a pretty happy guy. Everyone's in love but me."

The second the words were out, she winced. "I said that aloud, didn't I?"

The other three nodded.

"Crap. Sorry."

"Don't be," Annabelle told her. "Love is great. Except for when it's ripping out your heart and stomping on it."

"You, too?" Heidi asked.

"Oh, I'm the poster girl for picking the wrong guy. Trust me, if there's a selfish bastard within a fifty-mile radius, I'm all over him. Or I was. I'm in the process of retraining myself."

"How's that going?" Charlie asked.

"Slow. What about you?"

"Guys find me intimidating." Charlie shrugged. "Most days I like that." She glanced around the table. "So Heidi is dealing with her fear of cows, Annabelle's trying to get over falling for the wrong guy."

"Again and again," Annabelle added. "Let's be specific."

"Sure. I've given up on finding anyone because men are stupid." She turned to Nevada. "It's all up to you. You're going to have to represent us all on the road to happily-ever-after."

Nevada had been swallowing as Charlie spoke and now she started to choke.

"Me? No way. I'm not good at relationships."

"You're seeing Tucker," Heidi said. "Someone told me that at the grocery store, so it must be true. All the most accurate gossip comes from the grocery store."

Nevada felt a scream building up in her chest. "'Seeing' is a little strong."

"So, you're just using him for sex." Charlie touched her glass to Nevada's. "I can respect that."

"Can we talk about something else?" Nevada asked weakly.

Annabelle used her fork to slide several chips onto her plate. "Sure. That artist in town, Caterina Stoicas-escu, came into the library this morning. She's really interesting. Famous, but approachable. Do any of you know her?"

Nevada told herself that banging her head against the table wouldn't help. But this was a good reminder to be careful about what she wished for.

TUCKER STARED at his calendar. "Why?" he asked, suddenly realizing his perfectly good day was going to spin slowly down the toilet.

Nevada glanced up. "Why what?"

"Our appointment with the mayor. Why?"

"I have no idea. She didn't send an agenda."

"Of course she didn't. She wants to blindside us with something. That's what city officials do."

"Not here," Nevada told him. "She's happy about the construction. She wants the resort and casino. Because of the treaty with the last of the indigenous Máa-zib tribe, the city gets to tax whatever is built here. It's not a high percentage, but this is a huge project. Do you know what this is going to do for city revenues? I wouldn't worry about it."

He wished he could be as confident. In his experience, local government officials could be a pain in his ass. Until recently his biggest concern had been avoiding Cat. But being around her wasn't an issue now, which had set him free of the past. Things had been going great, and now this.

"We're up to date on the paperwork?" he asked.

"Yes. I double-checked that when she asked to see us. I've known Mayor Marsha all my life, Tucker. She's not out to get us."

He heard a car pull up outside. "I hope you're right," he said as he stood and crossed to the door. He stepped outside and walked down the two steps to greet the mayor.

As always, Marsha Tilson was well-dressed in a suit and low heels. Her white hair was in that puffy style women of her age seemed to favor. She had her purse over one shoulder and a folder in her right hand. He eyed the folder, knowing in his gut it was going to mean trouble.

"Good morning," the mayor said cheerfully.

"Mayor Tilson." He crossed to her and held out his hand. "Nice to see you."

"Please, Tucker. I've asked you to call me Mayor Marsha."

"Yes, ma'am," he murmured, before he could stop himself.

They shook, then she glanced around.

"You're making progress. The land is nearly cleared. I understand there is to be some blasting soon. If you would make sure you schedule it on a school day so we don't have too many young bystanders, I would appreciate it."

"Of course."

"Excellent." She motioned to the trailer. "Shall we?"

He wasn't exactly sure how she'd gotten control of

the conversation, but there she was, leading him inside his own trailer as if she were the hostess.

He climbed the stairs and walked in to find her settling on the chair by Nevada's desk.

"Cramped quarters," she said, taking the mug of coffee Nevada handed her. "I suppose you don't want to waste the money on an expensive office. Very sensible."

"Thanks."

He pulled up a chair and sat across from her. Nevada sank into her own seat.

The mayor set the folder on the desk. "The city council and I are very pleased with how things are progressing here. You're ahead of schedule, which is wonderful. The team you've brought in is an excellent addition to the town. They're well-mannered and eating out nearly every night." She smiled. "Something our local businesses appreciate."

Nevada shot him a "See?" look. He relaxed a little. Maybe he'd been wrong. Maybe there wasn't a problem.

"Mr. Janack, you've been a pleasure to work with."

"Tucker, please."

Mayor Marsha nodded. "Tucker." She glanced at Nevada, then back at him. "Which is why it pains me to have to come here and talk about something less than pleasant."

He held in a groan. Here it comes, he thought, trying to figure out what could have the good mayor's panties in a bunch.

"What's wrong?" Nevada asked. "All the permits

are in order, we're paying our fees, the plans have been approved."

The mayor reached across the desk and patted Nevada's hand. "Not to worry. I have no complaints about the construction. I wish the rest of my city business ran as smoothly. What I have instead is a more delicate problem. One I need your help with." She turned to Tucker. "You, especially."

He didn't like the sound of that. "All right," he said slowly. "What's the problem?"

"Caterina Stoicasescu."

"Cat?" Nevada asked. "What has she done?"

"More important," Tucker said. "What makes you think I can help?"

Nevada glanced at him. "Give it up. Our mayor knows everything."

He didn't know what to say about that.

Mayor Marsha drew in a deep breath. "Returning to the topic at hand, this must be fixed. On the surface, Ms. Stoicasescu has been nothing but generous. When we invited her to our artist series, we never dreamed someone of her caliber would attend. She's been delightful, giving interviews, speaking with students at the schools. She even taught a class at the college."

Tucker frowned. He didn't know about any of this. When had Cat gotten so involved with Fool's Gold? Nevada looked equally flummoxed.

"I didn't know," Nevada murmured. "She's making a place for herself here."

"I'm not sure about that. She doesn't seem to be the type to settle anywhere, however, she obviously has taken to the town. She's giving us a generous gift."

Tucker turned his attention back to Mayor Marsha. There was something about the way she said the words "generous gift." Something that indicated it was anything but.

"You're not happy about the gift?" he asked.

Marsha put on her reading glasses and opened her folder, then read from the paper inside. "Ms. Stoicasescu has been inspired by the positive female presence in Fool's Gold. As a thank-you for taking her in and making her feel as if she truly belongs, she wishes to give the community a gift. A sculpture that will celebrate the spirit of the town and the female energy that has made it so unique."

"Not the most gracefully worded press release," Nevada said, "but I'm missing the bad part. Is it the cost of the installation? We can hold a fundraiser. Cat's name is huge. We'll get donations from all over."

"I'm less concerned about the cost of the installation or insurance," Marsha said, removing her glasses. "It's the gift itself."

"I don't get it," Tucker admitted.

The mayor turned to her. "Cat wishes to celebrate all things feminine. Those were her exact words."

The mayor's expression tightened. If Tucker had to guess what she was feeling, he would say horror.

"How?" he asked.

"She's giving us a giant vagina. From the preliminary sketches, I would say it's going to be at least fifteen feet tall, and she would like us to place it in the center of town. Where the Thanksgiving diorama is now."

Nevada made a choking sound. Tucker found himself scrambling for words.

"A giant…"

"Yes."

What the hell was Cat thinking? A vagina? In the center of Fool's Gold. Now that he thought about it, he wasn't sure what that would look like. Would there be ovaries, too, or was that part of the uterus? He wasn't exactly an expert on female anatomy. He knew what he liked and what they liked and that had been the end of his exploration of the topic.

Nevada opened her mouth and then closed it. "Oh, my."

"Exactly," the mayor said. "We have tried to stop this by delaying the permitting process. However, Ms. Stoicasescu's assistant went on and on about freedom of expression and threatened to expose us to the national press as a town that is an enemy of art. We have already had to deal with the national press and it's not an experience I want to repeat."

"What do you want us to do?" Nevada asked.

The mayor closed the folder, put away her reading glasses, then rose.

"I want you to make it go away. All of it. Ms. Stoicasescu, her assistant and the vagina."

CHAPTER FOURTEEN

Tucker crossed the cleared land toward the side of the mountain. The blasting would take out about forty feet, which didn't sound like much. What he knew from having done this before was that the explosion would release tons of loose earth. Once that had been cleared, the side of the mountain would be stabilized and braced and the rest of the work could continue.

Digging for the water and sewer systems had already started. Massive pipes were being delivered in a few weeks and would be put in place. Having city water and sewer would make things easier, as far as doing the work and reliability, but it meant more permits and oversight. A trade-off.

He could see Nevada in the distance, talking to her team. The guys were nodding attentively, and one was taking notes. Tucker had to give her credit. She knew how to handle herself on the site.

"Hey, boss."

Tucker nodded as Jerry approached. The fiftysome-thing supervisor had been with the company nearly thirty years and had worked with Tucker for the past ten.

"The blasting crew is on their way. They'll arrive tomorrow. They'll go over everything, set up and be ready by Friday. Should be a good show."

"So I've heard."

The sound of female laughter drifted toward them. Tucker glanced toward Nevada and saw her laughing with her men.

"She's doing good," Jerry said. "A few of the guys weren't sure about reporting to a woman, and a local at that. But she knows her stuff. She's fair and easy to work for. Pretty, but what with you two being involved, no one's giving her that kind of trouble."

Tucker swung his gaze to Jerry. "We're not involved."

Jerry grinned. "Sure. Keep telling yourself that, boss. You'll start to believe it. Not that I blame you. Like I said, if you hadn't gotten there first, a lot of the guys would have made a play for her." The grin broadened. "Her sisters are getting married. You could make it a triple wedding."

Jerry laughed at his own joke and slapped Tucker on the back. "Want me to start a pool? You could make a lot of money betting with the guys."

"No, thanks," Tucker said, doing his best not to grit his teeth.

Their fake relationship had worked too well. They hadn't been dating but that didn't matter. They were barely seeing each other. Sure, they'd slept together, but that had been more an accident than anything else. Not that he hadn't enjoyed himself. He had. She was great. He liked spending time with her. Not just for the sex, although that was life-changing, but for the conversation. They got each other. She was funny and smart. He wanted to see more of her, but they weren't dating. Or involved.

Jerry waved and walked toward the group around Nevada. Tucker watched him go, not sure what he was supposed to do now. He'd made it clear that he didn't do relationships. He believed love made people into fools, and he wasn't going there again. Nevada understood that. They were on the same page.

At least he hoped they were. Now that he thought about it, he wasn't sure she did know the rules. What if she expected more of him?

The question had barely formed in his mind before a thin sheen of cold sweat broke out on his back. The last thing he needed was for everyone around here to think he'd misled Nevada. Her team would turn on him, and who knew what that would mean in town. So, they had to *talk about it*—words designed to make any man run for the hills.

But he had to make things clear. There wasn't going to be a triple wedding. In a year or so, he would move on to the next project. Sure, he would miss Nevada when he went, but that didn't mean he wanted to marry her. Or anyone.

Settling down had never been something he'd considered. He supposed at some point he should think about having a family. Traditionally that meant getting married. But even as he considered the possibility, he remembered how it had been with Cat. How he'd been unable to think, let alone to be his own man. She'd controlled him and humiliated him and there was no way he would do that again.

Determined to have it out with Nevada right that second, he started toward her. Before he'd taken more than a couple of steps, a police car came toward him. Fool's Gold Police Department was painted on the sides.

He waited while the officer behind the wheel parked, then got out.

"Tucker Janack?" the woman asked.

He nodded.

She walked toward him. "I'm Police Chief Alice Barns. Nice to meet you."

"Why do I doubt that?" Tucker asked, eyeing her.

She was of average height, in her forties and wearing a dark blue uniform. She looked more than capable of being in charge.

"I enjoy meeting folks," the police chief told him. "I'm a people person." She handed him a business-size envelope. "This is for you."

"What is it?"

"A summons to appear before the Fool's Gold City Council. They want Nevada there, too, just so you know."

"An official summons? Can they do that?" He wouldn't have thought a local body of government had that kind of power.

She smiled. "My being here says they can."

"Good point."

NEVADA HAD NEVER been called to the principal's office while in school, but if she had, she would guess it felt like this. She'd never attended a city council meeting before, so she didn't know how they usually went, but she assumed there was usually more than one agenda item.

She and Tucker sat at a large conference table with

seven women sitting across from them. Mayor Marsha sat in the middle, flanked by her council. No one looked happy.

Nevada glanced down at the piece of paper that had been put in front of her. There was the date, the time of the meeting, the word "agenda," followed by a colon and the phrase, "Vagina Issue."

With the meeting called to order, the mayor drew in a breath.

"I'm the longest-serving mayor in California," she said. "I've seen us survive earthquakes, snowstorms, grape blight and the recent catastrophic fire that nearly destroyed one of our schools. We've survived busloads of men and a reality show. The town and I will not be taken down by a giant vagina."

Nevada swallowed. "You mentioned that when you visited the construction site yesterday, but I'm still not sure what you want us…"

"Fix it," Mayor Marsha said sternly, interrupting. "You two knew Ms. Stoicasescu before. You're the reason she's here now. I'm holding both of you responsible."

Nevada wanted to protest that it wasn't her fault. That she had nothing to do with Cat or her gift choices. But the seven women staring at her didn't look like they wanted to have a discussion.

"Yes, ma'am," she said quietly, not sure what being responsible was going to mean, but aware that it wasn't good news.

Tucker leaned toward them. "If I may, Nevada isn't the one who had a relationship with Cat. This is my responsibility, not hers."

"Nevada and Cat are friends," the mayor said. "Nevada has shown Cat around town."

Nevada winced. So much for doing the right thing, she thought. It had come back to bite her for sure.

The mayor sighed. "I appreciate you defending Nevada. That speaks very well of you. At this point I don't care who fixes this, I just want it fixed and I want it on the record that we've had this discussion. There will be no giant vagina in my town. Do you understand?"

Nevada and Tucker both nodded.

"Good. Now you may go."

They stood and quickly left the room. Once in the hallway of city hall, Nevada leaned against the wall.

"If I weren't in the middle of this, it would be really funny."

"Tell me about it." He leaned against the wall opposite. "Now what?"

"We talk to her and explain the town doesn't want her gift." She wanted to say Tucker should do it, but Cat hadn't spent any time with him since arriving in Fool's Gold. "I'll do it."

"Are you sure? I can try."

"No. You're the ex. There's too much emotional baggage. She's my friend." Sort of.

"What are you going to say?"

"I haven't a clue."

NEVADA WENT TO THE GOLD RUSH Ski Lodge and Resort to look for Cat. The tiny, strange man who was her assistant said that Cat was working and gave Nevada the address of an industrial center on the edge of town. Nevada drove there.

The huge building had been subdivided into a dozen or so smaller light-industrial sites. The one at the end was nearly double in height. Thinking about how much room it would take to build a giant vagina, Nevada chose that one and knocked on the door.

No one answered. She rang the bell, then finally opened the door. She was met with a blast of music. Black Eyed Peas, she would guess.

Scaffolding filled the center of the huge room, just as it had back in L.A. when Nevada had first met Cat. It rose up to the nearly twenty-foot ceiling. Massive sheets of metal stood in a rack, and she could see the basic structure of the piece had already been started. Poles were strapped together to form a giant V. A pulley system would raise the metal up to the level of the poles.

Cat stood by a long table, cutting pieces of metal with wicked-looking shears. Heavy gloves protected her hands. Up against the wall was a sketch of what the piece would look like when it was done.

There were swirls and waves, intricate designs covering the feminine curves. If one could ignore the fact that it was a vagina, it was very beautiful.

Cat glanced up and saw Nevada. She smiled broadly, pulled off her gloves, then hit a button on a small remote. The music went silent.

"You came!" Cat hurried toward her and pulled her into a hug. "Don't you love this space? It's perfect."

Nevada hugged her back, then carefully stepped away. "I remember where you worked in Los Angeles. I still have trouble reconciling that everything is industrial here, but beautifully ethereal when you're finished."

Cat's green eyes glowed with pleasure. "It's my personal form of magic." She grabbed Nevada's hand and pulled her to the sketch on the wall. "I don't always know what I'm going to be doing. Sometimes I have to let the piece speak to me. But this time, I had a vision. It's so clear." She laughed. "I almost feel like I shouldn't have to make it. I can reach out and touch what it's going to be."

"It's amazing," Nevada murmured. "You're an inspiration, honoring the town in this way."

Cat leaned against her. "I have to. You're from here."

Oh, no. Not a place she wanted to go.

"There's just one problem."

Cat looked at her expectantly.

"It's the subject matter," Nevada said cautiously. "You're so brilliant and famous. Everyone will want to come see the piece, of course. But there's some concern that it's rather risqué for Fool's Gold."

Cat rolled her eyes. "Please. Don't be so provincial. My work celebrates the power of women."

Nevada supposed that a giant breast would be worse, but not by much. "Okay, but this is a family town. Parents don't want to have to explain what it is to their children."

"Why not? We should be proud of our bodies. There is beauty in each one of us." She drew her eyebrows together. "Are you saying the town doesn't want my gift?"

Her voice was low, almost neutral, but Nevada was getting a bad feeling in her gut.

"They are concerned about the vagina. If it were something else, maybe—"

"Something else?" Cat's voice was a roar. "They are daring to tell me what to create? They are interfering in my artistic process? Do they know who I am? Governments pay me millions of dollars for my work. Do you know how much the French are giving me for a piece? Work I have put off to create this, as a way to thank your town."

"Maybe if they're not appropriately grateful you should rethink doing it."

"Never." Cat stalked away, then turned. "How dare they! I am an artist. They have no right to refuse. No right to complain. It's a gift. You don't get to say what the gift is going to be. My piece will put this little town on the map. They should beg me to give it to them."

Her voice rose with each word until she was shouting. Nevada wasn't enjoying herself, but she wasn't actually nervous until Cat picked up the blowtorch and lit it.

"Okay, then," she said, hurrying to the door. "You think about it and we'll talk again later."

She scurried outside and hunched over when Cat screamed. The sound was still echoing in Nevada's ears as she jumped in her truck and sped away.

"LOOK AT THE BRIGHT SIDE," Tucker told Nevada. "At least now you don't have to worry about her wanting to date you."

"Shut up."

Nevada wished they were somewhere private so she could punch him really hard in the stomach. She knew how—she had brothers. But on the job site, with their crew around and the blasting team putting the final touches on their work, it didn't seem like the right time.

The good news was that watching the explosion and the subsequent crumbling of earth would probably make her feel better.

"Want me to talk to her?" he offered.

"Cat will probably attack you with a flamethrower. Which right now doesn't seem like such a bad idea."

Tucker grinned at her. "Don't be afraid. You could take her."

"She has tools and a vicious will. You should have heard her. She thought the town was ungrateful. If only that were enough to make her change her mind."

Nevada watched her men get into position. "I need to go."

"You'll feel better after the explosion."

"I hope so."

Blasting earth was a complex proposition. There were dozens of safeguards in place. Now she did a final check on her part of the operation, then settled in to watch the show.

"Um, boss?"

She turned and saw Jerry walking toward her, Cat by his side.

"You have a visitor," Jerry said, stating the obvious.

Nevada held in a groan. "What are you doing here?" she asked Cat. "Never mind. We have to move back. We're doing blasting."

She led the other woman back toward the trailer and got her a hard hat. Once it was in place, Nevada put her hands on her hips.

"Why are you here?" she repeated.

Cat stared at her, wide-eyed. Her full mouth trembled at the corners. "I knew it. You're angry with me."

"Not exactly."

Tears filled Cat's eyes. "I was so hurt by what you said. It was as if you stabbed me in the heart and then crushed my soul. The very essence of my being. What you asked me to do, how you want me to change... I thought you knew m-me." Her voice trembled on the last word, as if she were holding in a sob.

Nevada swore under her breath. She moved away from the trailer, motioning for Cat to keep up with her.

"I wasn't trying to crush your soul."

"How could you have said those things to me?"

"Telling you Fool's Gold doesn't want a giant vagina in the center of town is the truth."

"But it's my gift. It's who I am."

"Transcendent?"

The corners of Cat's mouth turned up. Nevada might not be into the girl thing, but she had to admit that Cat defined beauty.

"Yes," Cat whispered. "I want to give this to them because it's like giving it to you. Every time you see it, you'll think of me."

"You got that right."

Crap and double crap, Nevada thought. Someone called out the one-minute warning. She grabbed Cat and moved her farther back.

"I already have a vagina," Nevada said, unable to believe they were having this conversation. "Can you do something else?"

Cat shook her head.

Nevada sighed. "This isn't about you. I understand that you're giving us a gift, but don't you care that we don't want it?"

"You don't understand. When you see it completely, you'll be grateful. Everyone will be."

"No, we won't. We'll be horrified. Can't it be something else? A circle? The shape of a woman?"

Cat laughed. "Don't be silly. Of course it can't be something else. This is what I have to do. It's out of my control."

"Technically, it's not. You're the one building it. You're the one who—"

Then she was flying through the air.

She'd been partially aware of some kind of countdown, but she hadn't been paying attention. Who could notice anything else with Cat being her usual crazy self? That meant she wasn't paying as close attention as she should have been and didn't bother making sure they were back far enough.

One second she'd been talking, the next she was airborne, although not for long. The ground came up very quickly and turned out to be much harder than it looked. She slammed into it with a force that knocked the wind out of her.

For that heartbeat there was nothing, then she gasped for air, choking as she inhaled. Every part of her hurt. Her ears rang and her head seemed to be spinning.

"Someone has a lot of explaining to do," she muttered, cautiously sitting up.

She moved her legs, pleased that nothing seemed

injured. She drew in more breaths and found her head clearing.

Cat!

She saw her friend was also sitting, looking stunned. Thunder shook the earth. They both turned and watched part of the mountain fall away. A huge cloud of dust rose toward the sky.

"Are you all right?" Nevada asked.

Cat nodded.

"I should have been paying more attention," Nevada said, thinking she should also be standing, but it seemed too difficult.

"I'm fine." Cat crawled toward her. "Are you hurt?"

"No. Just shaken." She laughed. "Like a James Bond martini."

Cat grinned.

Nevada heard shouts from behind them. Great. Someone had noticed them flying by and was about to make a fuss.

"I'm not going to the hospital," she muttered.

Cat moved closer and put her hands on Nevada's shoulders. "You'll be okay," she said, then lowered her head and kissed her.

Nevada knew she might have some kind of post-explosion trauma thing going on, but she could still recognize a kiss when it happened. Warm, soft lips settled against hers. That's what she noticed first. Soft, not firm. Gentle. Cat's perfume surrounded her and those powerful artist's hands gripped her shoulders.

Nevada sat frozen, not sure what to do. Pushing away seemed the best option, but she didn't want to be mean about it. Nor could she figure out exactly where to push without giving Cat the wrong idea.

Before she'd worked out a plan, she heard some-one yell.

"Gold!" a man's voice cried. "Can you see the gold?"

Cat drew back. Nevada shifted away and told herself this would be an excellent time to stand up and run. Before she could, Tucker, Will and several of the guys surrounded them. She could hear someone yelling for the paramedics. Tucker knelt beside her and shook her slightly.

"What the hell is wrong with you?" he demanded, sounding furious. "You could have been killed."

He looked pissed and worried and somehow, in a twisted, girly kind of way, that made her feel ever so much better.

"I wasn't," she pointed out.

"Damned annoying woman," he muttered, before leaning in and kissing her as well.

This time the contact was familiar and arousing. As he straightened and continued to glare at her, she couldn't help smiling. Funny, after all these years, she'd suddenly become popular.

CHAPTER FIFTEEN

TUCKER STOOD OVER NEVADA as if warding off demons.

"I'm really okay," she said for the fourth or fifth time.

He continued to ignore her.

Just as disturbing as her near-death experience and the realization that she could have been killed by the explosion or subsequent slide was the fact that Cat had made her move. Tucker rarely had to work to keep a woman in his life. Knowing his competition was playing for the other side made him uncomfortable.

He was aware that he'd told himself he needed to back off where Nevada was concerned. That they were too involved. But right now he didn't give a damn about that. He wanted to stand over her, beating his chest, although he couldn't figure out what that would accomplish.

One of the firefighters raced over, the EMTs right behind.

"Are they hurt?" the firefighter demanded, dropping to her knees by Nevada and holding a penlight up to her eyes.

"I'm perfectly fine, Charlie," Nevada said, starting to stand.

"Don't even think about it," Tucker and the

firefighter snapped at the same time. Nevada kept her butt on the ground.

"I'm all right, too," Cat called, her expression bemused. "Doesn't anyone want to fuss over me?"

"I will." An EMT dropped to her knees and reached for Cat's wrist. "How are you feeling, ma'am? Dizzy? Does your head hurt?"

"Did you just say *ma'am?*" Cat closed her eyes. "I'm dizzy now."

Nevada chuckled.

Tucker glared at her. "Don't laugh," he commanded. "You might be hurt."

A second EMT joined Charlie. They examined Nevada while Tucker watched anxiously. He was aware of a group of men climbing up the side of the mountain and shouts about something he couldn't hear. There was a lot of activity he would have to deal with later. Right now Nevada was his main concern.

About two minutes later, the EMT removed the blood pressure cuff.

"You're fine."

Tucker was less convinced. "What if she hit her head?"

"I didn't," Nevada told him.

"You might not remember."

She rolled her eyes. "My head doesn't hurt, I don't have any ringing in my ears. I'm okay."

Cat was pronounced all right as well, but she didn't seem as anxious to get up. Nevada scrambled to her feet. She held out her arms and turned in a slow circle.

"See? Not broken."

Cat's EMT helped her to stand. The other woman reached for Nevada and clung to her.

"I can't believe we went through that today," Cat murmured. "We could have been killed." She gazed at Nevada. "We should go back to my hotel and rest."

Nevada slowly disentangled herself. "I don't think so. Tucker, could you find someone to take Cat back to her hotel?"

"Sure."

He waved Jerry over and told him to drive Cat back to her hotel. Cat protested, but eventually allowed herself to be led away. The EMTs went back to their truck.

Charlie walked over to Tucker and glared at him. "You should know better. She was standing too close."

Nevada shook her head. "Don't yell at him. It was my fault. I got distracted."

"Is that what you're calling it?" he muttered.

Nevada glared at him. "Don't start with me."

"You were kissing her."

He hadn't meant to say it, but the words came out before he could stop them.

Charlie blinked at them both. "Excuse me."

Nevada sighed. "It's a long story."

"I have time." She looked from Nevada to him and back. "But I thought…"

"Me, too," Tucker growled, not liking anything about this. In theory, the girl-on-girl thing was appealing. But not so much when one of the girls in question was his girl.

"Oh, really?" Charlie grinned. "How was it?"

"Different."

"Different good or different bad?"

"Are you asking for yourself?" Nevada raised her eyebrows. "Cat's entering her feminine stage."

"She's not my type and I'm not interested. Just curious."

Will hurried over to them. "Boss, you gotta come see this. When they blew the side of the mountain, a whole bunch of caves were exposed. There's gold in them. Statues and art and stuff. It looks old. Indian, maybe."

"Mayan," Nevada and Charlie said at the same time.

"The Máa-zib tribe," Tucker said, wondering what had been unearthed and how much it was going to delay construction. Surprises like this were rarely good news for the contractor.

"Can you take her to the trailer?" he asked Charlie.

"Hell, no. I want to see it, too."

"You heard them—I'm fine," Nevada said, walking toward the crowd. "How is this discovery going to mess everything up?"

"We'll have to find out. It depends on where it is and what will happen to it." He studied the blast area and the people swarming over the side of the mountain. If any more earth gave way, they were all going to fall.

"We have to get the area roped off," he told Will. "We'll need security." Not just for safety purposes, but if there really was gold... He swore. Nothing about this was going to be easy.

"It's at the far end of what's going to be the parking lot," Nevada pointed out. "That's good. Maybe the caves are past the property line. Then it wouldn't be your problem."

"I'm not feeling that lucky."

He put his arm around her. "Still okay? No headache or bruises?"

"I got a little banged up hitting the ground," she said. "Otherwise, I'm good."

They reached the base of the hill. Before they could climb up, a car drove toward them. Tucker recognized it and the older woman climbing out.

"I received a call," Mayor Marsha said as she approached. "We have ourselves a situation." She glanced toward the crowd on the hillside. "They can't stay there. The ground might not be stable."

"I'll get my men out."

"Good. I've already called Chief Barns. She'll post her people around the area until we can figure out what's going on." The mayor drew in a breath. "Is there really gold?"

"That's what I'm hearing."

"Because a giant vagina wasn't enough," the mayor mused.

"At least the gold will be a distraction," he offered.

"If you do your job and make the vagina go away, we won't need a distraction."

"Oh, right. Good point."

NEVADA LEFT WORK EARLY. Between the press, the police and interested people from town, the construction site was a busy mess. She would tackle what she had to in the morning. In the meantime she wanted a hot bath and some quiet time to process her new, complicated life.

While the tub filled, she kept having flashbacks to the last time she'd used it. That had been during her night with Tucker, the one that had curled her toes more than once. The man knew what he was doing, she thought as she climbed into the water. If the sex had been half that good ten years ago, she might have tried arm wrestling Cat for him. Not that winning would have made a difference. He'd been obsessed with the artistic beauty.

What a difference time makes, she thought, sinking into the hot water and smiling. Tucker had not taken Cat's kiss very well. He'd been more upset than she was. An interesting turn of events, considering it was her first girl kiss. But now there was a Cat problem and she didn't know what to do about it.

Turning her down went without saying, but how to do it? As much as the woman could infuriate her, she liked Cat and wanted them to stay friends. Tomorrow... she thought, stretching out in the water and letting the heat ease her bruised muscles.

When the water cooled, she got out and dressed. She was hungry and not in the mood to cook, which usually meant take-out. Before she could decide which restaurant, someone knocked on her door.

Nevada stared at the door, half-afraid to answer. She wasn't ready to face Cat. Their conversation would require a certain level of delicacy and preparation.

The knock came again.

Slowly, cautiously, she crossed the living room and looked out the peephole.

"Thank goodness," she said, pulling open the door.

Tucker leaned against the doorframe, looking handsome and capable. One corner of his mouth lifted. "Expecting someone else?"

"It crossed my mind."

"Mine, too. I've come to claim my woman."

It was a new century and she supposed she should object to the claim. Truthfully, though, hearing the words made her feel all gooey inside.

"What does that mean?" she asked.

"I'm taking you home with me. Pack a bag. We have dinner reservations in half an hour. I've already picked out the wine."

Wine sounded nice, as did spending the night with him.

"Give me five minutes."

Tucker's suite at the hotel had a living room with a sofa and two chairs, with a big bedroom beyond. She dropped her bag onto the bed, then turned to face him.

"Feed me."

He chuckled. "You never were one to play games."

"Not my style."

He took her hand and they went downstairs. Once in the restaurant, they were shown to a corner table. The wine was already open and poured, and menus sat to one side.

"Very well prepared," she said, sliding in.

He settled across from her. "I can be smooth."

"It's nice to have proof."

He leaned toward her. "How are you feeling?"

"Good. No headache. My back and butt are a little sore from the impact." She shook her head. "I can't believe I was so stupid and didn't pay attention to where we were standing. I know better. Are you going to write me up?"

"Not this time. But if you do it again, you'll be in big trouble."

"I won't." Not that there were any more explosions planned. "So, what did I miss?"

"Your mayor scares the crap out of me," he admitted.

"Don't feel bad. You're in good company. Mayor Marsha has a way of getting exactly what she wants."

"Quickly, too. The blast area is already blocked off. There are plenty of police standing guard. Extra security people have been ordered and will be arriving in the morning. Some famous archaeological team has been contacted to deal with the find. They're arriving tomorrow, too."

She sipped her wine. The full-bodied taste rolled over her tongue. The man knew how to pick wine, she thought, remembering Tucker had other talents, as well.

"What does this mean for construction?" she asked.

"The mayor swears we'll have our site fully back within two weeks. Even doubling that, a month isn't bad. We can put off the parking lot and focus on the other end. One of the advantages of working on a hundred acres. The big question is going to be who owns the gold."

"Did you get to see it?"

"A few pieces. There are carvings and statues, some jewelry. It's a pretty big find. I don't know anything about archaeology, but I'm pretty sure the people in khaki shorts are going to be happy."

"The find will also be good for the town," she said. "More tourists. We do love them and their dollars."

"Sure. And here I thought life in a small town would be boring."

"Never that."

He studied her.

She sighed. "I'm fine. Don't worry."

"I can't help it. You were hurt on my watch." He picked up his wine. "How's Cat?"

"I haven't talked to her."

"Do you want to?"

She raised her eyebrows. "Jealous?"

"Not completely. Just…dealing. It was my first live girl kiss."

"Mine, too." She shrugged. "I'm going to have to talk to her. I don't think she's genuinely interested in me. I think this is about her art. But I also don't want to hurt her feelings." She picked up her wine, then put it down.

"Oh, God," she murmured, mentally putting the pieces together. "We've all kissed each other. It's practically a threesome."

Tucker leaned back in the booth and laughed. The sound rolled over her, making her smile. Being around Tucker always made her feel better, she thought. Today she found the whole "safe and protected" thing pretty appealing, but it was more than that. She liked how he treated her as an equal and accepted her as part of his team.

She handed him a menu. "Brace yourself. I'm in the mood for steak."

"Go for it. You've earned it."

The server appeared a minute or so later and took

their orders. When they were alone again, Tucker poured her more wine.

"Do you know anything about Máa-zib history?" he asked. "I never knew they worked with gold."

"I didn't either. Most of the stories around here are about how they were a matriarchal society who didn't have much interest in men." She smiled. "Except for the business of getting pregnant."

"A romantic bunch, then." He took a sip of his wine. "My mother was the one with the most Máa-zib blood. If she ever talked about what she knew, Dad's forgotten and no one in his family ever told him stories. I asked him a few years ago and he couldn't remember her ever saying anything."

"You were young when she died."

"I don't remember her at all," he admitted. "There are a few vague images, but I suspect they come from my dad telling me about her, rather than me having memories of my own."

"That must be difficult."

"It's all I know. I can't miss what I never had."

Probably true, she thought, but sad. "If she hadn't died, would you and she have traveled with your dad? Or would you have been raised in one place?"

"I don't know. I never thought about it." He reached across the table and touched her hand. "I could have grown up in a place like Fool's Gold."

"There are worse fates."

"I like it here. More than I thought I would. There's a sense of community. Mayor Marsha can be a little rabid."

She grinned. "She's protective."

"I'm glad she doesn't carry a gun."

The feel of his fingers brushing hers ignited nerve endings all over her body. Later, she thought. While she was sure Tucker would agree if she suggested they move the party upstairs, she found herself wanting to wait. Not only for the sense of anticipation, but because this was nice. Spending time with Tucker—like a regular couple.

As soon as the ideas formed in her mind, she reminded herself there was danger in thinking like that. They worked together, which was its own complication, and he didn't believe in love. Not that they were at the love stage. Or even close to it.

Still, this was a good time to remind herself that getting involved would be stupid.

Jo LAY ON HER SIDE, her body heavy with satisfaction, her mind quiet for once. Will stretched out beside her, facing her, his hand on her hip, his expression intense.

"I could get addicted to you," she murmured.

"Good."

Not good, she thought. Far from good. Falling for a man—she knew the danger. Still, now that she'd given in, she couldn't convince herself to back off. Being with him was easy. Right. Talk about scaring the crap out of her...

Jake, her cat, jumped onto the bed. Being a typical feline, he ignored her and walked over to Will to be petted.

"Damn cat," Will muttered, scratching behind the cat's ears.

"You always say that, but you're very good to him."

"He's okay. For a cat."

She smiled. "You're a softie. So tough on the out-side, but it's just an act."

Instead of smiling, he kissed her.

"I love you."

His words fell into the silence. They were unex-pected and unwelcome.

Not love, she thought frantically, sitting up and pull-ing the sheet with her. Never love. They weren't sup-posed to get *that* involved.

His mouth twisted. "Judging by the panic in your eyes," he said gruffly, "this isn't welcome news."

She rolled off the bed and picked up her thong. After slipping it in place, she pulled on a T-shirt, then faced him.

"No. It's not."

"At least you're honest." He sat up, leaning against the headboard in her small bedroom. Pain darkened his eyes. "Want to tell me why?"

Annoyed that the scratching had ceased, Jake moved to the foot of the bed and began washing his face.

Will was a good man, Jo reminded herself. She'd always known that. He was kind and normal and he couldn't possibly understand. Telling him the truth meant losing him. Not telling him probably meant the same. She'd hurt his feelings, the one thing she hadn't wanted to do.

"You gonna spend the rest of your life hiding?" he asked. "What is it? Did somebody hurt you?"

She folded her arms across her chest. "It's not going to work. If I tell you, everything will change."

"No, it won't. I'm not that guy."

A claim he'd made before. But he was wrong. Everyone was that guy, she thought.

"Just tell me," he insisted. "I can't fix it if I don't know what it is."

"There's no fixing. It's my past and it can't be undone. It simply is."

He stared at her. "There's nothing you can say to make me turn away. I love you. That's not going to change."

He meant it. She could see it, and she almost believed him. But that would make things too easy, she thought sadly. She wasn't that lucky.

She stood there a long time before accepting the fact that she didn't have a lot of options. If she didn't tell him now, he would bring it up later. Either she gave in or they were done. She tried to tell herself that not wanting to lose him didn't mean she was weak, but she knew that she would be lying to herself. Somehow, when she wasn't paying attention, this man had become important to her.

A narrow straight-back chair stood in the corner of her room. She pulled it up closer to the bed and sat down. The past that she had done her best to put behind her flared up now, surrounding her.

"My parents died when I was pretty young," she began, studying her short nails rather than looking at him. "I was in foster care for a few years, different places. It wasn't great, but nothing too awful happened. I wasn't abused or anything. But I never belonged, if that makes sense."

She looked up and found him watching her intently. Her stomach tightened. Nothing about this was going to end well, she thought sadly. But it was too late now to come up with a lie.

"When I was about fifteen I was sent to live with a woman who was new to the foster care system. She was older—at the time I thought she was ancient. Now she seems less elderly." She managed a smile. "I think she was in her late fifties. Sandy. She was nice. Really nice. Sweet. She cared, which no one had for a long time. Then I met Ronnie. He was a year older than me in school, a bad boy. Sexy as hell, with tattoos and a motorcycle. I couldn't resist him. The day he kissed me, I knew I could die happy."

She looked at the blanket, at the floor. Anywhere that was safe.

"Being with Ronnie was exciting. Dangerous. One day we stole a couple of bottles from a liquor store. It was too easy. We got drunk. Sandy never knew, never guessed. Ronnie was so polite to her. She adored him and was happy for me. I felt bad, deceiving her, but that didn't stop me."

"I know that type of guy," Will said.

"Then you won't be surprised to know things escalated. We robbed a corner grocery a couple of towns over. Then held up a dry cleaner. They barely tried to stop us and the police had no clue who we were. Being bad like that was exciting and fun and something we shared. By day we were students and at night, we were Bonnie and Clyde."

She looked at him then and shrugged. "I'd only heard part of that story. I didn't know how it ended."

She drew in a breath. "We decided our graduation present to each other would be to rob a bank. Sandy was having me fill out college applications and said she'd put away a little money to help me pay for it. I couldn't believe it. I should have listened, I should have accepted the gift, but I wanted to be with Ronnie more."

"You robbed a bank?" Will sounded shocked.

"We tried. We did a decent job planning and would have gotten away, except the bank manager decided to stand up to us. Ronnie had a gun and…"

Now came the hard part, she thought. The part that haunted her. She could still remember the terror in the bank manager's eyes. The way he kept looking at the pictures on his desk. He had a wife and three kids. To this day, she could recognize those kids anywhere.

"We were so young and so stupid," she continued softly. "Ronnie was screaming at him to hand over the money and I—" Her throat tightened. "I went along with it, saying Ronnie would shoot him if he didn't listen. I was so scared, but determined."

She sucked in a breath. "The police broke in and one of the customers in the bank screamed he was going to shoot and someone fired, then they all fired."

She hadn't known a gun could be so loud. The sound had filled the small bank, echoing until it had seemed to explode in her head. The subsequent gunshots had seemed to go on forever.

She'd stood there, waiting to be killed—ignorant enough to think dying together would be romantic.

She dropped her gaze to her hands again. "There was so much blood," she whispered. "I didn't know how much there could be." She didn't have to close her eyes to see him lying there on the bank floor. She remembered that someone was screaming and the sound hurt her ears. It had taken so long to realize that person was her.

"They arrested me. My lawyer tried to get me to say it was Ronnie. After all, he was dead and couldn't say I was lying. But I wouldn't do it. I told them everything and then I pled guilty. I didn't want to have to face those people again at trial. I was sentenced and that was it."

She shifted on the chair, fighting tears. "Sandy came to see me. She was heartbroken. She kept saying it was her fault and I had to tell her it wasn't and I was so afraid she would abandon me, but she didn't. Not even when they sent me away."

Finally she looked at him. His face was carefully blank, his eyes expressionless. Better than jumping to his feet and calling her a murderer, she supposed, but not by much.

"They sentenced me to twelve years. I served nine. I was twenty-seven when I got out. That was nearly ten years ago. Sandy was sick and I stayed with her for the next couple of years, taking care of her until she died. She left me everything. I sold her little house and took the money and somehow found Fool's Gold. I bought this place."

She folded her arms over her chest again. "If I could take it back, I would. If I could give up my life so Ronnie didn't have to die like that... Such a waste for both of us. We were kids, but we still should have known better. I know I was lucky. The bank manager was shot but recovered and I had Sandy looking out for me. She never gave up on me. I don't know why. Anyone else would have walked away."

She paused, hoping he would say something. He didn't. Feeling uncomfortable, she added, "I learned my lesson. Obviously. Everything is different now, but I still carry that with me."

"I can see why." He rolled off the opposite side of the bed and started dressing.

She stood, careful to put the chair between them. Instinctively she knew she was going to need protection.

He pulled on jeans, then dragged on his sweatshirt. Finally he looked at her and swore. "I thought you'd been with some guy who beat you. I thought you were a Mafia princess or some crap like that."

She didn't flinch. Didn't let him know how his words cut through her.

"You don't have some noble past," he growled. "You're a criminal. An innocent man could have died because of you. A guilty man did die. That's not anything I want to be a part of."

He stepped into his boots, grabbed his jacket and was gone. Seconds later, she heard the front door slam and the uneven sound of his footsteps on the stairs.

She began to shiver. Not that the room was chilly. Instead the cold came from inside. It swept through her until she trembled so much she could barely stand.

She'd known what would happen if she ever told the truth. Known how it would end. She knew she shouldn't be surprised.

Tears filled her eyes. As she brushed them away she wondered if she would ever get to leave her past behind. Not that she wanted to forget. She would pay for what she'd done for the rest of her life and she deserved that. But somewhere along the line she'd changed, and she'd hoped that her future might change, too.

CHAPTER SIXTEEN

THE CONSTRUCTION SITE was pure chaos. Tucker stood beside the trailer and stared at what had once been a relatively quiet, orderly work area. Now there were police, state troopers, private security and tourists everywhere. The cleared area by the mountain had become a makeshift parking lot that overflowed with cars and trucks. Heidi Simpson had set up a stand selling her goat cheese, along with water, soda and sandwiches. He understood the need for everyone to make a profit, but wished they would all go away and leave him alone.

He felt his phone buzz in his shirt pocket and pulled it out.

"Janack," he said.

"You've made it to CNN," his father said. "I can't decide if I'm proud or horrified."

"Let me know when you decide," Tucker told him. "I know where I stand."

He went into the trailer so he could hear more easily, and shut the door behind him.

His father chuckled. "I can hear it in your voice, son. Bad?"

Tucker slumped into his chair. "I keep telling myself it could be worse. At least the find is at the far end of the site, just past our property line. We're not legally involved. As soon as the gold is taken away, things will quiet down. In the meantime, we're moving our equipment and men as far away as possible."

"Sounds like you have it under control."

"Nevada does. She volunteered to coordinate with the town on this."

"Always good having a local around."

"It is," he said absently, thinking Nevada's value went past simply being local.

He and his father talked about the job itself, and how long Tucker expected to stay ahead of schedule.

"Need me to fly in?" his father asked.

"I've got it covered."

"I know that, son. Keep me in the loop. Talk to you soon."

They hung up.

Tucker eyed the door, not wanting to go back outside, but knowing he had to. He'd barely walked down the steps when Nevada appeared at his side.

"Okay," she said, her eyes bright with amusement. "The archaeological team is on its way. Jerry radioed that their bus was coming up the road."

She motioned for Tucker to follow her to the lunch table where the guys ate. She pulled two pieces of paper out of her back pocket and spread them out.

"It will take us half a day to clear a temporary road through here." She pointed to the sketch she'd made. "I think it's worth it. We can move the equipment we need more quickly that way, and get right to work."

"What about that mess?" he asked, pointing behind them.

She glanced over her shoulder. "I'll have this under control by tomorrow."

"Impossible."

She laughed. "Trust me, Tucker. I grew up as one of six kids. This is nothing. I'm used to bedlam and anarchy. It would go faster if my mom were here, but I can do it by myself."

She continued to outline her plan, which was impressive. His father was right—having a local around helped. Tucker knew he was lucky to have her. And not just on the job site. She was an unexpected pleasure of being in Fool's Gold.

While he didn't believe in his father's choice of having women all over the world, Tucker hadn't lived the last ten years as a monk. There had been plenty of short-term, casual relationships. They'd been as easy to start as they had been to end. Almost from the beginning, he'd known they wouldn't work out, for an assortment of reasons.

With Nevada it was different. She understood his work and she understood him. They could talk about anything and spend long periods of time together. He trusted her, which wasn't something he often found.

"So?" she asked. "Do I have your approval?"

"And my gratitude."

"You can give me a small but tasteful present later."

Her impish smile made him want to pull her against him and give her that present now. But this wasn't the time or place.

Yet another car drove up, but this one made him groan. He recognized the lettering on the side.

"Police Chief Alice Barns," he muttered. "She brought the summons last time she was here. Do you think the city council is demanding our presence again?"

Before Nevada could answer, the police chief walked up. Tucker eyed her but didn't see any paperwork. That was something.

"Morning," Chief Barns said. "I'm letting you know that the extra security will be here for as long as it takes." She smiled. "I'm sure that makes you happy."

"My heart is beating faster as we speak," Tucker muttered. "Do we have an estimated time of completion?"

The police chief jerked her thumb toward the parking lot, where a battered van had pulled in.

"You can ask them. I have a list of their names. Want a copy?"

"No." He planned to be at the other end of the site until all this blew over. The idea of a hundred acres between him and them made him a happy guy.

"I'll take it," Nevada said. "I'll want to check their IDs, too, to make sure we don't have any treasure hunters muscling in. This find is part of Fool's Gold's history. No one is going to steal it on my watch."

"That's my girl," the police chief said approvingly.

Tucker watched as a half dozen or so khaki-wearing archaeologist types got out of the van. Most had on backpacks and carried tools and water bottles. One of the women walked toward him. She was tall, with dark hair and bangs.

Her gaze settled on him. "Tucker Janack?" she asked. "I'm Piper Tate."

They shook hands.

"I've worked with contractors before," she said. "I

know you want us off-site as quickly as possible. We want that, too. Our priority is the find and keeping it safe. We'll set up a round-the-clock team. Artifacts will go more quickly than human remains. Be grateful you didn't unearth a skeleton."

"Lucky me."

She gave a few more specifics. He noticed the police chief ducking out when the conversation got technical and wanted to go with her. Instead he nodded through a discussion of removing and cataloging artifacts and the rigorous designs of the boxes they would be using to transport everything.

When Piper finally excused herself to go join the others, Tucker saw that Nevada was laughing.

"What?"

"You've got to learn to fake it better," she told him. "You were obviously bored."

"It was a boring topic. I'm here to build something, not deal with old statues."

"I know someone who needs a little time on a back-hoe."

That did sound good, he thought. "I'm still stuck on what would have happened if we'd found a body."

"Go." She pushed him toward his truck. "I'll deal with this."

"Okay. Check in with me every couple of hours."

"I will."

He pulled his keys out of his pocket and had nearly made it to his truck when a familiar dark sedan pulled up next to the police chief's car.

"Sorry," Nevada whispered as Mayor Marsha got out.

Tucker hung his head. This was not his day.

He waited for the inevitable scolding as the mayor approached. A woman he didn't know exited the passenger side of the car.

"Annabelle," Nevada said, sounding surprised. "What are you doing here?"

Annabelle was petite, with red hair. She looked uncomfortable as she glanced around.

"I have a minor in tribal studies," she said with a sigh. "I specialized in the Máa-zib tribe. Somehow Mayor Marsha found out."

The old woman knew everything, Tucker thought. She must have some kind of network in town.

"I want Annabelle to keep an eye on the archaeology team," the mayor said briskly. "My office is fielding dozens of calls from museums all over the country and a few from Central America. Everyone wants to know about the find and some are even trying to put in a claim." She smoothed the front of her suit. "Of course the Máa-zib lived here, so we'll have a say in what happens to the artifacts. The Smithsonian called. I tried to interest them in Ms. Stoicasescu's giant vagina, but they passed."

"I would have liked to have heard that conversation," Tucker said in a low voice.

Nevada elbowed him in the ribs.

Mayor Marsha narrowed her gaze. "What are you doing today, Mr. Janack?" she asked.

"Getting on with building. Nevada is coordinating with everyone up there." He pointed to the crowd swarming the side of the mountain.

The mayor shook her head. "I'm getting too old for this," she murmured. "Maybe it's time to retire."

"Don't even think about it," Nevada told her. "Come on. We'll go see if you can taste some goat cheese."

The three women walked toward Heidi's stand on the edge of the parking lot. Tucker edged toward his truck. As he reached it, Nevada glanced back at him and grinned.

He climbed inside, thinking that it was nice for someone to have his back. Later, he would be sure to return the favor.

TUCKER FINISHED HIS WORKDAY hot, sweaty and in a much better mood than he'd started. He didn't even care about all the cars, the archaeologists picking over the site or the gaggle of security guards rushing around everywhere. He was going back to the hotel, where he would shower, then head over to Nevada's place and spend the evening with her.

He stepped into the trailer to check his email, only to find Will looking for him. He hadn't seen the man all day and, staring at him, he knew why. Will looked haggard. His skin was pale, his eyes bloodshot. He obviously hadn't slept. Slumped shoulders emphasized that whatever it was, it was bad.

"What happened?" Tucker demanded. "Who died?"

"No one." Will looked at him. "I want to transfer to another job. I don't care where. I need to get out of here."

There was only one reason for a man to look like that and want to leave town, Tucker thought grimly. And that reason was a woman.

"Jo?"

Will nodded.

"Want to talk about it?"

"No." Will sighed. "You were right. Love makes us all fools. I believed in her."

Tucker didn't know what to say to that. On the one hand, Will had been happy with Jo. On the other, the bad ending was inevitable.

"Okay. Let me see what I can do."

"Thanks." Will started toward the door, then turned back to him. "I thought she was the one. I was wrong. Love is for suckers."

THE DAY HAD BEEN A GOOD ONE, Nevada thought happily as she stepped out of the shower and reached for a towel. While she would have preferred to spend her time actually building something, keeping the job moving forward while dealing with a whole new level of crazy had been interesting, too. Plus, she'd spent a little time with Heidi and now understood more about goat cheese than anyone else she knew.

She put on body lotion, then dressed. She'd just reached for her blow dryer when her phone rang.

"Hello?"

"It's me," Montana said with a sigh. "We have boyfriend trouble."

There was a tradition in town. When one of the women got hurt by a man, her friends rallied. Liquor and plenty of sugar got the dumpee in question through the first painful night.

"I'll be there. Who is it?"

"Jo."

Not a name Nevada had ever expected to hear. "What? No. She's dating Will. He's a great guy."

"Not anymore. I don't know any details. Just that Charity found Jo crying in her bar."

"That's horrible. I don't understand." Will adored Jo. He'd chased her until he'd caught her. They were so happy together. "Give me twenty minutes."

"Okay. I have a few more calls to make."

Nevada hung up and quickly dried her hair. She got her keys and a jacket, then headed outside. She'd just stepped onto the house's front porch when she ran into Tucker.

"Hey, I was on my way to see you," he said. "Want to get dinner?"

"I can't." She looked at him. "What happened with Will and Jo?"

Tucker shoved his hands into his front pockets. "I don't know. He said it was over and he wants to transfer to another job."

She felt her mouth drop open. "No. He's leaving? What happened?"

"I didn't ask."

Typical man. "Did you have anything to do with this?"

"What? No. How could it be about me?"

She wasn't sure. "You're always saying relationships are bad and that being in love makes a man an idiot. Is that why Jo and Will broke up?"

His gaze narrowed. "No. Will figured it out on his own. Something he found out about Jo. Why don't you put the blame where it belongs?"

"I am. On him."

"Sure. When in doubt, blame the guy."

"If you don't know what happened, how do you know it wasn't him?" She paused, but Tucker didn't speak. "I have to go and help a friend," she told him.

"Fine," he grumbled.

"Fine," she snapped back.

They glared at each other, then Tucker turned and left. Nevada slammed the door, but the act wasn't very satisfying, probably because of the ache in her gut. The one that told her Will and Jo's breaking up had reinforced every stupid idea Tucker had about love.

WITHIN AN HOUR, Jo's house was overflowing with friends, food and margaritas. Charlie and Montana had each arrived with two bags of ice, and the blender had been going nonstop ever since. Charity and Pia coordinated the arriving trays, plates and bowls of food, sorting them by type. From what Nevada could tell, there was enough ice cream to feed a football team. There were cookies, a pie, two cakes, bags of M&M's and frosted brownies.

For those who preferred the salty side of things, bowls of potato chips and tortilla chips sat next to nuts and dip. The closest they came to healthy was a token container of baby carrots.

Nevada carried a pitcher of margaritas into the crowded living room. Jo sat on the sofa, Annabelle on one side of her and Liz on the other. Dakota rocked a sleepy Hannah. Finn was away on an overnight flight.

Nevada filled empty glasses, then set the pitcher on a sideboard. Pia and Charity joined them.

"I wanted a girls' night out," Pia said with a sigh. "But not like this."

Charity nodded. "It's so awful."

Nevada agreed. Jo had been in Fool's Gold for several years. No one had ever seen her on a date or even showing interest in a guy. And that wasn't because no one had asked. She'd finally given her heart to someone only to have it trampled.

Annabelle put her arm around Jo. "It's okay to let it out."

Jo blew her nose. "I've been crying for hours. I'm not sure how much more 'cried out' I can get." She wrapped her arms around herself as if she were cold.

Liz reached for the blanket on the back of the sofa. Annabelle helped her drape it over Jo.

"This is stupid," Jo said, looking up. "I'm fine."

"You're not at your sparkly best," Pia pointed out. "That's okay. We've all been there. You've helped us, now it's our turn." She glanced around the room. "Okay, I'll be the one to ask. What happened?"

The room went quiet as everyone turned to Jo. Nevada settled on an ottoman by Heidi.

Jo's face tightened. She looked both scared and defiant. Nevada expected her to say she wouldn't talk about it, but Jo surprised her by saying, "I think it's time for me to tell all of you about my past."

Over the next few minutes, she told the story of falling in love and getting in too deep.

"I know what I did was wrong," she added when she'd explained everything. "That bank manager could have died because of us. Ronnie *did* die. I can't take it back and I can't make it right. I'm not asking to forget.

I'll never do that. I'm not even looking for forgiveness. I just want to stop beating myself up. But maybe I shouldn't. Maybe serving my time and living with regret isn't enough."

"It's enough," Montana said firmly. "You made a mistake. It was a horrible one, but you've learned, you've served your time and now you're a great part of our community."

The other women nodded.

"I don't understand," Nevada said slowly. "Will is a sweetie. Why would he have acted like that? Why wouldn't he understand?" She couldn't reconcile what Jo had told her with the man she knew.

Jo shrugged. "You'd have to ask him."

Nevada planned to, first thing in the morning. There had to be something else going on. Something they didn't know.

"Here," Dakota said, standing and handing Hannah to Jo. "Pregnancy bladder. I'll be right back."

Jo started to take the baby, then pushed her back toward Dakota. "I can't."

"Why not? You hold her all the time. She adores you."

That was true, Nevada thought, watching the way the little girl smiled at Jo and waved with excitement.

"You heard what I said," Jo told her, more tears filling her eyes. "You can't leave your kid with me after that."

"Oh, please." Dakota handed the baby back and walked away.

Jo held Hannah in her arms. "I don't deserve this."

"Why not?" Charlie demanded. "You were a kid and

you screwed up. In my mind, it's how we take responsibility that counts. If you were sitting there telling us all the reasons it wasn't your fault, I'd be pissed. But you know what you did was wrong, you've done your time and you're being a good person now. Isn't learning to do better the whole point? Don't we want the people who commit crimes to feel remorse and rejoin society as good citizens?"

Liz squeezed Jo's arm. "You're punishing yourself enough for all of us. It's time to stop."

"Will doesn't think so."

"Will's a jackass," Charlie said. "Most men are."

"I was falling for him," Jo admitted in a small voice. "I thought…" She sniffed. "I was a fool."

Seeing her normally strong friend so defeated made Nevada feel as if the balance of the world had shifted. Nothing about this felt right. As soon as she got to work tomorrow, she was going to talk to Will and get it figured out. Yes, what Jo had confessed had been a lot for anyone to take in. But Nevada couldn't believe he'd walked away without a word. There was a puzzle piece missing and she was going to find it.

THE FOLLOWING MORNING didn't go as smoothly as Nevada would have liked. She woke up with a hangover, a testament to whomever had made the margaritas. A long shower, coffee and aspirin didn't do much to take the edge off. The only thing that was going to help was drinking lots of water and the passage of time.

The drive to the job site ended with nearly half a mile of bumpy dirt road. Not only did the ride upset her stomach, it increased the intensity of her headache.

By the time she walked into the trailer, she was ready to inflict her pain on others. Luckily, Will was at his desk.

An unwilling victim, she thought grimly. The best kind.

"What were you thinking?" she demanded, her voice a little quieter than she would have liked. Unfortunately, she couldn't stand to talk any louder. "What is wrong with you? I trusted you with my friend and you hurt her."

Will stood and faced her. He looked nearly as bad as Jo had, without the proof of tears.

"It's not what you think," he told her.

"You beg her to tell you about her past, hear about the mistake she'd made as a kid, and then dump her?"

He shifted from foot to foot. "You don't understand."

"Explain it to me."

He stared at her. "I can't."

"You won't."

"Same thing."

"It's not the same thing. Why are you doing this? Why are you acting like this? It's not like she's not sorry. It's been something like nineteen years and since then, she hasn't done anything wrong. Who the hell are you to judge her?"

She wanted to hit something, mostly him. She wanted him to get it.

"Are you complaining about the woman she is now?" she demanded. "What part of her character are you judging?"

Tucker was at his desk as well. Although he was listening, he didn't say anything. Smart man. She would deal with him later.

"You don't understand," Will began.

"You're right, I don't. Any of this. You might be disappointed in her, but that's nothing when compared with how disappointed I am in you. I trusted you. Jo trusted you. But you're a sham and you're a jerk."

Will stiffened, but didn't respond. She turned her back on him and walked over to grab her hard hat.

"Nevada," Tucker began.

She turned to him. "Really? You want to get in the middle of this?"

He studied her for a second, then shook his head.

She walked to the door and paused, hoping Will would say something. Maybe offer an explanation or an apology. There was only silence, so she left.

CHAPTER SEVENTEEN

"You've been avoiding me."

Cat's words were delivered in a matter-of-fact tone, but still made Nevada wince. Mostly because they were true.

"Things got complicated," she said by way of feeble excuse. "After the explosion, with the gold being found and everything. There was a lot to coordinate. Then one of my friends was dumped by her boyfriend. It sucks."

"Men can be pigs," Cat said.

They were walking through the Halloween Festival, a celebration of all things fall and gifty and spooky. Booths piled with sweaters and jewelry nestled next to carts stacked with pumpkin cookies and caramel apples.

"I agree," Nevada murmured, thinking she wanted to shake Will until he finally told her why he was being such a butthead. She was also annoyed with Tucker, mostly for standing up for his friend, and being male and guilty by association. Seeing as he was reasonably intelligent, he'd stayed out of her way. A good plan, because she was starting to miss him.

"I've been working," Cat said. "Losing myself in the art. It's very effective. No matter what I'm feeling, I channel it into what I'm doing. It's probably why I've never had a committed relationship. I've never been able to hang on to intense feelings long enough."

Nevada looked at her. "That's very insightful."

Cat smiled. "I have depths."

"You do."

The air was crisp and scented with woodsmoke, the sky blue. The leaves had changed and now were falling everywhere. No one could keep up with the piles of crunchy leaves, so they collected in colorful piles.

Cat paused by a booth selling scarves and studied the color. "I'm glad knitting is popular again. Traditional crafts provide a creative outlet for women. As our society increases our connection with technology, we risk losing the simple pleasures that bring beauty to our lives."

Nevada felt her mouth drop open. She consciously closed it and told herself it would be rude to ask if Cat had had any recent alien encounters. Besides, it was unlikely she'd been possessed by pod people, which meant there had to be another explanation for all the discerning statements made this morning.

Cat picked out a delicately knit scarf in shades of green and put it around Nevada's neck.

"This color will suit you," she said. "I know you believe your eyes are brown, but they're actually made up of dozens of colors. Wearing green close to your face will make your eyes look more hazel."

"Thank you," Nevada said, both touched and confused. "I didn't know that."

Cat shrugged. "I'm an artist."

She chose a deep red scarf for herself, then paid the owner.

When they walked away, Cat reached for her hand. "Stop resisting me."

All the warm fuzzies from the morning fled, leaving behind a vague sense of panic.

Nevada waited until she led them around the carts and booths to the relative quiet of a tidy alley behind the stores on the main street. Then she pulled her hand free and faced Cat.

"I can't," she began. "Be with you in that way. I like us being friends, but nothing more."

Light touched Cat's face, as if the sun itself wanted to be closer. She was simply that kind of person.

"You don't know that," Cat told her, apparently not the least bit hurt by the rejection. "You haven't tried. One kiss isn't enough to judge by. Come back to my hotel room. We'll make love and then you can decide."

Oh, there was an invitation, Nevada thought, taking a step back. "No. I can't. I don't want to. Cat, I'm not that kind of girl."

"You might be."

"No, I'm not."

Cat looked at her for a second, then leaned in to kiss her. Nevada took another step back.

Cat drew in a deep breath. "You know this is me, right?"

Despite everything, Nevada laughed. "Yes, I know that."

"Fine." Cat linked arms with her. "I don't understand your decision, but I'll accept it. Reluctantly."

"You're sure?"

"Yes. I don't have to be told twice."

True, Nevada thought humorously. She had to be told many more times than that.

"You're making this all so much more difficult than it has to be," Cat grumbled as they walked back to the festival and strolled by booths. "Have I mentioned I'm entering my feminine phase?"

"More than once."

"Then you can see how being with a woman is important to me."

"I can. Want me to ask around for you?"

Now it was Cat's turn to laugh. "I don't need help to find lovers." She paused. "It's your loss."

"I have no doubt."

They stopped by a display of earrings, then moved on.

"At least I have my work," Cat said with a sigh. "I'm so happy with how the piece is turning out. The vagina is so beautiful. The curves, the contrast of the stark metal with the feminine form. I'd thought of going more stylized, but why try to disguise what it is? Reality trumps illusion. I should be done in less than a week."

Nevada thought of Mayor Marsha's instruction that she and Tucker fix "the vagina problem." This wasn't going to be good news.

"You're still giving the sculpture to the town?"

"Of course." Cat squeezed her arm. "There's going to be an unveiling and everything. I want you to be there."

"Oh, goodie."

A WEEK AFTER SPILLING her guts and getting her heart stomped on, Jo still felt unsettled and sad. She wasn't sleeping very well, she couldn't eat and if she kept crying as much as she had been, she would turn into a mummy. A body simply couldn't continue to lose that much water on a daily basis.

She forced herself to go through her daily routine, mostly because she'd put too much into her business to lose it all now, especially because of a man. But pretending to laugh with people, holding conversations, wasn't easy. She wanted to curl up somewhere and be unconscious until she'd healed enough not to hurt so bad.

It was her own fault, she acknowledged, walking into the grocery store and grabbing a basket. She knew better than to let some guy into her world. While the situation with Ronnie had been disastrous for completely different reasons, the results were the same. She and men simply didn't mix well.

She'd been doing so great, too, she thought grimly, heading to the display of fresh pasta. Making a life for herself, fitting in. She loved living here, loved everything about the town. Now she wondered if she'd gone and screwed it all up. Everyone would know what she'd done now. The girls had seemed so understanding when she'd told them, but once the truth about her past sank in, would it change how everyone felt about her?

She moved down the aisle. Up ahead she saw a familiar older woman with styled white hair.

Jo came to a stop, knowing she didn't have it in her to face Mayor Marsha right now. The older woman had been supportive from the moment Jo had moved to Fool's Gold. She'd trusted Jo. No doubt now Jo felt she had broken the mayor's trust.

Jo started to turn around, but she was a second too late. The mayor saw her. Their eyes locked, then Mayor Marsha pushed her cart toward Jo.

She had nowhere to go, she thought. Nowhere to run. Besides, why bother putting off the inevitable. The mayor was a direct sort of person. She would make it clear if Jo wasn't welcome in town anymore.

"Jo," Mayor Marsha said as she approached. "I'm so sorry about you and Will. He seemed like a nice young man. Obviously I was wrong about him."

Jo nodded and braced herself for the inevitable "but." Instead the mayor walked around her cart and held out her arms, inviting a hug.

Jo stood in place, her basket hanging at her side.

Mayor Marsha didn't hesitate. She crossed the last few feet and pulled Jo close.

"It's all right," she said quietly. "You'll get over him. It may take a long time, but you'll heal. We all do."

Jo nodded, telling herself she wasn't going to start crying again.

The mayor stepped back. "Is there anything I can do?"

"You mean like helping me pack?" Jo asked before she could stop herself.

"Oh, child." The other woman reached for her again. This time the hug was stronger, as if she would never let go. When she straightened, her blue eyes were filled with tears.

"Don't you think I have things I regret in my life?" Marsha asked. "Horrible deeds, bad decisions? I lost my own child because I was too proud and stubborn. She ran away and never came back, all because of me.

We each have shameful acts in our past. You were punished for yours. Don't you think I wish someone would punish me and then say I was done? At least I would know the debt had been paid in a way that was significant to someone."

"I don't understand," Jo whispered.

"No one wants you to leave. You're one of us. An important member of this community. We love you, Jo. You are as much a part of the fabric of Fool's Gold as any other person. I'm sorry your young man couldn't accept your past. In time I hope you'll see that's his loss, rather than yours. He could have won you. What a prize. He's too proud or too foolish to see that, but we're not."

Jo felt the tears on her cheeks. "Thank you."

"You're more than welcome. Now, put that basket away. I'm making you dinner tonight."

"I DON'T WANT to fight with you," Tucker said.

Nevada faced him across her threshold, torn between wanting to slam the door in his face and a desperate need to be in his arms.

"Will hurt my friend."

"You don't think he's hurting, too?"

She knew there was an argument to be had, but not one either of them was going to win.

"Nevada, I miss you."

Words that weakened her resolve. She stepped back and let him in.

"WERE YOU TEMPTED?" Tucker asked.

Nevada dug her spoon into her bowl of pistachio

ice cream. Dressed only in a robe and socks, sprawled out on her sofa with a hunky, barely dressed guy after amazing sex, she felt good. Better than good. Ice cream simply moved the moment from a ten to a ten and a half.

Tucker nudged her with his foot. "I asked you a question."

"I heard."

"You're not going to answer it?"

"You think you're being funny, but you're not. You already know the answer. You just want me to say I'd rather have sex with you than Cat."

His grin was unrepentant. "I was hoping for more than that."

"What? That I'd rather have sex with you than with anyone else?"

"That works."

"It's amazing you and your ego can both fit in the construction trailer," she told him.

"I mostly leave it outside."

She licked her spoon. "You know, now that you mention it, my parents always told me to try something before making up my mind about it. Maybe I should have taken Cat up on her offer. She must be great in bed. You were mesmerized by her."

Tucker moved with lightning speed. One second she was holding her bowl, then next it was on the table and he was diving toward her, tickling her sides with his nimble fingers.

"No!" she shrieked, laughing and squirming. "Stop. Stop! I'll be good."

She wiggled, trying to get away, but only succeeded

in shifting under him. He lay on top of her, his dark eyes bright with amusement.

"Say uncle," he commanded.

"Kiss me," she said instead.

"That works."

His lips were cold from his ice cream and tasted of the cookies-and-cream he'd been eating.

"Had enough?" he asked.

No, not really. She wasn't sure there was enough where Tucker was concerned. Being with him made her happy. Really happy. Happy, as in…

She stopped short of thinking the *L* word, but knew it was there. Lurking.

Not that, she told herself. She couldn't fall for him. Tucker wasn't interested in more than a fun relationship. While she knew he'd learned the wrong lesson from Cat, she didn't know how to help him unlearn it. The danger signs were obvious and, if she was going to save herself, she had to seriously back off.

"Can I have my ice cream now?" she asked.

"Sure."

He kissed her again, then sat up. He pulled her into a sitting position and passed back her bowl.

"Better?" he asked.

She forced herself to take a bite and smile. "Perfect."

But the ice cream settled uneasily in her stomach.

In an effort to distract herself, she searched for a safer topic.

"The last of the gold should be gone by Tuesday," she said. "Once they started crating it, the process went faster than I would have thought. With the artifacts taken away, the tourists will leave, along with the ar-chaeologists."

"About time," he grumbled. "It's good that Piper Tate is damned efficient."

"Did she scare you?"

"Some."

She laughed. "I think she would be fun to work with. She knows what she wants and she goes for it."

"Not always a good quality in a woman."

She raised her eyebrows.

Tucker dug into his ice cream. "Pretend I didn't say that out loud."

"I will if you tell me what's happening with Will."

Tucker slumped back against the sofa. "Anything but that."

"Okay. Let's talk about how we feel."

Tucker gave an exaggerated shudder. "You win. Will came to me a few days ago and said he wasn't sure he wanted to transfer."

"He's been avoiding me."

"Why wouldn't he? You've been yelling at him for days."

"He was wrong."

"You don't know that." Tucker wasn't smiling any-more. "He's entitled to what he thinks about the situation with Jo. Just because you're okay with her past doesn't mean he has to be."

"You're taking his side?"

"I'm saying you don't get to dictate the terms of his choices."

"All she did was tell him the truth. She didn't want to talk about her past. She told him he wouldn't accept it and he promised he would. Nothing changed about her, except he now has new information."

"That makes him wrong?"

"He shouldn't have said he would be okay with anything she told him."

"Okay, I'll accept that," he said. "But just because Will doesn't like that Jo spent years in prison, for a crime she *did* commit, let's remember, doesn't make him a bad guy."

"Maybe," she said, grumbling. "I don't like it, though."

"Neither do I," Tucker said. "He's unhappy, you're unhappy. It doesn't make for a comfortable working situation."

This was the second good point Tucker had made in as many minutes.

"I should probably stop glaring at him," she admitted.

"That would help."

"It's not professional."

"True."

"This is not a time to be agreeable," she told him.

He put down his ice cream and faced her. "Jo's your friend and you're being loyal to her. That's great. Will is my friend. I'm staying loyal to him. You're right, what Jo did happened a long time ago, but it's still relevant. He doesn't talk much about his childhood, but I do know his dad was in and out of jail when Will was a kid. That can't have been easy. Jo telling him about her past probably pushed some buttons."

She hadn't considered that. "You could be right."

He grinned. "Let me know when you decide."

JO FINISHED UP at the bar. It was after two in the morning. She was usually home by now, but these days she found herself working later and later.

She still couldn't shake the feeling of sadness, but at least she'd let go the sense of impending doom. She no longer believed she was going to be run out of town at any second. Mayor Marsha's kindness had gone a long way to dissipate her fear. Her friends were faithful and supportive. Getting over Will would be an ongoing journey, but at least she would take it to where she belonged.

She locked the front door and walked through the quiet streets to her house. The nights were colder these days. The days shorter. Fall had arrived. There was already snow on the mountains. Fool's Gold was beautiful in every season, but she thought it was at its best in winter.

A police car drove by. The female officer waved at Jo, who waved back. Twinkling lights beckoned from the windows of Morgan's Books. The flags that hung from the streetlights were decorated with turkeys and horns of plenty. She'd already received three different invitations for Thanksgiving.

Home, she thought, telling herself that contentment would be enough. This was home.

She turned onto her street and crossed to her house. As she walked up the path, something moved on her porch. The shadow stepped into the light and became a man.

Will.

The harsh bulb wasn't kind. He looked as bad as she felt. Tired, drawn, sad. Or maybe that was just her mind's way of trying to make her feel better. Maybe he wasn't hurt at all. Maybe he was leaving and he'd just stopped by to make sure she knew she wasn't good enough for him.

She squared her shoulders. He might have battered her heart, but he wasn't going to break her.

She climbed the steps and stopped in front of him.

"I need to talk to you," he said.

"What more is there to say?" she asked coldly.

"You told me about your past," he told her. "I want you to hear about mine."

She believed in being fair, so she nodded once and unlocked the door.

When they were inside, she motioned for him to take a seat on the sofa. She stayed far away, choosing the safety of the club chair by the fireplace.

"Go ahead."

Will had shrugged off his jacket. He wore a chambray shirt and worn jeans. His hair needed cutting and he hadn't shaved that day. Scruffy, she thought, trying to be scornful. Only he looked good and she was painfully glad to see him.

Maybe he was going to tell her he'd been wrong, her heart whispered. Maybe he was sorry. She told herself not to hope, but it was difficult not to wish him back into caring about her.

He leaned forward, his elbows resting on his thighs, his hands hanging loose. Instead of looking at her, he stared at the floor.

"My dad was one of those guys who could charm anyone," he began, his voice low. "Women loved him, especially my mom. She would do anything for him.

God, she loved him. I loved him, too, but I figured out pretty fast he wasn't like other dads. He didn't have a regular job. Instead he was always looking for his next chance at easy money."

He paused, then glanced at her. "Easy money. That's what he called it. He was too good to work for someone else. He used to say men like him were meant for better things than a factory job. If he'd put half as much effort into something that paid regularly rather than chasing the next scam, our lives would have been a whole lot better." He cleared his throat. "He was a con artist. My father cheated honest people out of their money. He was in jail more than he was out, but he never learned, never changed. When he got out, he already had a mark in mind."

Jo folded her arms across her chest. "That must have been difficult for you."

"It was. I wanted to move away, to never see him again, but my mom wouldn't listen. She loved him and was convinced one day he would change. He broke her heart over and over again with his damn promises. She always believed him, no matter what I said. I vowed I wouldn't be like him. I would always do the right thing. And I promised myself I wouldn't be like her. I wouldn't allow myself to be tricked over and over again."

She felt a chill and closed her eyes. So much for him knowing he'd been wrong. So much for any hope that they could work this out.

"I don't believe people change," he told her. "I saw that in my dad and with his friends. They weren't interested in being other than what they were. Jail time didn't do anything except give them time to plan the next con. When you told me what you'd done, I couldn't believe it. Here I'd gone and fallen for someone just like him. I was my mother all over again."

The unfairness of the words made her want to stand up and scream her defense. But it wouldn't matter. Will saw what he wanted to see. It just wasn't the whole picture.

"Only I was wrong."

The soft words barely penetrated. She stared at him.

"I was wrong," he repeated, straightening. "You changed. You're not that teenager anymore. You've made a life for yourself here. I can see your character in everything you do. You're not like him." His gaze intensified. "I'm sorry, Jo. I shouldn't have said what I did. I reacted harshly, without thinking."

She let his words wash over her as she tried to figure out what she was feeling. Relief, certainly. Maybe a little hope. But she'd trusted him and it had hurt when she'd revealed her darkest secret and he'd left. Sure, he was back now, but how could she trust him not to leave again?

"I believe in you," he continued. "I believe in us. I want this to work. Please give me a second chance to prove myself to you."

For once there weren't any tears. Resignation settled on her as she accepted the truth of the situation—she wasn't willing to be vulnerable again, to be hurt again. Being alone was easier.

"I'm sorry, Will," she said, rising to her feet. "I resisted getting involved with you for a reason. I knew it wouldn't work out. I didn't want to tell you about what happened to me, about what I did, because I knew you wouldn't be able to deal with it. I was right. You couldn't."

He stood. "No. I don't accept that. I was a jerk. I handled it badly. But I figured that out. I'm here. Isn't that what relationships are about? Working things out together?"

"In theory. The truth isn't that simple or easy. I've been alone a long time now, Will. And maybe that's for the best." She held up her hand. "I'm not punishing you. I'm just accepting that having a man in my life isn't going to happen for me. It's better for me to be alone."

His mouth twisted. "Safe," he said. "Risk nothing, lose nothing."

Anger started deep inside. She welcomed it, knowing the emotion would give her strength.

"Easy for you to judge," she told him. "You weren't the one who was told you weren't good enough."

He swore under his breath. "So, that's it? I don't get to make a mistake? You expect me to forgive you, but I don't get the same treatment?"

"I didn't hurt you. I hurt someone else a long time ago. What I did had nothing to do with you. But you did hurt me. You extrapolated from an event you had no part of and used that as an excuse to walk out. We both have our own demons to deal with. Which one of us is going to get hurt next?"

She waited for him to yell at her, to escalate the fight. Instead his shoulders slumped, as if he'd just been loaded down with a weight he couldn't carry.

"Don't," he said quietly. "Don't do this, Jo. I know

you're pissed and you have every right to be. If I could take it back, I would. If I could not screw up, I would. You're not my dad. I get that. But at first, I was so surprised by what you said. I thought…" He shook his head. "I guess it doesn't matter what I thought. I can't convince you. You're going to see what you want to see."

He started to the door, his steps uneven. When he got there, he turned back to her.

"You're wrong about one thing. It's not that I got mad and handled it badly. That could happen to anyone. It's what I did next that says who I am. I wanted to leave town—I asked Tucker for a transfer to another job. But I couldn't go and I couldn't let go. I worked it through. While I hurt you, it wasn't on purpose. I've admitted my mistake, I've learned from it and I'm doing my best to apologize."

He opened the door. "I'm not the best-looking guy around and there are plenty richer. But I'm still a good man who loves you. I even like your damn cat. It's not the screwing up that defines a person, Jo, it's what he does afterward that says who he is. You know that better than anyone, because you're the one who said that to me."

With that, he walked out.

She heard his steps on the porch, the slight hesitation in his stride from his limp. Then that faded and there was only silence. Something warm brushed against her leg and she reached down to stroke Jake. The cat stared up at her, his yellow eyes seeing far more than usual.

"Don't," she whispered to herself. "Don't say anything. I can't forgive him. I can't let him back in my life. What will he do the next time?"

There was no answer—only silence and a hard, thick pressure on her chest. She couldn't breathe, couldn't speak, could only feel the emptiness that was her future.

Even as she wanted to go to him, her mind screamed out that she couldn't trust him. That he would hurt her again and no one was worth those tears. Her heart whispered that, yes, crying was inevitable. It was impossible to feel love without also feeling pain. But the price was worth it. *He* was worth it. That if she let him go, she would regret it for the rest of her life.

The need to protect herself battled with the hunger of her heart. Twisted and torn, her heart fought rational thought. Then she was moving. She flung open the front door and raced across the porch. She hurried down the steps, along the path until she reached the sidewalk. Frantically she looked in both directions, trying to figure out where he was.

Then she saw him nearly at the end of the block.

"Will!"

She called out loudly, aware that it was late and she wasn't being a good neighbor, but unable to stop herself. The figure in the distance paused.

She ran toward him, nearly flying as she covered the distance. When she got close, he held out his arms and welcomed her home.

She flung herself at him and hung on as if she would never let go. He held her even tighter. Once again she couldn't breathe, but this time it was for the best reason of all.

"Will, I…" she began.

He silenced her with a kiss. "Later."

"But I have to tell you—"

"No, you don't." He released her from the hug but kept his arm around her. "Come on. It's cold and you're not wearing a jacket."

She stepped in front of him and grabbed him by the shoulders. "I'm trying to tell you I love you and all you can say is I'm not wearing a jacket?"

He smiled then. A slow, sexy smile that made her stomach turn over and every part of her burn.

"I love you, too, Jo. Let's go home."

CHAPTER EIGHTEEN

TUCKER HEARD A FAMILIAR sound from outside the trailer. Tires on dirt and gravel. Funny how he could pick out those particular tires from all the others. Not funny in a good way, though, he thought, wishing the construction trailer had a back door.

With nowhere to run, he was forced to stay behind his desk and hope for the best. After all, he was a grown man. He could stand up to what was outside. He didn't have to be afraid.

But all the logic in the world didn't stop him from wincing as he heard footsteps on the stairs, followed by the turning of the handle. He braced himself for the onslaught.

The door opened and Mayor Marsha stepped inside.

"Good morning, Tucker," she said cheerfully.

"Ma'am."

She was as well dressed as ever, in one of her suits, the skirt hitting exactly at the middle of her knee. Her white hair was in that puffy do she seemed to like so much. Despite the warmth in her gaze, he knew this wasn't a social call.

He stood and walked toward the coffeepot. "The gold is all excavated," he said, pouring her a cup.

"Cream," she said when he held it out.

He added cream, stirred, then took it over to her.

She'd settled at the small table in the back. He passed
her the coffee. For a second, he thought about making
a run for it, but knew that wouldn't work. She would
simply hunt him down. Better to face her now and get
it over with.

"Thank you," she said before sipping the coffee.
"Having the gold gone must be making your life here
more peaceful."

"I didn't love the tourists."

"I imagine not." She put the mug back on the table.
"I've been keeping track of the progress you're making on the site. Impressive. I have every confidence
this facility is going to be an excellent addition to the
Fool's Gold community."

"We appreciate the support from you and the city
council. Some cities wouldn't want the casino so close."

Mayor Marsha smiled. "I'm sure that's true, but I'm
not concerned. If anyone becomes difficult, our police
department is more than capable of handling the situation. The additional tax revenue is more than worth
the effort. The occupancy taxes for the hotel alone are
going to fund a new high school. Children are our future, as they say."

"So I've heard," he murmured, wondering when she
would drop her next bombshell. Unless she was here
to nag him about Cat's giant vagina. A gift he'd yet to
figure out how to undo. Not that he'd tried especially
hard. He frowned as he realized he hadn't seen much
of Cat since her arrival. And to think that at one point
in his life, she'd been his reason for breathing. Time
really did heal.

"The last two years have taught me a valuable lesson," the mayor told him. "We haven't been vigilant enough in our planning here in Fool's Gold. We've let outside events guide us. That disastrous reality show is just one example. Now the gold find. It's not that we could have predicted either, but we should have been better prepared. To that end, I'm starting a committee of business leaders. People who understand about fore-casting and projections. Our purpose will be to provide a new kind of leadership for us all. I'm looking for sug-gestions for myself and for the city council."

"Sounds like a good idea," he said, wondering when she would get to the part that would make him uncom-fortable.

"I'm glad you think so. I'd like you to be a part of the group. Perhaps even head it up."

She was good, Tucker thought. He hadn't seen that one coming.

"I appreciate the invitation, but I'm not the right person."

"Why not?"

"I'm not a permanent resident. Once the job site is up and running, I'll head on to the next project. I'm in town a year at most."

The mayor pressed her lips together. "I don't under-stand. I was under the impression this was the last job you'd be running. That once this was done, you would be taking over the company."

She was better than good at getting information, Tucker told himself. She was practically a witch.

"How did you know that?"

The older woman sighed. "I know everything,

Tucker. I would have thought you'd know that by now. Aren't you taking over the company?"

"Yes, but—"

"And once you're in control, you can locate the head-quarters anywhere?"

"Sure, but—"

"And isn't it true that you're not completely happy with living in Chicago and were thinking of moving the office somewhere else?"

He sprang to his feet. "Wait a minute. I haven't talked with anyone about that. I haven't even made up my mind."

She stared at him pointedly until he settled back in his chair.

"Fool's Gold would be an excellent place for you to settle your company. We're very supportive of business. Housing is reasonable, the schools are some of the best in the country. You should think about it."

He couldn't get past her knowing things he'd barely articulated to himself. He hadn't told Will or Nevada. He'd discussed moving the company with his father. Once. Three years ago. In Argentina.

"Who are you?" he demanded.

"I'm someone who pays attention. Please, don't go reading any more into what I said than that. It's obvi-ous you're looking for something more than the vaga-bond lifestyle you've known since you were a child. You find the town charming. You came here because of Nevada. Now that the two of you are together, think-ing you want to stay is the next logical step."

If he hadn't already used up the drama of jumping to his feet, he would have done it again. While he couldn't disagree with anything she'd said, even he hadn't put all that together in a reasonable way.

But he wasn't staying. He'd never planned on staying. Staying meant taking things to the next level with Nevada. He wasn't interested in that. He didn't believe in happy endings or forever. Love was…

"I can see by your expression you're not ready to commit to being in town longer than the job requires," the older woman said. "I hope you'll change your mind. You need us, Tucker, even more than we need you."

With that, she collected her purse and left.

He continued to sit at the small table, trying to figure out what had just happened. Talk about unexpected and just plain weird, he thought. Sure, he liked Nevada and he liked the town, but staying? Moving the company here? That wasn't going to happen.

He wasn't looking for permanent. Not personally or professionally. Sure, he would be taking over the company, but he still planned to go around the world for the big jobs. Maybe not to be in charge, but he wasn't going to become some guy, stuck in an office. He needed more.

As for Nevada, he knew he'd screwed up there. Let things get too far. He'd been trying to back off before, but then Cat had happened. As always, having her around was like dealing with a natural disaster. He'd reacted to the situation and now Mayor Marsha thought things between him and Nevada were more than they were.

That made him wonder if Nevada thought the same thing.

He stood and returned to his desk. But once he was there, he found himself restless. He swore.

He didn't want to hurt her. She was great and he really liked being with her. She got him and he got her. They were a good team, both in and out of bed. He liked watching her move, he liked making her laugh. He wanted to be around her.

Sure, he trusted her more than he'd ever trusted another woman and maybe, if things had been different, she would have been the one. But they weren't different. He knew what would happen if he gave in to love. He knew the price and he wasn't going to pay it. Not again. Not for anyone.

TUCKER'S LONG MORNING turned into an even longer afternoon. Nevada showed up after lunch, flushed and chilled from working with the guys. She talked about how the digging was going and which pipes had been delivered. Rather than pay attention, he watched her, trying to figure out how badly he would miss her when he was gone.

"Are you even listening?" she demanded.

"Sure. To every word."

"I don't think I believe you. You have the strangest look on your face."

Will's arrival was the perfect interruption. His second in command bounced into the trailer, grinning like a fool.

Nevada glanced at her watch. "Nearly two. Guess you're not an early riser anymore."

"I called."

"You left a cryptic message on the voice mail saying you'd be late. Not exactly the same thing."

"Good enough for the likes of you two." Will crossed the small trailer, grabbed Nevada by the waist and spun her in a tight circle. "Congratulate me. I'm engaged."

"Woohoo!" Nevada flung her arms around him. "Finally. I was tired of being mad at you."

Will laughed and released her, then walked over to Tucker and held out his hand.

"I'm the luckiest guy ever," Will told him.

Tucker did his best to conceal his shock. Will engaged? They'd always been nomads together.

"Congratulations," Tucker said automatically.

"When did this happen?" Nevada asked, hugging him again.

"Last night. Technically, early this morning." Will laughed. "She made me work for it, though. I'll tell you that."

"Married." Nevada clapped her hands together. "I'm not sure Jo is the big wedding type. Are you two going to do something in town or run off and get married?"

"Whatever she wants is good with me."

Will sounded happy. Or whatever was beyond happy, Tucker thought, confused by the rapid change of events.

"You'll be staying here," he said.

"Yup." Will chuckled. "If I don't, Jo's gonna hunt me down. Gotta love that in a woman." He sighed. "I'll finish the job, then look for work in town." Still looking pleased with himself, he laughed. "I guess I'm giving my two-year notice."

Will leaving the company? Just like that? For a woman?

Nevada walked to her desk and picked up a stack of magazines. "My sisters left these for me," she said, waving the bridal magazines at him. "Want to look them over?"

Tucker waited for his friend to make the sign of the cross and then run for the hills. Instead Will grabbed them.

"Sure," he said with a chuckle. "That'll get her attention. Hey, is there a jewelry store in town? I need to buy my woman a ring. A big one."

"I know just the place. Jenel's Gems. Jenel will be able to help you find the prefect ring."

Will tucked the magazines under his arm, then headed for the door. "I'm out of here, boss. See you tomorrow."

With that, he was gone.

Tucker stared at the closed door, not sure what had just happened. Everything was getting out of hand and somehow he had to figure out a way to stop it.

"THIS IS REALLY SUDDEN," Nevada said, not sure how she felt about Cat's announcement. Despite everything that had happened, Nevada wasn't sure she was ready for Cat to leave. They'd barely become friends. Well, as much as anyone could be a friend with Cat.

"I've created and now it's time for me to move on," Cat told her.

They were in front of the Gold Rush Ski Lodge and Resort. A long, dark limo idled next to them, the driver and Herbert, her assistant, already loading piles of luggage.

"You know the sculpture is finished," Cat said. "You'll be the one to present it to the town."

"Lucky me."

"I knew you'd enjoy being the one."

"You'll miss the unveiling," Nevada reminded her, thinking there was a whole lifetime of things she would rather do than be in charge of giving her hometown a giant vagina.

"I've done the important part," Cat told her, then touched her shoulder. "Come with me."

"Cat, you know I can't."

"No." Cat's green eyes darkened. "You don't want to. There's a difference."

Nevada bit her lower lip. "I'm sorry. I know this is important to you, but there's no way I can be in that kind of relationship with you."

"Your loss," Cat said lightly.

"Tell me about it."

Just then Cody, one of the college guys who rented from Nevada, walked up.

"Hey," he said, handing Herbert a duffel bag. He slid into the back of the limo.

Nevada looked from the open door back to Cat.

"No way."

Cat's smile turned mischievous. "He's not you, but he gets me through the night."

"He's a boy."

"Yes. All that youthful enthusiasm and energy. He's good for at least three times a night and I'm teaching him exactly how to please me. There are worse fates."

"He didn't give notice that he was leaving," Nevada

said, knowing she should probably be more worried about Cody's future than her rental income.

"He'll be back and, in the meantime, I'll pay his rent."

Cat leaned in and kissed her. Nevada didn't turn away in time, or maybe she felt she shouldn't. Either way, Cat's soft lips pressed against hers, then lingered for a heartbeat before she drew away.

Cat sighed. "If I could convince you."

"It's not just the girl thing," Nevada admitted. "It's that I want something permanent. Like what my parents had. A forever kind of love. My sisters have found it and I'm hoping it's out there for me, too. You're amazing, Cat, but you don't do long term. You can't. Not with your gift."

Cat's eyes filled with tears. "You're right," she whispered. "My art always comes first. Eventually I'd feel confined and my work would suffer."

Nevada realized that for once, they were both speaking the truth. Even if she was interested in Cat, the other woman couldn't give her what she wanted.

"I'll miss you," Nevada told her.

"And I'll miss you."

They hugged.

When they straightened, Cat smiled at her. "If I could have loved anyone, it would have been you."

Nevada touched her cheek. "I'll bet you say that to all the girls."

Cat climbed into the limo. Herbert shut the door, then scurried around to the passenger seat and got in. Seconds later, the long, black car drove away.

Nevada stood there in front of the hotel. The afternoon was clear, but the forecast called for snow that night. It was perfect weather for a fire and maybe a man in front of that fire.

But she wanted more than that. Telling Cat the truth had opened up something inside of her. Something she'd been afraid to admit.

She did want more than a lover. She wanted a husband and a family. She wanted to have roots and traditions. She wanted to hear the man she loved tell her he loved her back. She wanted to know they would be there for each other, no matter what. She wanted it all.

THE DRIVE TO THE WORK SITE had never taken so long or seemed so short, Nevada thought as she parked her truck next to the trailer. She'd had enough time to try to talk herself down, all the while considering what she was going to say.

She knew there was risk involved, that the conversation could go very badly, but still she had to try. She owed herself that.

She walked into the trailer. Tucker was on the phone. He smiled when he saw her and motioned he wouldn't be long. A few seconds later, he hung up.

"What did Cat want?" he asked.

"To say goodbye. She left."

"What about the statue? Did she change her mind?"

"No such luck. It's finished and she wants me to present it to the town."

"Better you than me. Mayor Marsha isn't going to be happy."

A problem for another time, she thought, walking toward him.

She took the seat next to his desk and drew in a breath. She was shaking a little and thought she might have to throw up. Not the best combination, but waiting would only make things worse.

He drew his eyebrows together and touched her cheek. "You okay?"

She nodded. "I have to tell you something."

"You're running off with Cat."

"No. Although she did ask."

"You have to give her points for persistence."

"I do." She looked into his eyes. "Tucker, I know your relationship with Cat was difficult. That you were obsessed with her."

He leaned back in his chair. "Tell me about it. What a mistake."

"It was, but you were a kid."

"Nearly twenty-three. I should have known better."

"How? You'd grown up all around the world, never settling in one place. You didn't know what it was like to just date someone. To have a crush and then get over it. Then you met Cat, and even someone with a whole lot more relationship experience couldn't have handled her very well. You did the best you could."

He looked uncomfortable. "Why are you saying this?"

"Because you learned the wrong lesson. Love isn't a trap. Love is a gift. It makes us stronger. Look at Will. He's a great guy and loves his job and his life, but have you ever seen him happier? He's walking away from all of this because he wants to be with Jo."

"That's his decision."

"Do you think he'll regret it?"

"I don't know."

"Yeah, you do."

He shrugged. "Okay, he's happy. So what?"

Here it was. The moment of truth. Did she have the courage to say it? To put herself out there? Until this moment, she never had. She'd always taken the safe road, made the easy decision. The biggest risk in her life had been applying for this job. Now it was time to take the next step.

"I love you," she told him. "We're good together. I want you to stay and be a part of my life. I want us to have a future."

She paused, not sure if she could continue or not. As she was trying to make up her mind, she saw horror enter his eyes. Instead of being happy or intrigued, he looked angry.

"Don't start," he said, standing. "Dammit, Nevada, why do you have to do this? I told you before. You said you understood. Don't you get it? I'm not interested."

With that he walked out.

She stared after him, her heart pounding, her mind unable to absorb what had just happened so quickly. Then she heard the rumble of his truck, the spray of gravel and he was gone.

NEVADA DIDN'T TELL ANYONE. She couldn't. Pain and shame were an uneasy combination she wasn't willing to share. She finished her day, went home, got through the night and returned to work the next morning. She didn't cry. She also didn't sleep or eat. She was numb most of the time, but when the pain came, it was like knives.

She walked into the trailer telling herself she was getting her hard hat, but secretly she wanted to see Tucker again. Tucker, who hadn't called. Instead she found Will at his desk.

He looked up when she walked in. His look of concern warned her, but couldn't begin to prepare her.

"Nevada," he said. "I don't know...." He cleared his throat. "He just..." Will crossed to her. "I'm sorry."

She got it then. Reality slammed into her, nearly knocking her to her knees. She looked around the trailer, seeing what was still there, noticing what was gone.

"He left," she said flatly.

"I'm sorry," Will repeated.

Tucker was gone. He hadn't called in sick or left to meet with a subcontractor. Instead he'd fled Fool's Gold completely. Without a word.

She knew without asking that he was never coming back.

CHAPTER NINETEEN

DESPITE MAYOR MARSHA'S best efforts, people found out about the unveiling ceremony. Nevada had noticed the lack of signs and postings in the online events calendar. For a town that prided itself on keeping its citizens informed, the powers that be had been completely silent when it came to the original sculpture by Caterina Stoicasescu.

Nevada appreciated that she wasn't asked a lot of questions. She'd managed to get through the past few days by sheer force of will. She'd done her job, and when it was time to go home, she went back to her place, curled up in bed and got up again in the morning.

Some nights she cried. Others she laid in the dark, waiting for the pain inside to lessen just a little. One night she'd actually slept, which would have been a blessing, except she kept dreaming about Tucker.

Before realizing she was in love with him, dealing with her sisters' double wedding had been a little uncomfortable. Now it was going to be a nightmare. While she'd never imagined she and Tucker would join them as a couple, she'd counted on having him around. Later, she'd imagined a whole lot more. Now all of that was gone. Lost.

Because the construction site was outside of town,

no one was used to seeing him around very much. Word of his departure hadn't spread. The guys on the site knew, but they weren't going to talk, not to people in town or even to her. They were just a little protective on the job, and they watched her cautiously, so she figured out that they knew.

Will kept his distance. Perhaps because he didn't want her asking him questions or maybe because he felt bad that he was so happy. Nevada planned on telling him she was glad he and Jo were together. That having her heart broken and losing the man she'd probably loved for the past ten years wouldn't change that. Just because she wasn't getting her happy ending didn't mean she wasn't interested in other people being together.

If she felt guilty about anything, it was keeping the truth from her family. Not so much her brothers, but her sisters and her mom. They would want to be there for her, to offer comfort. Her friends in town would feel the same way. But she couldn't face one of those huge "the guy's a jerk" events that inevitably followed. Until she figured out how she was going to survive the loss, she had to manage her heartache alone and get through the unveiling ceremony without anyone figuring out there was a problem.

The mayor had scheduled the event for three in the afternoon—just when most of the schools were letting out. Nevada guessed her plan was that the mothers and kids would be busy and unable to attend, and most businesspeople would be at work. That left only a small group of the community who would be available to attend.

Sure enough, when Nevada arrived in the center of town, there were only a handful of residents milling around the fabric-covered statue.

"You're here," the mayor said, crossing to Nevada. "I want this to be brief. No fanfare. I'll just speak a few words, then we'll expose the damn thing to the world."

The older woman looked more resigned than happy. While Nevada hadn't seen the completed piece, she'd seen the sketches and knew it was everything the mayor wanted to avoid.

"I'm sorry I couldn't talk her out of giving this to the town," she said.

Mayor Marsha shook her head. "Ms. Stoicasescu is very stubborn. No one could have changed her mind. I can only hope someone will vandalize it quickly and we'll be forced to take it down." She smiled. "After all, we have an insurance policy to cover that sort of thing."

"Have you seen it?" Nevada asked.

"No. I couldn't stand to watch while they installed it." She glanced up at the fabric blowing in the light breeze. "I shudder to think what people are going to say. I hope the media doesn't find out about this. They'll be back in a heartbeat."

She glanced at her slim watch. "All right. Let's get this over with."

The mayor walked to the microphone that had been set up next to the covered sculpture.

"Good afternoon. It is with pleasure that I present the work of Caterina Stoicasescu. This gifted artist has given the town an original piece. To quote her, it represents all that is beautiful and feminine in the town of Fool's Gold."

The mayor pressed her lips together, then nodded at a woman in a city park uniform. She pressed a button, and a pulley system was activated. Over the low hum of the engine winding the rope, the heavy canvas rose higher and higher.

Nevada stared at the slender supports, then the bottom of the piece came into view.

The metal curved into a near point. Random squiggling designs decorated the sides. As the cover exposed more, the V shape was more pronounced. At the top, two bulging pods sat on either side of the curving V.

Nevada tilted her head as she stared. To be honest, it wasn't all that vaginalike—probably a good thing for the town.

"What is it, Mommy?" a little boy asked.

"I have no idea," his mother replied, sounding puzzled.

"Thank God," Mayor Marsha murmured.

For the first time in days, Nevada laughed.

TUCKER'S FATHER'S OFFICE was about the size of a bus terminal, with sweeping views of Lake Michigan. Tucker generally enjoyed visiting Chicago. He liked the feel of the city, the restaurants, enjoyed the people. But this time he wasn't interested in his surroundings. Instead of enjoying the view, he paced in front of his father's desk.

"I can't go back," he repeated for the third or fourth time. "I'm totally at fault. I shouldn't have gotten personally involved. I know better. I didn't mean to, but she was there, you know? Just there."

He paused and looked at his father, who was simply watching him.

"She's beautiful. That's part of it. Not traditionally gorgeous like Cat or some model, but there's something that grabs you, and then doesn't let go." He jammed his hands into his jeans pockets, then pulled them out. "She's good at her job. The guys like her a lot. They respect her. And she's funny. I have a good time with her."

He stopped in front of his father's desk. "So, you see why I have to leave."

"No," Elliot Janack said slowly. "I don't."

"I can't be with her. I know what she'd want. Love. Marriage. Forever."

"Why is that bad?"

Tucker started for the door, then turned back. "I never told you what happened with Cat. Caterina Stoicasescu. That artist? We did the installation for her about ten years ago. It was the first time you put me in charge of a job. I fell for her, Dad. I fell hard."

Haltingly, he detailed his obsession with the irresistible artist and how difficult it had been to break away.

"I don't want that. Sure, Nevada is great and I'm going to have a hell of a time getting over her, but I can't be that man again."

His father nodded. "So, what's the plan?"

"I take on another job. Prove myself. I know you're disappointed that I'm not staying on to finish up the Fool's Gold resort." He shook his head and swore. "Finish. It's not even started. The pipes are just now going in. There's a lot to do. Will's a great guy and capable, but this is bigger than anything he's ever done. He's going to need help."

Elliot leaned back in his chair. "Why do you think you have anything to prove?"

"I have to earn my way into the position. You're not going to leave the company to me just because I'm your son."

"That might be a concern if you were someone else, Tucker. But you've been capable of running Janack Construction for years. Everyone else knows that—I've been hoping you'd figure it out, too. The only reason you're not in charge now is that I haven't been ready to step down. I didn't ask you to run the Fool's Gold project to prove anything. You said you were interested, so I gave it to you. You've already earned my trust, and you've always had my love. I'm proud of you."

Tucker felt like he was a kid again, all long legs and awkward gestures. He swallowed. "Thanks, Dad."

"You're welcome." His father motioned to the chair in front of his desk. "Ready to have a seat?"

"Sure."

He sank onto the soft cushion, then wanted to jump up again. He couldn't just sit still. He needed to be doing something. Get busy. Or run.

He pushed the last impulse away. He wasn't running. He was making an intelligent choice. There was a difference. Not a big one, but it was enough.

"When your mother died," his father began, "all that kept me going was knowing I had to take care of you. I couldn't stand to stay here, there were too many memories. So I took you wherever the work was. All over the world. I told myself that you would enjoy living in different places, meeting different people. And you did. But while you gained a lot, you also lost out."

Elliot leaned forward in his chair. "You didn't get to have the same friends year after year. You never stayed in a school long enough to play sports or fall for the girl. I'm not saying there weren't women. I still remember that incident with the ambassador's daughter when you were seventeen."

Tucker grinned. "Hey, that wasn't my fault. She's the one who crawled into *my* window to wish me happy birthday."

His father smiled. "Point taken. But while there were different girls, you never stuck around long enough to fall for any of them. Until Cat."

Tucker studied his dad. "You say that like you knew her."

"I knew of her. One of the guys on the crew called me and told me what was going on. He said you were in over your head, but I figured it was time you learned about life and love. So I stayed away."

Tucker grimaced. "They knew?"

His father laughed. "You weren't subtle. You fell hard, got your heart broken and learned your lesson, just like I'd planned. Only it was the wrong lesson, son. Love doesn't make you a fool. Some of us are blessed with several partners we can love, while others never find anyone. But the lucky ones find that one person who changes everything. For me, it was your mother. I love her as much today as I did when I proposed. I would rather have had her those few years than have loved anyone else for a lifetime."

Elliot's mouth twisted. "I would give all this away."

He motioned to his office. "I would sacrifice everything but you to have her back just for a day. To love is to be blessed. What you had with Caterina was…"

"An obsession," Tucker said grimly. "I've heard."

"But you don't believe. You think you can't love and still be who you are. You think the price of love is too high. You're wrong. Love is worth everything. Not that I'm going to be able to convince you," his father added.

"Probably not."

Elliot nodded. "Fair enough. Let's get together in the morning and talk about the next step. We can start the transition for you to take over the company now or find another job you want to run."

That was more than Tucker had expected. "Thanks, Dad." He rose.

"You're welcome."

His father stood and walked around his desk. The two men hugged. Elliot put his hands on his son's shoulders.

"Your mother would be very proud of you. She loved you."

Tucker thought of the vague memories that had no real form and wished he could have had her in his life longer. But she'd been taken without warning, leaving behind a little boy and a grieving husband.

Tucker left.

Once he was in the hallway, he crossed to the elevator and pushed the button to go down. He kept a small apartment in the city. Getting some sleep seemed like a good idea. Then he'd give some serious thought to what he wanted to do next. Getting out of the country sounded good. He would stay busy. Forget. Because there was no going back.

SOMETIME AROUND THREE the next afternoon, Tucker decided to throw his TV out the window. There was nothing on the damn thing. Despite the fact that he hadn't slept in two days, had spent nearly three hours working out in the gym in his building and had walked most of the city, he couldn't relax, couldn't focus and couldn't find anything to watch on television. He needed to be in a rain forest somewhere. Maybe a decent jungle fever would put his world into perspective.

He got up from the sofa and crossed to the small kitchen. In the refrigerator he found beer and leftover pizza. Neither appealed. Still restless, he walked toward the bedroom. Maybe if he took a shower he would get sleepy, or at the very least, forget.

He was halfway there when someone rang his doorbell.

Nevada!

He knew it was her, he thought, as he jogged to the door. She'd come to knock some sense into him. To yell at him and tell him why he was wrong. She would convince him and he'd let her and…

He opened the door only to find Cat standing in the hallway of the condo building.

"Oh," he said, disappointed and frustrated. "It's you."

"I'm not that happy to see you, either," she snapped, pushing past him. "I feel horrible. I haven't been working. I'm lost and nothing helps."

She stepped into the middle of his living room and faced him. Misery pulled at her face and her mouth was a full pout.

"I hate this," she said, then stomped her foot. "I miss

Nevada and I miss that stupid little town. What little creativity I felt is gone. But now I don't know what to do. Cody was a disappointment."

"Who's Cody?"

"Oh, one of the college boys renting a room from Nevada. I thought he would help, but he doesn't. Then I remembered how good you and I were together, so I came here. You have to fix this, Tucker. I need you."

Her voice was a whine, her expression petulant. She was a child who hadn't gotten her way. After stomping out of the party, she regretted what she'd done and wanted to go back.

"Sorry. I can't help you."

"You can, but you won't." She crossed to him and put her hands on his chest. "How can you resist me?"

"Easily," he said without thinking, knowing it was the truth.

The truth slammed into him like a professionally thrown fastball. It hit his gut going ninety-seven miles an hour and knocked the wind out of him.

"I love her," he said.

Cat's big green eyes narrowed to angry slits. "What did you say?"

He pushed her hands off his chest and stared into space. "I love her. I have for a while. I didn't love you at all. Being with you was like being a junkie waiting for my next fix. I could never match the previous high but I was sure the lows were going to kill me. Nevada isn't like that. Every time I'm with her, I feel better and stronger. She gives everything."

He turned in a slow circle, not sure where to go or what to do. "She told me she loved me and I left. What the hell was I thinking?" He grabbed Cat's upper arms. "She said she loved me. What am I doing here with you?"

His car keys were on the small table by the drawer, where he always tossed them. So was his cell phone. He picked up both as he headed out the door.

He was halfway down to the parking garage when he realized he probably should have packed something, or closed the door to his condo. Whatever, he thought with a shrug. Cat would shut the door behind her. Or maybe not. Either way, he didn't care. This wasn't his home—he didn't belong here. He belonged with his woman and, by God, he was going back to her.

NEVADA THOUGHT maybe she should get a pet of some kind. While the self-sufficiency of a cat was appealing, maybe a dog would be better. Some kind of mixed-breed rescue dog who could come with her to the job site. She logged into the Fool's Gold Animal Shelter website with the idea of looking at pictures. Maybe staring into big, brown dog eyes would make her feel better. Eventually something would have to.

She missed Tucker. She wanted to be strong and brave and say that she was over him. That he'd been an idiot to leave, and if that was how he treated her declaration of love, then she was better off without him. It was possible that one day she would actually believe that, but today wasn't that day. Today, or rather, tonight, she ached. The hole where her heart used to be endlessly reminded her of what she'd lost.

She clicked on the dog pictures, then just as quickly left the site. It wasn't responsible to get a dog now—

while she was grieving. She had to figure out how to deal with her loss. Then, when she felt better, she would decide if she was ready to take on the responsibility of a pet.

Very rational and mature, she told herself. Her mother would be so proud.

The phone rang.

She glanced at the clock and saw it was after ten. Had something happened to someone in her family?

She glanced at the caller-ID screen and her throat went dry when she read Fool's Gold Police Department. She pushed the talk button.

"Hello?"

"Nevada, this is Chief Barns. No one is dead."

She drew in a breath. "Good to know."

"That said, I have a problem. I need you to come to the town square right away. No one's hurt. Don't worry about that, but there's…a situation."

"What does that mean?"

"It'll be a whole lot easier to show you."

With that, the line went dead.

Nevada had no idea what the police chief was talking about, but she wasn't going to get any answers just waiting. She got up and pulled on boots, then shrugged on a heavy coat and gloves. It was barely above freezing this late at night.

She jogged through the quiet residential streets, grateful it wasn't windy or wet out. As it was, her ears were freezing by the time she rounded the last corner and could see into the square.

Streetlights illuminated the benches, the bushes that were mostly naked this time of year and the police car parked just to the left. The floodlights that had been installed for the giant vagina shone up on the weird sculpture. They also showed a ladder, a man on that ladder and the sparks of a blowtorch.

Chief Barns stepped out of the shadows and walked toward her.

"I don't understand," Nevada said, confused by what she was seeing. "Is he—"

The man moved then and she recognized him. Tucker. Tucker? What was he doing here? Was he back?

"Seems to me some vandal is dismantling that eyesore," Chief Barns said cheerfully. "The good news is Cat believes in simplicity of assembly. It went together quickly and should come apart just as easily. In the morning, one of my officers is going to find that it's missing. What a shame. There's going to be a lot of paperwork with this one."

Nevada could only stare at the man on the ladder. "You're not going to stop him?"

"Why? I don't see anything."

"What will happen to the piece?"

The police chief shrugged. "Rumor has it the whole thing is going to a sculpture garden in San Francisco. I'm sure they'll appreciate it more than we do here."

The chief slapped her gloved hands together. "I need to get home. One of my boys is studying for a history test tomorrow and I need to ride herd. You have a good night."

With that, she got in her police car and drove away.

Nevada walked slowly toward the statue. Sparks were flying, then one side of the giant vagina fell to the ground. She instinctively braced herself for the sound of metal crashing into concrete, only to realize there was padding in place to protect the pieces.

"Tucker," she yelled.

He turned and looked at her, then turned off the blowtorch. He hung it over the rung and started down.

She stood there waiting. Her heart thudded rapidly as she battled hope and fear and a twisting kind of nausea in her stomach.

When he reached the ground, he tore off his protective gear and swept her into his arms.

His mouth was hot and hard and claimed her in a kiss that made her toes curl. She hugged him back, holding on as if she would never let go.

"I'm sorry," he said, pulling back enough to speak. "I was an idiot. Worse, I was the jerk who hurt you. I'm sorry, Nevada. I shouldn't have left, except I had to. It was the only way for me to figure it out. But I'm back now and I'm never leaving. I talked to my dad on the way out and I'm moving the business here. I want to be here with you, in this town."

He stepped back and took her hand in his. "I love you, Nevada. I have for a while. You were right—what I had with Cat wasn't love. It wasn't anything good. But I couldn't see that and I never wanted to go there again. Because of that, I nearly lost you. I hope you'll give me another chance. We belong together. I want to spend the rest of my life making you happy. Say yes."

She was floating. Honestly, she could feel her feet leaving the ground. This couldn't be happening, only it was. He loved her. Tucker Janack loved her.

Warmth and promise and happiness filled her. She stared into his dark eyes and knew that they would always have each other. That their future was going to be more wonderful than she could imagine.

She smiled. "You haven't asked me anything," she said, her voice teasing. "What am I supposed to answer?"

"What? Oh. Right." He dropped to one knee. "Nevada Hendrix, will you marry me?"

Right there, in the night, with the stars as witness, in front of a giant vagina. Only in Fool's Gold, she thought happily, pulling him to his feet.

"I love you," she whispered, before kissing him. "Of course I'll marry you."

He picked her up and swung her around, then set her down slowly and kissed her.

This was perfect, she thought, kissing him back. They held each other close, before he turned back to the statue.

"I need to get this finished."

"I'll help," she said. "It'll go faster that way and then we can go home."

EPILOGUE

5:45 p.m. New Year's Eve
Gold Rush Ski Lodge and Resort

A LIGHT SNOW had been falling all day. Just after sunset, it had taken a turn for the serious. White carpeted the parking lot and roads. The valets checked the guest list one more time to confirm that everyone had arrived. As all the guests would be spending the night at the hotel, getting the roads plowed could wait.

In the smaller of the two ballrooms, chairs had been set in neat rows, dividing the space into sides for the bride and groom. Make that brides and grooms. A few folks from South Salmon, Alaska, who knew Finn Andersson mingled with former patients of Dr. Simon Bradley. Elliot Janack, Tucker's father, introduced himself to Sasha and Stephen, Finn's twin brothers.

Max Thurman settled on the brides' side, Dakota's adopted daughter, Hannah, in his arms. While Max wore a dark suit, the baby was dressed in a pale pink dress with lace shoes and a crown of tiny pink roses in her hair.

The Hendrix brothers, except Ford, who'd been unable to get leave, were in attendance. Ethan sat next to his wife, Liz, their three children next to her. Kent and his son would sit beside them after escorting Denise to her seat.

The townspeople settled on both sides of the aisle, to make sure the numbers were even. With the Hendrix triplets finally settling down, there was no point in upsetting anyone. Better for the men to feel they were a part of Fool's Gold.

The Gionni sisters, still feuding, sat across from each other. Eddie Carberry and Gladys Smith settled next to each other. Mayor Marsha walked in with her granddaughter and grandson-in-law, Charity and Josh Golden, their beautiful daughter in Josh's arms.

Pia and Raoul Moreno each had a twin daughter. Morgan, the man who owned the bookstore, sat next to them and reached for one of the girls. He was still waiting for his daughter to give him a grandchild. The McCormick family took up an entire row. Janis and her husband, Mike, still looked at each other like they were on their honeymoon, despite having been married more than thirty years. Daughter Katie and her husband, Jackson, were expecting their first child in the spring.

Jo and Will slipped in a side door.

"Is my hair okay?" Jo asked anxiously.

Will kissed her. "You look amazing."

She smiled at him and leaned close. "Thanks, but do I look like I just had sex? I think people would find that tacky."

"No. They'd be jealous."

As she sat next to him, the diamond ring on her left hand winked in the light. Neither of them were interested in a big wedding like this. Sometime in the next few weeks, they would take off for Las Vegas and make it all legal.

Charlie, Annabelle and Heidi walked in together.

"Nice," Charlie said. "A little fussy for me, but nice."

"It's beautiful," Annabelle said with a sigh. "It almost makes me wish I was more romantic."

Beside them, Heidi nodded. "I've sworn off men, but I could almost go for this."

They walked up the aisle and found seats behind Mayor Marsha, Charity and Josh.

Denise Hendrix sighed with contentment, watching the guests settle. Despite the speed with which everything had been arranged, the whole wedding had turned out perfectly.

The fragrance of roses and lilies mingled with the scent from tall, tapered candles. Romantic music drifted from the small orchestra in the corner. She was willing to admit that might have been an extravagance, but it wasn't every day a mother saw three of her daughters marry.

She stepped into a side hallway and went to check on the larger ballroom, where the dinner would be held.

Controlled chaos reigned. The cake decorator was setting out the last of the cupcakes. Rather than have three cakes, the girls had decided on different cupcakes for each of them. The colors of the frosting ranged from pale pink to deep red. The flavors—chocolate, spice, coconut and vanilla—reflected in the decorations on each cupcake.

A bar was set up in each of the corners. With no one having to drive, champagne and cocktails would flow. She watched ice being delivered and glasses unloaded.

Appetizers would circulate for the first hour, then dinner would be served, followed by dessert and chocolate-covered strawberries. There was a dance floor by the orchestra and a net filled with balloons that would be released at midnight.

Denise pressed her hand against her stomach, telling herself not to be nervous. Everything would go perfectly. She smiled to herself, then returned to the smaller ballroom. Once the girls were ready to begin, she would be seated next to Max—the one place in the world she most wanted to be.

"I'M WEARING A TIARA," Nevada said, studying herself in the mirror. "I can't believe it. I work in construction. How did this happen?"

Dakota leaned forward and adjusted the headpiece. "It belonged to Tucker's grandmother and he wanted you to wear it. Were you going to say no?"

"Obviously not."

"I think you look beautiful," Montana told her.

"We all look beautiful," Nevada said, knowing it was true. Somehow they'd managed to pull off a triple wedding that reflected all their styles.

Nevada's dress was simple. Strapless, with a plain, fitted bodice and a slim skirt. Her romantic indulgence was the bow in back that flared out into an elegant train.

Dakota had chosen beaded chiffon—an empire style with a deep V that highlighted her suddenly impressive cleavage while concealing her baby bump. Montana's dress was feminine, with tiers of cascading silk and lace.

Nevada had on Tucker's grandmother's tiara. Dakota wore a simple veil, and Montana had a loose, almost Edwardian updo decorated with tiny flowers.

The door to the brides' room opened and Denise walked in. "Everyone ready?" she asked, before pausing, her fingers covering her mouth. "Oh, you're so beautiful. My daughters."

Each of them rushed to her and she hugged them tightly.

"I love you."

"I love you, too."

"Don't cry, we'll smear."

"I can't believe we're doing this!"

They posed for the last few pictures, then Denise passed out their bouquets.

"Everyone is here," she said. "Dinner is going to be lovely. I'm just so happy." She drew in a breath. "I wish your father was here to see you three."

"He is, Mom," Montana told her.

Denise brushed a tear away. "I suppose you're right."

They all went out into the hallway. While Denise was escorted to her seat next to Max and Hannah, the sisters waited together.

They had already decided the order in which they would walk down the aisle. Dakota had gotten engaged first, so she would lead, Montana would follow and Nevada would bring up the rear.

The music changed to the "Wedding March." The guests rose.

Dakota started walking as slowly as they'd practiced. Everyone she knew and loved was here tonight. She met Finn's gaze and smiled at him. He smiled back.

A wave caught her eye and she saw their daughter grinning at her. Baby Hannah. Life had blessed her in every way possible.

Montana went next, loving how her dress rustled with each step. She felt like a fairy princess in a castle, and waiting for her was her very own handsome prince. Simon watched her, as serious as always. His love reached across the few yards separating them and drew her closer.

Later tonight, when they were alone in their suite, she would tell him what she'd learned that morning after peeing on a stick. Until then, she would do her best to convince him she was drinking champagne when she really wasn't.

A baby, she thought happily. Maybe she would have twins!

Nevada waited until Montana reached the end of the aisle before starting her walk. Tucker's gaze never left hers.

Cat had sent her regrets, something that had secretly relieved Nevada. Who knew what the beautiful but temperamental artist could have done at an event like this. She'd sent a gift, something she'd made herself. It was upstairs, still wrapped. Nevada and Tucker had decided they were going to need a whole lot of champagne before finding the courage to open that present.

Nevada was still several feet away from her sisters when Tucker broke ranks. He came toward her, causing several of the guests to chuckle. He took her hand and led her the rest of the way.

"Just so you don't change your mind," he whispered.

"I won't. Not ever."

He looked around and smiled. "I guess that makes six of us."

When all three brides and all three grooms were in place, the minister began.

"Dearly beloved…"

"I'm going to cry," Heidi whispered.

"Me, too," Annabelle said softly.

"I don't believe in crying," Charlie told them, even as she sniffed. "This is the worst. It's making me feel all soft and romantic."

"Me, too." Annabelle sighed. "I want to find somebody."

"Oh, yeah." Heidi drew in a breath. "Me, too. But I think all the good ones are taken."

The mayor was sitting in front of them. She turned and smiled.

"Next year, ladies. I have a feeling. Just you wait and see."

* * * * *